A Compilation of

Short Stories and Other Writings

By

Michael R. Wright

Volume I

A Dedication To...

...All my Family here and on Facebook.

Since November 11, 2018, our Facebook page has grown to over thirteen thousand members. I've come to somewhat of a crossroad in this whole writing ordeal. I have a dilemma. I write and share my stories for free because that is what I think is the right thing to do. Many of you have suggested that I put together a book of short stories and put it for sale. The thought of selling them makes me a bit uneasy, but many of you have said that some of the stories have helped you in one way or another. Also brought to my attention, was the fact that only the folks on Facebook with cell phones and computers could benefit from them. There are folks all across our nation in retirement homes and assisted living centers, and even living home alone, with no means to read the stories.

So I have decided to take your advice and make a book of short stories. To keep it inexpensive, and to speed the process, I have bypassed the commercial publishers, and have self-published it. The Writings of Mike Wright will remain on Facebook, still free for all to read my stories as I write and post them. If you want to buy a copy for your night table or coffee table, that is up to you. I don't care either way. This is not about making money; it is about trying to spread a little hope, love, and good will to others. There is one favor I would ask. If you have the means to buy a book and donate it to your local senior center or nursing home, etc., that would mean more to me than you could ever imagine.

Anyway, I will keep you all in the loop as I continue my mission to give everyone a tiny break from the daily hustle and grind of life. My deepest heartfelt thanks and gratitude to you all, for the encouragement and support you give me each day with your comments, likes, and messages. You have lifted my heart, and together we can lift many more. May your days be blessed beyond all understanding with Love, Happiness, and most of all, Peace.

Your friend always,

Mike

Table of Contents

A New Year's Miracle
(Genre: Seasonal/Love)

It was New Year's Eve. My wife and I were planning on going to her sister's house for dinner, and to party a bit to ring in the new year. It was getting very cold, and the temperature was dropping all day down into the single digits. The power was out due to the storm from the day before and the only electric we had, was from the generator.

Molly looked at me and said, "Maybe we should stay home. If that generator goes out and it gets any colder, we could lose some of the animals in the barn."

Our home had coal and wood for heat, but the barn had just an old electric heater that was set to come on at forty degrees. It was just enough to keep it from freezing. Still, at floor level along the walls, a bowl of water would freeze solid when it was as cold as it was then. I too, was a little worried about them.

"You have been excited about this night for two months," I said. "You should go. You haven't seen your sister in almost a year. I'll stay here and take care of everything. You go and have a great time. Just promise me you will bring me a big plate of leftovers."

After a minute Molly agreed. I saw the excitement flow back into her eyes and her whole being. I continued the chores while she got ready. Her sister lived about three hours away, and further up into the mountains. I filled the tank on the Subaru. It was all wheel drive and great for navigating the mountain roads in winter. Molly was a good driver, and the roads had been cleared and sanded well.

"I'm ready," Molly said.

"You're all gassed up. Wear your seatbelt and drive safe. I want you to relax and have a great time. I'll see you next year," I said with a smile. "It's 2:00pm now," I said. "I'll expect a call around five."

"You know I will," she said.

I gave Molly a big hug and a kiss. I watched as she drove down our long driveway toward the road.

Okay, back to work, I thought. *If I'm staying here, I still have chores to do.* I filled the coal stove, and brought in a few armloads of wood for that stove also. We use a coal stove in the basement, and a wood stove on the first floor. The coal burns twenty-four-seven all winter. We use the wood stove to regulate the temp in the main living area.

After tending the stoves, I went out to the barn to check the animals. The wind had picked up considerably and I thought about Molly. *I do wish I had gone with her.* We were so in love.

Even after thirty-two years together, we were best friends.

I puttered around the barn for quite a while, cleaning and tending to the animals. Feed, water, and the like. Everyone was doing fine. I headed back to the house. I was getting hungry, and it was dark now, and Molly should be calling me any time.

I entered the house, and first thing was to light the lanterns. It was pitch black in there. Then, I put some cold ham and potatoes in the iron skillet and put it on the top of the wood stove. I put a few raw carrots in there too. I opened the flue and the small vent at the bottom to create a draft so the stove wood get good and hot. I refilled the coffee percolator with water and coffee, and onto the stove it went. Thank god for the stoves.

I went downstairs and got the water pot off the coal stove. We always keep it there to have some humidity in the house. The stoves tend to dry out the air something fierce. I took the water pot and filled the kitchen sink. I washed myself up good, and cleaned the few dishes from our lunch.

As I sat down by the stove, my cell phone rang. "Right on time," I said as I answered.

Molly laughed. "I'm here safe and sound," she said. "Everyone says to tell you they love and miss you. I most of all," she added.

"I love you too, Babe. Have a good time."

"I will," she said. "Will you be alright?" she asked.

"I'll be fine," I told her. "I have dinner on the stove and everything is in good shape for the night. I'll see you tomorrow when you get home. Don't forget to call me when you leave."

"I won't," said Molly. "I love you."

"I love you too. Give everyone my love and big hugs."

"I will," she said.

"Okay, Babe, love you."

I hung up and leaned toward the stove. The ham was just starting to sizzle. I could smell it and boy did it smell great.

As I was eating, I could hear the coffee bubbling away. I used to tell the kids that the pop pop poppity pop sound is where they got the name Popop. Most folks never heard a real percolator. I have used mine ever since I was a young man. I used to bring it on camping trips, now it sits atop the wood stove all winter long. Our main cook-stove is electric. We used to have gas, but one winter the valve froze outside and wouldn't work. I switched over in the spring. It appears everything has its flaws.

The smell of coffee now filled the air around me. I finished eating, drank my coffee, and decided to hit the hay. I took the coffee pot off the stove and set it on the hearth. Then I grabbed the lantern and made my way upstairs and into the bedroom.

No sooner than my boots dropped out of my hand and onto the floor, I heard the generator begin to sputter. "Damn, I knew I forgot something. I forgot to gas up the generator. I'm glad it sputtered now, rather than when I was asleep and wouldn't hear it. After all, that is the whole reason I had to stay home alone," I laughed out loud. The animals.

I put my boots back on and down the old creaking stairs I went. Put on my coat hat and gloves and opened the door. The temperature on the thermometer nailed to the porch said five below zero, and that is without the wind factor.

I went to the shed and got a five gallon gas jug. I keep two filled so I don't have to hand pump it from the tank every time I need gas. I walked behind the barn to where the generator sits. It stays outside under a lean-to. The fumes would kill the animals and even people if it was inside.

I filled the tank. It took the whole five gallons. I put the cap on and headed back to the shed. When I walked out from behind the barn, a wind gust caught me and nearly knocked me to the ground. The empty gas container flew out of my hand like someone pulled it. Man was it windy. I picked up the gas jug and put it in the shed. I walked back to the barn. The generator was running full clean and at full speed again. It would last all night now.

I came to the front of the barn and opened the door. One last check on everyone. All was good. The animals were comfortable and set in for the night. I left the barn and closed the door. The latch was old and flimsy. *I need to fix that one day*, I thought. With that, I headed to the house. Sleep was looking really good now.

I took about three steps and wham! I was knocked to the ground, and it felt like my leg was on fire. A huge gust of wind ripped a big limb off one of the big pines on the side of the barn. It was on my leg, and had me pinned to the ground in the snow. The limb had punctured my leg near the ankle and I was impaled. I was literally nailed to the ground. The pain was excruciating. There was however, very little blood.

I could not move. I was stuck to the ground, on my back, in the worst pain I ever remember. I began to feel sick. I was nauseous. I was cold. Very cold. The wind was howling over my body and all I felt was icy cold. I was gonna yell for help but to who; I was alone. My phone was on the arm of the chair where I ate by the warm stove.

The tree limb was huge and too heavy for me to move. I tried over and over to lift it. It was big. Each time I tried I could feel it rip at my leg. *I am gonna freeze to death,* I thought.

I turned my head, threw up, and fell unconscious.

"Wendle, wake up. Wake up, Wendle."

I could barely open my eyes. My leg was on fire again; the cold had gone. I was as warm as toast. My eyes opened more and it was bright, so bright. "Where am I?"

Molly was kneeling next to me. She leaned close and kissed me. "Help is coming," she said.

I began to feel some kind of weight on my entire body. "What is going on?" I asked.

"You have been trapped under a tree limb since last night," she said.

"I remember now," I told her. I tried to sit up but could not; the weight held me down, so too did the limb which had me pinned and impaled. My eyes now more clear and focused, and fully awake, I saw our two oldest sheep laying on me. "Why didn't you just get me blankets?" I asked.

"I just got home," said Molly. "It is three in the afternoon. Dolly and Kendall were already laying on you when I got here. I called the ambulance right off and then woke you up."

I looked toward the barn door. It was wide open. The flimsy latch was broken and there were two hoof print dents in the door. Sometime after I fell unconscious, our horse, Jacob, kicked open the door and the girls came out and laid on me. Our animals saved my life. I began to cry.

Molly went into the barn and told me that Jacob's stall door was smashed to bits. He was still in the stall. *The sheeps' stall door is also shattered,* she said. Molly looked at me and began to cry too.

With both hands I began to rub Dolly and Kendal. They pushed their heads back toward my hands and I just cried harder.

The paramedics came and I was on my feet within a month. Molly and I decided that Dolly and Kendall would become pets. Jacob, well, he is like a son. They have seen me prepare for market many times, and yet, they still chose to return the love we have shown them during their stay with us. I guess there is a moral to our miracle. If you raise your stock humanely and with love, they don't mind their sacrifice. Better to have been loved, than never loved at all.

The Snow Fridge
(Genre: Seasonal/Family)

I could smell the hot cocoa and grilled cheese, drifting out from inside the house. The power was out, and our mother was cooking on the wood stove. Mom had opened the window just a little, because it was really hot inside. It was in the single digits last night after the storm, and our father had the coal and wood stoves both burning. He goes a bit overboard from time to time. It is either too cold, or too darn hot. Shannon and I were outside, but we were warm.

Shannon is my sister. We had our snowsuits and boots on, and were in the yard building an igloo. The snow was about a foot deep, and really good packing. We had been working on it all morning. I heard the back door open and mom came out onto the deck. "Lunch is ready," she told us.

Shannon dropped her snow box, and ran toward the stairs. "Last one in's a rotten egg!" she hollered as she dashed up onto the deck.

I put by box upside down on the wall and tapped on it. The block of snow slid cleanly out onto the wall, and I followed her into the house to eat. Dad had made us each a snow brick box. They were rectangular cardboard boxes, with clear packaging tape completely around them, in and out. He did a great job making them. They lasted a long time. Even when the snow was wetter, the cardboard stayed dry. We used them a few times over the winter that year.

We took off our clothes, and hung them near the fire in the living room. Dad had strung a rope across the hearth area, just for our wet clothes. Our boots went on the floor. Mom had already put our sandwiches on our plates, and hot cocoa into the cups.

"MMMMMM," said Shannon as she took a big gulp. Mom always used extra chocolate and whole milk. Sometimes, she even used half milk, and half heavy cream. Either way, it was always the best.

I went for the grilled cheese first. Smelling it outside in the yard had made me as hungry as a horse. I ate it in three bites. Mom knew us well. She put a second one on my plate, and refilled Shannon's mug. It's funny, food always tastes better after being outside playing and working hard. "Thanks, Mom," I said.

"Yea," said Shannon. "Thanks, Mom."

"You're welcome guys," said mom with a smile.

Just then, Dad walked in. "I just talked to the plow guy," he said. "Apparently, the power will be off for a few days. There is a lot of damage from the storm. Lines are down all over the county."

"Oh boy," said Mom.

"It's a good thing we have the stoves to keep warm and cook on."

Mom was always on the ball. Her mind was sharp. "What about the food?" she said. "How will we keep it from spoiling?"

"Well," said Dad, "we can put it down in the garage.

"But it will all freeze there," insisted Mom, "and I'll have to walk all the way down to the garage for everything.

Dad was staring out the window into the yard in a daze. Then suddenly he spoke up and said, "I have an idea."

"What are you thinking?" asked Mom.

"I'm thinking about my stomach," replied Dad. I laughed and so did my sister. Dad was funny. Mom brought him two grilled cheese on rye bread with bacon on them. That was his favorite, and a cup of coffee. Mom always took real good care of us all. She was tops.

"I see you two have been working hard on that igloo," said Dad. "If you two can make a house out of snow, maybe we can make a refrigerator too."

Mom looked at us and smiled. Dad bit into his sandwich and let out a sound of pure pleasure. Again we laughed.

"After lunch," said Dad, "I'll need everyone's help."

Mom sat down next to Dad, and we all ate our lunch. By the time we finished eating, our clothes were all dry, and nice and warm.

"Okay," said Dad, "let's get moving."

Mom did the dishes. She used the big pot of hot water on the wood stove, to half fill the sink. Shannon, dad, and I got dressed and went outside. Dad took a piece of plywood from the garage, and carried it up onto the deck, and leaned it against the rail.

"What is that for, Dad?" I asked.

"To block the sun," he said.

We began shoveling all the snow on the deck into a big pile against the plywood. Dad was right. The sun was on the plywood and not the snow pile. We packed it hard with every shovelful we added. When the deck was cleared, the pile was just the perfect size. Dad asked me to go to the shed and get the small gardening hand tools, so we could dig out openings for the fridge. Shannon and I both went. We had to shovel a path to the shed, and around the door so we could open it. We grabbed the little hand shovel, and the three fingered pointy thing. We then scurried back through our path, and up onto the deck by dad.

Dad dug and dug. Sometimes he used the pointy thing to scratch at the hardest packed snow. After about an hour, Dad had two good sized holes dug deep into the pile. He also dug a hole under the pile on the left side, right down to the deck.

"What is that hole for?" I asked.

"That will be the freezer," he said.

"Freezer," I asked, confused.

"Yes," said Dad, "the cold and wind will come through the spaces between the deck floorboards, and keep the frozen foods frozen. As long as the temperatures stay like they are now," he added.

At one point, I looked over at Shannon. She was just standing, gazing at our unfinished igloo. She looked sad. She saw me looking at her. "It will never get finished now," she said. "It will be dark soon."

I put my arm around her shoulder and said, "Ya know, Shannon, an ice box for the food is more important, and we can finish the igloo tomorrow after school."

"But," said Shannon, "what about the animals?"

"What animals?" I asked her.

"The wild cats," she replied. "They will freeze."

Dad overheard her and came to where we were standing. He looked into the yard at the roofless igloo. "Let's finish the fridge," he said, "and then we can all go finish the igloo."

Shannon jumped up and down, "Thank you, Daddy! Thank you, Daddy!" she said again, and wrapped her arms around him.

"Back to work," he said.

"Get your mom," Dad said. "We are done."

"Mom, Mom!" I yelled as I opened the kitchen door.

Mom already had her coat on, and had all the food in boxes. We made a line from the door to our new snow refrigerator. Mom brought out one box and handed it to me. I handed it to Shannon, and she handed it to Dad. Dad unloaded the food into the holes in the snow pile, and Mom brought out the next box. The frozen foods were the last to come. Under the pile and into the freezer they went. When all the food was inside, Mom took a picture, and then Dad used white towels to cover the openings.

Immediately, Mom said, "Okay, let's get going. We have a lot of work to do."

She had apparently overheard our earlier conversation. We all looked at her and smiled as we stampeded down the deck stairs, and into the yard. Shannon and I packed the boxes with snow, and Mom and Dad tapped them out onto the circled wall, slowly tapering them inward on each level, and rubbing them in smooth and tight. Before we knew it, Mom had the final block on the top.

"It is finished!" exclaimed Shannon. "It is finished!"

"No, not just yet it's not," said Dad. He and Mom disappeared into the house, and were back in a flash. Dad had another white towel in his hands, and it was all cut up. He hung it on the igloo opening, and the hanging cut strips became the door. Mom had two bowls of cat food. One was dry food, and one was from a can. I think it was tuna fish actually. She put the bowls just inside the opening. "Now it is finished," she said.

Shannon hugged Dad and then threw her arms around Mom, hugging and squeezing her too. I had a big smile on my face. The day was a success. We built our igloo, and our new snow refrigerator. There is nothing you can't accomplish, if you just stick together.

The power was out just over a week, and all our food stayed fine. No predators even came on the deck. I think they ate the cat food we put out each night. Two wild cats made it their home for a few weeks that winter. If you look closely at the picture, you can see the gallon jugs of milk, eggs, bacon, and lots of other stuff. It was much bigger than it looks. Thanks Mom and Dad for all the memories. We have continued making them with our kids and grandkids. Missing you more these days, but I know I will see you soon. May all the families on Earth, hold each other close, and may peace and happiness, fill every heart.

May You Fly Free!
(1924-2019)
(Genre: Family/Poem)

And as her eyes closed for the last time, a new inner sight opened. She could see everything. It was like standing on the highest mountain top. Nothing would ever impede her view again. She saw new life. A new beginning. It was more beautiful and vibrant, than anything she had ever seen in her entire lifetime here on earth.

Suddenly, she realized that she had not even moved from her bed. A feeling of complete, and utter freedom overcame her. There was nothing to keep her down or hold her back. It was amazing. Peace, beyond all reason was hers. She lifted her head, and saw some of her loved ones by the bed crying. "It is alright," she told them, but they could not hear her. She then sat up, and held each one of her family members firmly. They did not realize, that she was still there with them.

Wings began to emerge from deep within her. Her hands and arms, slowly withered and disappeared. Her new wings were as white as the driven snow, and ran the entire length of her body. From this day forward her hugs would be complete. They would totally encompass each of those she held. One last time, she hugged each of her loved ones who were at her side. Her huge bright wings covering and protecting them forever.

"Mary," she heard a voice call, "I'm here."

She spread her wings wide for the first time ever, and began to fly. The ceiling opened like magic, as she rose from the bed and up into the air. As she looked down, she saw her cocoon, now an empty shell, lying on the bed, and her family gathered there, so saddened by her having left them. With a flap of her wings she flew high into the sky. She made one last visit to each and every one of her loved ones, wherever they were, wrapping her wings around them for comfort, and bidding a final farewell.

Again she heard the voice call. "Mary, I am here."

She knew her family would be alright, and floated toward the beautiful sound of the voice. She flew higher and higher, and as she did, everything became brighter and brighter.

"Where are you?" Mary asked.

"Here," said the voice.

With another strong flap of her wings, she pushed even higher. Her mind expanded to an immeasurable size. She could see and understand everything.

As she continued upward, other angels began flying near her. "Hi, Mary," they said. She was overcome with the most awesome and powerful love you could ever imagine. Mary was still with her loved ones, but it was those who had gone on home before her. She could still see and feel her family on Earth. It was as if she was everywhere.

Another angel approached Mary. He looked deeply into her loving eyes and said, "They will all be fine. Welcome home, I've been waiting for you." He lifted his wing and gently put it around her, and together they flew.

May you find peace and comfort this day, knowing that, one day, you too, shall grow wings and fly. Godspeed!

This writing is dedicated to my Aunt May, who flew the night of February 6th, 2019. She is the last one of a generation. May her children, grandchildren, and great grandchildren, remember her always. Peace!

Life After Death
(Genre: Family/Death/Spirituality)

I believe our dreams are a part of both sides of life. The part where we are active and alive here in the physical, and also the part of life going on around us in the supernatural. They call it supernatural because it is quite super.

Life after death. Many folks don't believe our souls live on, but I for one am sure of it, and I think that our dreams float between both realms. Let me try to explain.

It all started many years ago when I was just a young boy. My parents were dead, and I lived with my grandparents, Ma-mom and Pop. They were wonderful. They took really good care of me, and we were all best friends. One night, while I was asleep, I woke to the sound of voices talking in the living room, and my Ma-mom was crying. I got up from my bed, and made my way down the hall toward the commotion to see what was happening.

When I entered the room, Ma-mom came and picked me up and held me tight. "Pop went to heaven," she said as she squeezed me even harder. I felt her tears falling on my neck and running down my back. I had heard of heaven but I really did not understand what it was. Just then two more men entered in the front door with a skinny bed on wheels, and went into Pop's room. A few minutes later, another man took Ma-mom and me back into the hall by my room. My head was still on Ma-mom's shoulder and I watched the first two men wheel the bed back out. It was completely covered with a white sheet. I know now that Pop was on it. Although then, being only six years old, I had no idea what was going on.

Out the door they went. The man let Ma-mom and me back into the living room. Two of our neighbors came inside. They each hugged Ma-mom and said they were so sorry, and that everything would be alright. "We are here for you," they said, "if you need anything, don't hesitate to ask."

Ma-mom thanked them. She put me down and then put on the kettle to make tea. All the men now left, and it was just me, Ma-mom, and the two neighbors. I listened as they talked about heaven, death, and peace. I remember that part the most. Death and peace.

The next day there was no Pop. He was gone. He never came back, well not in human form anyway. I started to miss him right away. We had always spent the days together, the three of us, cooking, playing in the garden, and going to the market; we even played cards. Some times in the evening Pop would turn on the radio and we would hear a story. I could tell Ma-mom was missing him too. We talked a lot about him, and I think that made her feel better. One day I was telling her that Pop had visited me in a dream. She perked right up and was all ears.

It was the third night after he had died. We had dinner, and Ma-mom turned on the radio. It was a repeat of the last story we had all heard together. I saw tears in her eyes, but she did not cry out loud. After it was over, I went to bed. I don't remember falling asleep, all I remember is the dream. I was in the garden with Ma-mom planting seeds. Pop was with us. 'That is too deep,' said Pop to me. 'You want them to grow right?'

'Yes,' I said.

'A half inch is all you need,' he said. Pops made the holes with his finger, and I dropped in the seeds. Then he showed me how to gently cover them with dirt, and pat them down firmly with my hand.

'Thanks for the help, Pop,' said Ma-mom.

'I love being here in the garden with you two,' he said smiling. Then the two of them stood up and hugged, and each grabbed one of my hands and together they lifted me up to join in the embrace. It was great.

When I finished telling her, Ma-mom smiled. She liked my dream. "I think your grandfather is telling us something," she said. "I think that he is saying he is right here with us."

I looked around but he wasn't there. I wondered if she was alright. Maybe she was seeing things.

As the years passed, Pop was always visiting me in my sleep. Just like with the seeds, he taught me things. Sometimes the dreams made no sense at all, but others, were on point. It was always just me in the dreams. I had no age, or face; it was just me. Although, in most of my dreams I could fly. In some dreams, I saw people I knew, or had seen at school or at work, or maybe in the market, but there were others that I had never seen before. And the places I found myself were extraordinary; places I had never been to, or even seen. Of course there were a lot of places I did know also.

As I got older, Pop came less and less to visit me in the night. I will never forget him. Ma-mom passed when I was in my late teens. I shared all my dreams of Pop with her over the years we were together. She always told me that he lived in heaven and was watching over us. My dreams somehow confirmed that for her. I knew I was with him in my dreams, but when I was awake, I was not so sure. Ma-mom didn't visit me like Pop. She was in some dreams, but they were mostly memories flashing in and out. When Pop was there, it was like a new day each time. By the time I was 22 years old, Pop stopped visiting. My dreams were now of school, work, and girls.

Sometimes an occasional nightmare. I was alone in life and on my own.

I struggled through the days searching for love and happiness. They were not an easy thing to find. I did, however, find a lot of heartache. Maybe love was not mine to have. Depression began to settle in. I found my days dim and overwhelming. I had lost all my motivation. Then the visit.

Pop showed up one night, and Ma-mom was with him. They were sitting on my bed just looking at me. Tears filled my eyes. I reached out to hold them, but my arms just swung empty through the air. I woke up crying. When I finally fell back to sleep, we were together again, but in a new garden. A much bigger garden. There were others all around, and everyone was happy, even me. It was the best I had felt in years. Pop told me not to worry about love so much, that one day I would have more love than I knew what to do with. I didn't understand.

When I woke up, I tried for hours to fall back to sleep. I wanted to feel good again, like in the dream, like I used to feel. Sleep evaded me and I went on with my day. I thought a lot about what Pop said about love. I decided I would just work and try to do things I enjoyed. I went hiking, canoeing, and camping with some friends; I even joined a softball team at the local pub.

I wound up falling in love with a girl at a pizzeria. We had won our game, and stopped for a slice to celebrate. She was working behind the counter. The cutest little thing I ever saw. I asked her for a date and she accepted. Two years later we married. I guess Pop was right. I was so in love. The years past and we had kids. They grew up and we grew older. Love and hate battled our life together but we never gave up. Today we are at peace for the most part and in love. Not the blissful, lustful, star-struck love of younger years, but a deep love, with happiness, trust, and comfort in one another's arms. No matter what happens, we go on. In fact, when I think about it, we are just like Ma-mom and Pop.

The grand kids are getting older now and so am I. Pop has begun to visit me again. We talk a lot more these days. Last night we were sitting in the park on a bench. It was a beautiful day. Pop looked just like he did when I last saw him alive in our home, and I was just still me. Ageless, with no face. I was just me. I asked Pop, "Why is it I can fly in my dreams but not in real life?"

He looked at me and stood up and just lifted himself into the air. "Because," he said, "while your body sleeps, your soul flies with angels. One day," he said, "you will be here full time."

"But," I said, "why didn't I fly with you for so many years in between?"

Pop looked at me. "You already know the answer, don't you?"

I thought for a moment. "Is it because I was so busy and worried about life that I didn't relax enough to be able to let go?"

Pop touched his nose like in the charades game we used to play. I laughed. "So that's it, if I had just let go and not worried so much. I looked over the bench toward Pop; he was gone.

I stood and started walking home when I saw the ambulance pass by. My wife flew to me, and kissed me gently on the lips. "I'll see you soon," she said. I walked a little further and saw that the ambulance was at our house. I heard the men at the door and my eyes opened.

Empty your mind of worry and fear, for the best is yet to come. There are no conditions, we will fly together. Unconditional love awaits us all.

Hold Each Other Tight
(Genre: Love)

There is no better feeling on this planet, than to be held tightly in the arms of someone you love, and who also loves you, while your arms are around them, tightly holding them back, and pulling each other as close as you can. This is not something that everyone gets a chance to feel in this life. Even fewer of us, experience it on a regular basis. When we are young and fall in love, yes there is much loving embrace, but as the days filled with life go by, the hugs slowly fade away, replaced by rut and routines, driven by the desperation to succeed in life. Jobs, big homes, money, children, ego, all seem to play a part in stealing away the true love we all so richly deserve, and desire.

If I could give the young people of this world one piece of advice it would be this: For two full minutes each day, every day, no matter what you are feeling or going through, put your arms around your partner and hold each other close and tight. Then for one minute, just look into each other's eyes in quiet. And then again, hold one another close for two more minutes, just breathing and relaxing in each other's arms, letting the true healing take place, each and every day.

Our youth deserve the best chance we can give them.

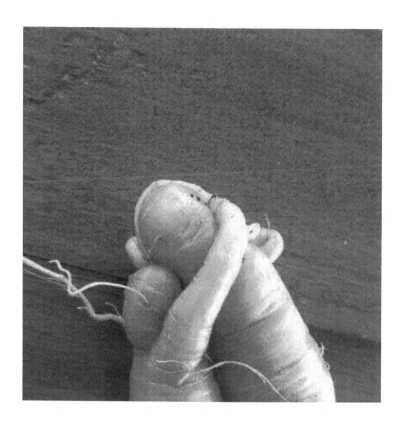

A Parent's Prayer
(Genre: Family)

Please, oh please, take away the sickness and pain of my child; give it to me instead.

Let me suffer all the ills and heartaches in front of them.

Please, oh please, let their lives be happy and healthy, filled with joy and prosperity.

Let me endure all the injustice for them.

Here, I am. They are mine.

No matter how old I get, this is my prayer.

Dear Mom/My Dearest Child
(Genre: Family/)

Dear Mom,

I know we can't see each other right now, but one day, we will be together again. Life has a funny way of pulling loved ones apart, and we are no different than anyone else who suffers loss. I guess I never realized just how quick the end could come. All of these unsettled feelings and emotions that we never took the time to deal with. Who knew one of us would be taken away so fast. I want you to know, that I admire you more than anyone else on Earth, and I miss you so very much. You gave birth to me, and raised me with such love and patience. You taught me to be a kind and gentle person, and to always respect others. Even though I wish we had had more time together, I know that passing on is a part of life, and not a punishment dished out by some unloving God.

I think about you a lot, and I hope you think about me too. I'm sure we have both shed our fair share of sad tears, but it's time for us to heal and think about all the good times we shared in life. The angels are watching over us both, and all of our family and friends. I love you, Mom. You were my hero, and always will be. Please forgive me for not always being there for you. I did my best, but sometimes I feel it was not enough. It's Mother's Day on Earth again. I hope you can feel me in your heart. Happy Mother's Day Mom, I love you!

Your Loving Child

My Dearest Child,

I will always love you. You did just fine. We all entered life with no training and learned as we lived. I was always so proud of you, even though I didn't say it all the time. We have all taken some bad turns in the road of life, but somehow we managed to get back on the right path. I remember the good times and the bad. Together, they were the greatest adventure of all. Have no regrets, for as we have learned, life is lived in the blink of an eye. I miss you more than you could ever imagine, but one day we will be together again. And thank you my precious, for thinking of me. Wipe the tears and sadness away, for love holds us together for all eternity.

I love you,
Mom

Tomcat
(Genre: Pets/Homesteading)

Quite a long time ago, I bought and began raising chickens and ducks. One day while I was building their coop, I noticed a stray cat lurking in the far back corner of the yard. He was all grey with those raccoon-like markings on him, and man was he big. His fur was smooth and it appeared he was well taken care of. Each day at some point while working in the yard, I noticed he was still around. I was a little worried he was waiting to get his paws on the baby chicks. I quickly added a run. A run is a fenced in area, where the birds are safe to roam around without getting caught by any predators. The new run was flimsy, but it would suffice for now, and keep the cat at bay. I didn't see him again after that for quite some time.

The chicks grew and turned into healthy egg layers. Each morning, I would go out back to feed and water them. I collected the eggs, and around noon, I would let them out to forage the property freely, in search of worms, bugs, and whatever greens they might want to eat. It was wonderful. Nothing ever harmed my birds. I was feeling pretty good about the whole experience, until late one night, or should I say, very early one morning.

It was just after I had collapsed in the yard from heat exhaustion. I was okay, but the doctor told me I had to keep hydrated for now on. "No excuses," he said. "Drink lots of water."

I did as he ordered and I was in great health. Although now, I always had to pee. I woke up at least twice each night. Once around midnight, and then again around 2:00am. One morning during my 2:00am dance, I heard the ducks quacking a bit. I went to the window, and sitting by the run, I saw that big old Tom cat. He wasn't as pretty this time though. His fur was dirty and roughed up, and he looked like he had been fighting.

"I knew it," I said to myself. "That cat wants my birds." I had seen him on occasion early in the morning leaving the yard, but never gave it much thought. Ya know, now thinking back, each time I saw him, he always looked rattier than the time before. He even smelled like a skunk. I put on my pants, boots and shirt, and went outside to shew him away. He walked over to the edge of the woods, and then turned his head toward me. After a glaring look, he turned his head frontwards and jumped into the woods. *Good riddance*, I thought. *You're not getting my ducks or my chickens.* "You're all safe now girls," I said to the flock. "Go back to sleep." I proceeded back into the house, took another pee, and back to bed I went.

I started a new routine. Every time I got up to go, I would pass the window and survey the yard to make sure everything was fine. I began to see the cat every night. I was worried he was gonna get in the run and hurt the girls. Night after night I chased him away and went back to sleep. He was spraying his scent all around the coop and run. It stunk. I guess he was marking his territory. *Not on my watch,* I thought, *these are my girls.*

I was laying restlessly awake, knowing he would just come back and try to get in the damn run. I should have built it stronger, but winter was setting in and I was too old to do it in the cold all alone. One night after chasing him, I laid in bed thinking. *I know, I'll buy a pellet gun and shoot him in the butt. He'll surely get the message then.*

The next day I went to the local Walmart and bought a gun. When I got home, I practiced shooting old soda cans off a chair down in the back yard. Then I shot some more from the window. I was actually very good at it. I was ready. *When I see that damn cat again, I will just give it a good sting.*

That night when I woke up for my midnight run to the John, I couldn't get back to sleep, so I sat in my chair by the window with the pellet gun in my hands. Sure enough, just after 2:00am, I spot old Tom cat walking around the run from the side behind the coop. I lifted the gun and aimed for his hind section. I just wanted to scare him enough to stay away. When he sat down near the run, I gently squeezed the trigger. Pop.

"RRRRaaayyyaaaaaoooouu," screamed the cat, and dashed off faster than ever. I felt a bit bad, but it had to be done. He was a threat to my birds.

The next night, I looked outside and he was nowhere in sight. Then the night after that, and the night after that. I did it. My girls were safe again.

It was on the fourth night free of that old scroungy nuisance cat that it began.

I woke up, and went out to feed and water, when I saw a pile of feathers inside the run. One of my chickens had been eaten alive. I figured the cat had come back for revenge. The following night, I stood guard at the window. *This cat is not going to get the better of me,* I thought. I waited until day break, but nothing. Three nights in a row, I sat glued to that window, ready to take him out, but only peace and quiet.

I was tired the next night and just slept. When I went out in the morning, one of my ducks was lying on the ground inside the run. The breast and entire neck had been eaten. *I have had enough. I have to find this cat and kill it, or trap it maybe and relocate it far away.*

I opened the coop door to fill the feeders, and there were mice eating the feed off the floor.

They scampered away fast. I noticed also, some weird holes in the dirt inside the run. *Maybe a snake,* I thought. I asked a friend of mine about the holes, and he immediately said, "Get a cat; you have rats too." It was strange, two years and I never had mice and rats, not that I saw anyway. I thought about old Tom cat. Maybe I was wrong.

I needed to know. I bought a large live trap to catch the cat. I also made a tin can and bucket mouse trap. I couldn't use poison, I didn't want the girls to die or get sick. The mouse trap was just a five gallon bucket with a wire running through it, and a tin can. I spread peanut butter all over and around the can. When the mouse crosses the wire to the can in the middle, the can spins, and the mouse will fall into the bucket. I set it up inside the coop. I set the live trap, baited with cat food, near the run. I slept through the night. I didn't even have to pee. I was getting things done. *I will catch the cat, and the mice, and everything will be safe again.*

I was up extra early and feeling great. I made coffee and had a bite to eat, then out to feed and water, and, check the traps. No sooner than I opened the back door I could smell it. Sure enough, there was a big skunk in the live trap. I wondered why he was here and not the cat. I wasn't gonna try to move the cage with the skunk, I didn't want to get sprayed. I moved slowly and bent down to open the trap and let it free. The skunk began to turn around to spray me. I talked ever so softly saying, "It's okay buddy, you're okay. Easy pal, I'm gonna get you out of here." He stood still as I opened the trap. With the latch in place I stood up slow and moved away. In a minute or two, the skunk ran off into the woods. I went into the coop and there in the bottom of the bucket were five mice. Them I drove across the main road and into the forest about a mile away.

I set the live trap again that night, and caught a huge opossum. It was one ugly creature. It was all teeth. That guy I brought about four miles down the river. He'd be better off there than in my yard. I set the trap again and again, but there were no more takers. The cat never showed up. About a week after I stopped setting the trap, I lost another duck. I would have no choice but to rebuild the run in the spring. The cat was smarter than me.

I was back to waking up again at night to pee. I heard a chicken barking and clucking something fierce. I jumped into my clothes and out the door I ran. I was down the deck stairs in two leaps. I stumbled and fell as I hurried across the yard to the coop door. Just as I opened it, a giant raccoon blew right past me and was gone in seconds. It had killed yet another one of my flock. I looked in the bucket and sure enough, more mice.

I sat on the coop steps bewildered. *I am losing this battle,* I thought. *Why are these animals all after my ducks and chickens? It was safe for so long before this all started.* And then it dawned on me. *Tomcat!* He didn't want my chickens or ducks at all. He was catching the mice, and protecting his food source. That is why he smelled like skunk and was always so beat up. What had I done? I had misjudged the cat entirely. Man did I feel dumb. It hurt me to think I had shot him with my pellet gun. I wondered where he was now.

I stood, and headed back up the deck stairs. I turned and gazed over the yard one last time to make sure I didn't see the raccoon. I caught sight of a set of yellow gleaming eyes, right at the edge of the wood line. I looked hard and steady. *It must be the coon,* I thought. I went in and got my pellet gun, and opened the window as quietly as I could. I set my sights on those eyes. I was about to pull the trigger when suddenly the animal jumped forward, out of the woods, and into the yard. It wasn't the raccoon at all, it was the old Tom cat. His fur was shiny and clean. He wasn't beat up at all. He looked just like he did the first time I saw him, while I was working on the coop.

I felt bad I had been so mean to him, and so quick to judge. I lowered the gun and went into the kitchen. I still had cat food left for the traps, and filled a small bowl with it. I went outside and placed it near the run. I went in and turned off the light, and sat in my chair and watched.

Tom cat, that's what I named him, ate the food. Each night I would set out the bowl and he would come and eat it. Within a few weeks, I began to smell his spray again. The mice and the holes in the dirt slowly disappeared, and nothing seemed to bother the girls anymore. That was almost twenty years ago. Good old Tom cat and I became pretty good friends over the years. He would sleep inside during the day, and at night, he stayed outside working hard. He was always all beat up looking, but he was well fed, loved, and cared for. He passed away, when I had had him for sixteen years. He was lying near the wood stove all warm and comfy. I still miss him today. Nothing could ever replace good Old Tom Cat.

A Blessing in Disguise
(Painting a Picture)
(Genre: Family/Motivational)

Laying on the ground in the middle of the woods, just relaxing and looking up at the splendor of all that is good, is such a far cry from living on the filthy, cold streets of the city, at the mercy of human beings, who believe you to be the dirt they walk upon. Looking back, had it not been for Sam, I and many others would have found ourselves at Death's door, homeless and hopeless, with nowhere to turn, living in the endless cycle of poverty and despair.

For me, it began many years ago. I was stuck and couldn't find my way out. I kept hitting dead ends. I finally got down on my hands and knees and stuck my head through the stalks. There was this girl in the next row. She was beautiful. She was also stuck at a dead end. She was a little upset and had tears in her eyes. I crawled through and stood up.

"It's okay," I told her. "I'm lost too. We can do this together, I know we can."

It took us all day, but finally we made it out. I think we got out the way we came in, at least that is how it felt.

We talked the afternoon away lost in the maze. We became friends in just a few hours. I kissed her on the cheek and said goodbye.

"Here is my phone number," she said, "I'll be looking forward to hearing from you soon."

Who would have ever thought that we would have found true love there? We were married a year later.

I was on top of the world. Newly married to the most wonderful girl ever, a nice home in the country, and a wonderful job.

I was blessed with all the promise life had to offer. Even a baby on the way. We were so in love. We had parties in winter, spring, summer and fall.

When we weren't entertaining, or enjoying our lives together, I would be hard at work, keeping up our happy lifestyle. It cost a lot. A lot more than I could have ever imagined.

I got the call about one in the afternoon, while at a business lunch with some very important clients. My darling wife was in labor, and on her way to the hospital.

I needed this account. I couldn't just walk out. This was our bread and butter. If I lost this account, I could lose everything.

I stayed for another hour and then politely excused myself.

"My missus is in labor," I said, "I have to get to the Hospital."

"Get moving man," said one of the clients. "Family comes first."

I was stunned to hear him say that. He was always all business. Maybe it was the many drinks he had talking, but I took my que, and hit the road toward the hospital.

It was only an hour I thought, I bet she is still in labor. And after all, I could say I hit traffic, that's why I'm late.

Unfortunately, I did hit traffic. I didn't get to the hospital until around four thirty. I ran through the doors and up to the delivery room. I asked for my wife.

"Please wait here while I get the doctor," said the nurse.

The obstetrician came out, and over to where I was standing. His eyes were aimed low, and his face was sullen.

"What is it?" I asked a bit impatient. I could see something was wrong. He slowly lifted his eyes until they met mine.

He put his hand on my shoulder and said, "There were some devastating complications during the delivery, your wife and daughter did not survive."

My heart, no, my entire being imploded. I stood frozen, numb, I couldn't comprehend the words he was saying.

"I'm sorry for your loss," he said.

My mind was reeling, *I wasn't there for her*. I fainted and collapsed to the floor.

After the funeral, I tried to go back to work. Life now, was all wrong. I couldn't help but blame myself.

I should have left immediately when I got the call. With all the traffic, I would still have never made it, but I should have left right then. I should have taken that whole week off from work. I should have been there no matter what.

I couldn't eat or sleep. Days, then weeks passed, and I couldn't shake the horribleness that filled my mind and soul.

I began drinking to try and sleep. It didn't help. I took all kinds of pills trying to escape the pain that overwhelmed me, but guilt was consuming my every moment.

Finally one morning, I went to work. Everyone, I thought, was staring at me.

They knew I didn't rush to the hospital the minute I got the call, I put money first.

I sat in the chair in my office with the shades closed. I looked at my desk, but all I saw was confusion. I couldn't focus. I stayed until four pm and then left. That was the last day I would work.

I sat around the house in a deep dark depression, caught up in a self-pity party.

The weeks turned into months and I was not getting any better. Bills piled up, and the house was in utter disarray.

One morning, they turned the electricity off for failure to pay my bill, and I just left the house dark and gloomy. It was befitting to my soul.

I had lost about 35 pounds by now, and looked like a beanpole. I was a wreck. One night, I downed a whole bottle of scotch, and a handful of pills. I tried to end it all. Instead, I woke up under a pile of garbage in an alley, in the city, right where I belonged.

I have no recollection of how I got there. Two young homeless kids were laughing at me. Both of them were all dirty and scroungy. They held in their hands, whatever belongings I had. My wallet and ID, and my last thirty five dollars.

"Give me my stuff," I said.

"No," said one of them, "This is for Mama." Then they ran off.

The sun peaked between the buildings, and crossed over the alley way. It felt good on me while it lasted.

I got up and began walking. And walking, and walking. I was aimlessly drifting through the city streets.

When nightfall came, I found another alley and crawled behind and under some more garbage. Sleep continued to evade me.

My eyes closed, but all I saw was my wife and daughter, on the delivery bed, cold and blue.

I did lose consciousness for an hour or two each night, but there was no rest or comfort to be found. I was in hell.

Time passed, and I began to beg passerby for loose change. Anything to get something to eat and drink.

Some folks spit on me. Others said, *get a job you bum*. And still others, just put their noses in the air, and walked on by as if they could not see or hear me.

Every so often, a tourist from out of town, would drop a couple of coins into my tattered coffee cup.

I began to meet others who shared my misfortune of being destitute, and lived out on the streets. Some, were fakers. They panhandled all day and then went back to their apartments at night.

I, like most of the others, slept where ever I could find a bit of cover. The garbage piles became my home.

I learned about street life and survival one day at a time. After about three years living on the street, I knew most of the other homeless people. I became friendly with some, and others were to be feared.

Sleep came easier these days, as time was healing my injured soul. It was a tough life. Battling rats for table scraps behind diners, or in garbage bags on the sidewalks, and fending off other bag people, who wanted your coat or shoes.

I wondered how the youngest members of the street could survive under these conditions.

Then I thought about the kids who robbed me, my first morning here in hell. When I had demanded my belongings back, they said no, they were for Mama. I wondered now, were they homeless, or did they come out only in the day like the fakers from a home?

My curiosity got the better of me, and I wandered through the streets to the alley I had first awakened in.

I lingered there for over two weeks, waiting and watching, until I saw one of the kids. He was stealing fruit from a street vendor. I snuck up from behind and grabbed him. He struggled and kicked, screaming *let me go*. I held him tight.

"Calm down," I said, "I want to talk to you." The vendor looked at me. "Get away from here you dirt bag," he said. "This fruit cost money."

I reached into my pocket, and pulled out three quarters I had from begging. I gave them to the vendor and said, "I hope that covers the cost."

He took the money and waved his hand for us to leave, with a look of disgust on his face. I turned, kid in hand and left.

"What are you gonna do with me?" asked the boy.

"I have questions," I said. "Answer them honestly, and I will let you go. What is your name?" I asked.

"Ben," replied the boy.

"Hi Ben, it is nice to meet you, I am Joseph."

"I remember you," said Ben. "Me and my friend Greg took your stuff a couple years ago."

"Yes," I said, "That is what I want to ask you about."

"We gave it to Mama," he said.

"Yes, I know," I said, "Is Mama your mother?"

"No," said Ben, "She is Mama to a whole bunch of us. She takes care of us."

"Does she have a house," I asked?

"Well, said Ben, "Not a house, but an old abandoned store where we sleep at night. It is warm, and safer than the street. We bring her whatever we can, and she feeds us all by dividing it up fairly."

"What about the money you panhandle or steal?" I asked.

"She uses it all for us. Milk and food. Sometimes we get socks when winter comes."

"She sounds like a good Mama," I said. I thought for a second about my wife. She would have been a good Mama too.

"I would like to meet her," I said to Ben.

"I don't think that is possible," he said. "She has rules. She does not like, or want strangers around, unless they are kids."

"I see," I said. "Okay then Ben, thank you for sharing this information with me. You may go now, as I promised you."

Ben looked at me puzzled. "Thanks Joe," he said, then turned, and scurried away down the street.

The store front was an old paint store. It appeared to have been abandoned during the great depression.

It was one of the oldest buildings I had seen so far here in the city, but I could tell it was structurally sound.

It was ragged and worn, but there was not a loose brick to be seen. Even the old plaster inside was intact, except for some holes caused by pilferers.

You could still see the numbers carved in the brick. 125. The name was painted on. But it was so old and worn, I could only make out a few of the letters. *Abra--- -rom--n Pa--nt-ng Co.* And, from the rooftop, it had a clear view of the river.

I had watched the place for a few days now. Ben had no idea that I had followed him home, after letting him go the day we talked. I figured it was the best way to find the answers I was looking for.

It was weird. I was being drawn to this kid, and to Mama, and to this place. There was something in my soul brewing, but for the life of me, I didn't know what it was, or why. I'm just a dirty, worthless, homeless bum, I thought.

The kids came and went from sun up, until sundown. After dark it was always quiet. No one came or went at night. Except for Mama.

She was a small younger woman probably in her late twenties. She would leave after eleven P.M, and return by two A.M every single night.

She would carry out two old empty carpet bags, and when she returned they were filled. With what, I didn't know.

I was more than curious to know what she was up to, so one night I decided I would follow her. Eleven on the nose, her small figure appeared in the doorway with the bags. She was wearing a shawl, covering her head and arms. I could not see her face. Her dress was dark blue and long. It reminded me of my grandmother's.

She walked across the street, and ducked into a small alleyway between the buildings. I was as quiet as ever, as I followed her. I waited for her to exit the alley, and then I bolted through and stopped at the end.

My eyes scanned the area, and watched to see where she headed next. When she was a good distance up the road, I came out of the alley, and again walked slow and careful in her direction.

It was not long, before she entered a small all night market. Now I had the chance to get really close to her. I was just another customer in the store. It was the best cover ever.

I watched as she picked through the cheaper overly ripe fruit. She put the best looking ones into the basket. Then she got milk. Next she was by the meat section.

She was talking to herself, as if deciding which meat she would buy. She put something in the basket, but I could not see what it was. Then she walked the aisles and grabbed a couple of cans of beans, and some wilted vegetables.

As she headed to the checkout, she stopped and turned. She looked directly at me. Our eyes met. *Was I that obvious?* I asked myself. *Did she know I was watching and following her?*

Her gaze turned back to a rack by the cash register. I walked back down the aisle I was in, still watching her in the mirror at the end of the aisle.

She quickly, almost guiltily, grabbed a small box of cookies, and shoved them into the basket.

My heart began to beat a bit faster. I thought of all the kids she was taking care of. My initial thought of Mama when Ben had told me about her, was that she was probably taking advantage of them somehow. How wrong I was. I was just like the people on the street. I thought the worst of her. Tears filled my eyes, as I realized how deep even my preconceptions and stereotypes were.

She was now haggling over the price of the fruit and vegetables.

"They are wilted," she said, "And should be discounted."

The vendor then gave her a lower price, and I saw a quick smile cross her face. I continued watching as she paid the cashier for her purchase. It was mostly all in coins.

She filled the two bags, and off she went, headed back in the direction we had come.

About two blocks from the market, on a small dark side street, two men, (they definitely looked homeless, but I did not know them), approached Mama.

"One man said something to her, but I could not hear what it was he was saying. Mama shouted "NO!" and turned to walk away.

The other man blocked her path. He knocked one of the bags from her hand, and onto the ground. They were going to rob her, I thought. Suddenly, the other man grabbed her from behind, and the first man began to grab at her dress.

For a second I was frozen with fear for her, and in the next, I was on top of the men. I punched and kicked them with everything I had.

Mama kicked one of them hard in the groin. He fell to the ground, as I punched the other in the face, breaking his nose. His blood began to flow.

He ran, and the other guy got up and ran after him.

"Are you all right?" I asked her.

"I am," she replied. "Thank you for your assistance," she added.

I bent down and picked up her groceries and refilled the bag.

"I'm sorry this has happened to you," I said. She looked up at me. "Why are you following me?" she asked.

"I...I'm. I'm not.. "

"I know you are," she said abruptly. "And," she continued, "I have seen you watching my home for the past week."

I looked into her eyes. "Yes," I said, "You are right. I don't know how to explain."

"Try the truth," she said, "It is usually the best."

"I mean you no harm," I said to her. "It is a long story, and I'm not even sure of the answer."

Mama looked at me. "Carry one of the bags and walk with me. Tell me your story."

I shared everything from losing my wife and daughter, to my life here, homeless on the street.

I told her how I felt drawn to the boy Ben, and somehow, through him, to her.

"I don't know why," I said, "But I have this feeling inside, that I am supposed to be here with you and the children."

As we neared the old rundown store where she lived with the kids, she said, "I have been waiting a long time for you to come."

My eyes opened wide in disbelief. "I don't understand," I said.

"I," said Mama, "Lost my husband and son in a car accident when I was a young bride. I wound up here caring for these poor unfortunates. One night, while I was sleeping, I had a dream of a man who would come, and together we would build something great. I believe this man is you."

Tears filled my eyes again. My heart leapt in my chest, and my soul was floating higher than it had been in years.

"But build what?" I asked.

"I do not know," said Mama, "That is where you came into the dream.

Mama allowed me to enter her home. It was run down, but it was clean and tidy. All the kids were sleeping.

I was amazed at how well this woman was caring for these young ones, with almost no income at all.

She had books that she would use to teach them to read and write. Even math was on their daily curriculum.

She had a small camping type stove, which was fueled by a small propane tank, like the kind plumbers use for their torch. Mama was putting the groceries away.

"What will you do with the milk?" I asked. Mama showed me a very small refrigerator.

"A man brought this here for us a long time ago. It is a refrigerator out of an old camper van. It, like our little stove, is powered by the propane tanks. I can get four tanks for two dollars at the store, and they last a long time."

"They go faster in the winter," she said, "as I sometimes use the stove for a little extra warmth for the kids. You can sleep there," she told me, pointing to a corner on the far side of the room. "Here is a blanket."

The blanket was old, but it was comfortable none the less. It was far better than being under the garbage piles. I was asleep in no time at all.

I woke to the smell of cooking food. It was the first time I smelled that in almost four years. The kids were hovering over the books, and doing the lessons, which Mama set out each morning.

Two of the boys however, were hovering over me.

"What are you doing here?" asked Ben. Greg was looking at me intently. "He looks familiar," Greg said.

"Yea," said Ben, "This is the guy we found under the garbage pile in the alley a few years back."

"Remember, I told you about him grabbing me about week ago."

"Yes," said Greg, "I remember."

"So," said Greg, "What are you doing here?"

"Get to your lessons boys," interrupted Mama. The boys immediately did as they were told. I was stunned how all the children obeyed her so quickly, and without question.

"This is Joseph," said Mama. "He will be staying with us for a while. Listen to him as you would me. He is going to help around here also." Mama looked down at me laying on the floor.

"You will need to get up earlier than this," she said.

"Yes ma'am," I quickly answered. I got up and folded my blanket, and set it on the shelf.

"Breakfast is ready," she said, "Come and get it."

One by one the children filled their small bowls and ate. Afterward, each wiped their bowl clean and set it in their small cubby space.

There were two walls filled with cubbies. They were used to store the paint cans when the store was active years ago.

"Okay kids," said Mama, "Out ya go. No stealing and no hurting anyone. Ask nicely and bring home what you can."

Off they went. I counted eighteen kids. Fifteen boys and three girls.

"You too Joe, there are no free rides here. You will have to earn your keep if you are to stay."

I said "Okay Mama," and followed the children out the door.

It was a bright sunny fall morning. The streets were filling with people and the holidays coming fast. This was a better time for us living in the street. People felt guilty this time of year. They would bring food and clothes, and pass them out for free. Sometimes socks, sometimes new underwear. Used coats were very welcomed items.

People came from outside the city with cars and vans, bringing hot soups, sandwiches, and even turkey dinners around thanksgiving.

I wondered about the conversation I had with Mama. What could I possibly build with her? Why was I even here?

I thought about how I would panhandle today. Would I just sit and beg, or was there another way?

I decided to try a new approach to separate people from their coins. I got a piece of cardboard from the trash, and made a small sign.

"I will work if you have a job me, but please help me to eat."

I set it up on the sidewalk next to my old cup. All day I sat and watched the people walk by. I was invisible. One frail old guy, walked past at least twenty times. I thought for sure he was gonna dump some change on me, but nothing.

It was near dark and I was getting ready to head back to Mama's. I had almost three dollars in the cup. I was ashamed to go back with such a little amount.

It was not even enough to feed me, no less the kids and Mama. I started to walk back toward my old garbage piles, when the frail old man approached me. He reached into his pocket. I knew it. He was gonna give me some cash.

He looked at me and asked, "Can you paint?"

I stuttered my answer. "Y ye ye yes, I can."

He took his hand out of his pocket and handed me five dollars.

"This is an advance," he said. "I have some old kitchen cabinets that I need painted. Is there a place that I can bring them, where you can do the work?" he asked.

Was he crazy? I was homeless. Anyone could see that. I thought about Mama's place. Then like a ton of bricks it hit me. Mama's place.

"Yes sir," I said. "There is an abandoned paint store just a few blocks from here. I could do the work there."

"I know the place," said the old man, "I will deliver the cabinets in the morning."

"I...I don't have any paint or tools," I said.

"I'll bring what you need," he said, "Don't you worry."

With that, the old guy turned and walked away. I looked at the five dollar bill he gave me, and on it was written, *Sam*.

I looked up in the direction of the man, but he was nowhere in sight. I was now worried that Mama would be angry with me. I had no right to agree to anything with regards to her home.

With eight bucks in hand, and the prospect of some work, I headed back to Mama's.

It was well after dark when I entered into the house. The kids were asleep, and Mama was in her chair, reading.

"I made you a small plate of dinner. It is on the table. There isn't much, but it should fill your stomach for tonight."

I ate it up in seconds as I was very hungry. Funny thing, it filled me completely. It even gave me a warm feeling all over.

"Thank you," I said. "That was the best meal I have had, in a very long time."

"You're welcome," said Mama. "How did you do today?" she asked.

Like all the children had done earlier, I handed her what I had.

She looked up at me and smiled. "Eight dollars, not bad. Maybe I can pick up a little extra food tonight when I go shopping."

I knew now, why she went out every night. First there was only the money of the day, second there was really no room for storage. The fridge was so, so tiny. But all in all, it was a good system.

I did worry about her going out alone though. I suggested that we go together. She agreed. The kids were safer here than out in the street, and besides, her system had worked well for a long time. She looked at the fiver.

"How is it you have a whole five dollar bill? Did you run into Rockefeller or something?" she asked, laughing.

It was the first time I had seen her laugh. She looked incredible. It seemed she was happy.

"No I said, just some old guy who said he has a little painting I can do for him. The five was an advance."

"A job!" she exclaimed. "My, I am impressed."

"Well," I said, "We will know for sure in the morning. He is supposed to bring the project here. I hope you're not angry..."

"Angry?" she asked with a big smile, "This was a paint store after all, it is very fitting. Maybe the boys will want to help."

"That would be awesome," I said, relieved that she was not mad at me.

We talked for an hour and I fell asleep in my corner.

At eleven o'clock, I woke up and went shopping with her. When we returned, I grabbed my blanket and went right back to sleep.

I was up before everyone. I was excited about painting the cabinets for the old man. Mama woke up second.

"Well that's more like the man I need around here," she said smiling. "How did you wake up before me?" she asked.

"I'm really excited," I said.

"So am I," said Mama. She turned the small knob on the camp stove and lit the burner. "I'll have breakfast ready soon," she said.

The children began to wake. Ben and Greg were the first up. I was going to tell them about the painting job, then I thought, what if the old man doesn't show up? Just then I heard a truck outside.

"That'll be for you Joe," said Mama beaming. Ben and Greg jumped into their clothes and followed me outside.

"Good morning sir," I said.

"My name is Sam," said the old man.

"Hello," I said, "My name is Joseph."

"It is very nice to meet you Joseph. I have the cabinets here, along with some paint and various tools you may need for the job."

Ben and Greg, and some of the other children, helped me unload the truck. We carried the cabinets and supplies into the building, and to a big room which was probably a showroom at one time. After the truck was unloaded, Sam and I shook hands.

"I'll see you in a few days," he said. "Do a good job."

"I will," I replied boldly.

Sam hopped into the truck left. I found it kind of odd, that someone trusted me, a homeless person, with a job, when they had no knowledge of me at all.

"Breakfast is ready," said Mama. I dismissed the thought and went to eat with my newfound family.

The children ate and finished their lessons. Ben and Greg, followed me into our new workshop.

All the others went out to forage in the streets. I remember hoping they would all have a good day, and bring home as much as they could.

Greg reached into a bag and pulled out some tools. "What's this," he asked?

"That is a scraper," I said. "We need to scrape off the old paint."

"Here are two more," said Ben.

We went through the tools and I explained to the best of my knowledge what each one was, and what they were used for. I found two old two by fours, and set three cabinets on them.

Ben and Greg watched as I began to scrape the paint.

"Can we do some too?" They asked.

"Certainly," I said, "Each of you take a cabinet and get to work."

We spent hours scraping the paint from the cabinets. There were fifteen in all. Mama brought us some water, and a small snack for lunch.

Usually, there is no one home at lunchtime except Mama. I think she gave us her food.

My hands had blisters and were sore. I said nothing, because the boys didn't complain, not even once. It was a long day.

As the other children straggled in, they came to see what we were doing. I guess it didn't look very impressive, as they each in turn, went back into the living area, and left us be.

When I heard Mama say dinner was ready, we set the tools aside, and went to eat.

When we finished, Ben and Greg wanted to get back to work. Tomorrow I said. We need to rest.

I fell asleep early, and woke as was usual now, to shop with Mama, and then back to sleep. In the morning when I woke up, Ben and Greg were already in the work room.

"What's next Joe?" they asked.

"Well boys, we need to get the cabinets as smooth as possible. When we paint them, we don't want any nicks or dings. We need to sand them."

Sam was smart. He had sandpaper and small sanding blocks to do the job right. I showed the boys how to sand.

"Always sand with the grain."

"What is grain?" asked Ben.

Greg's ear perked up. I think he too wanted to know the answer.

"Look at the wood," I said. "Do you see the lines in it?" They both answered yes.

"Okay," I said, "That is the grain. It is the age rings in the tree. When you sand wood, it is best to always sand with the grain. You see the long lines that go up and down the wood right, well that is the direction of the grain."

"Sanding it against the grain would take much more work to get smooth, and the wood will look ratty. This is most important when using stains. Stain sinks in, allowing you to see the finished wood. Paint covers the grain, and you don't see it, but it is much easier to sand smooth with the grain. It saves energy and time."

The boys and I sanded the cabinets down to bare wood. We used lighter sand paper at the end and they were smooth as a baby's bottom.

"I'm tired," said Ben.

"Me too," said Greg.

"Yea me three," I said, "We have done a lot of work in two days."

When the other kids began to filter in, they were not so quick to leave. The bare wood cabinets looked great.

They were all feeling the soft smooth wood. Everyone was beginning to get interested.

We ended the day as usual. Dinner, and conversation of the day's events. Stories from the streets, and now from our new workshop.

The third day, two more children stayed behind to help with the cabinets. I looked at Mama. She looked back at me. I was worried about food, and losing two more incomes was going to hurt.

She smiled at me, and nodded her head toward the shop.

"Okay kids, let's do this. First thing," I said, "is to prime them. Primer is used to help the paint adhere to the surface."

Next, I showed them how to mix the paint. Sam had brought four cans of all white eggshell finish. The brushes were made of synthetic fiber. They were great for water or latex based paints.

We had latex, so all was good. The kids and I painted the cabinets. Also with the grain, wherever possible. We gave them two coats.

With the extra hands, things moved along much faster now. When dinner came, we were finished.

As the kids entered the shop, you could hear the oohs and aahhhs. Mama came in to get us all for dinner.

"Very nice job," she said, "They look brand new."

Dinner was kind of light. Mama and myself forwent the meal, and let the children eat it all, so they were nourished. We would survive.

Mama and I went outside while the kids ate. I told her, now that we were finished with the cabinets, I would hit the streets in the morning, and take the others back out with me. Our project was finished.

I laid on the floor under my blanket wondering when Sam would return for the cabinets, and mostly wondering, how much he would pay us for our work.

I dozed off and slept. I dreamt of Mama's house. The front was bright pink with new paint. It looked wonderful. I saw Ben and Greg on ladders working hard trying to finish it before Mama got home. It was dark out. Mama was shopping.

I woke up and shook my head. I looked around and Mama was gone. She had gone shopping without me. I must have been really tired.

I suddenly thought of my wife and daughter. It was the first time in quite a while. I got that horrid feeling in my stomach.

I jumped up and out the door. I ran across the street and through the alley. Panic was setting in. I rounded the corner of the building, and there was Mama.

Startled to see me, carrying only one bag, Mama was done shopping and on her way home.

"What's wrong?" she asked. "You are all pale, as if you have seen a ghost."

I put my arms around her for the first time. "I was so scared," I said. "I woke up, and you were gone."

"You looked so peaceful sleeping," she said, "I just wanted you to get a full night's sleep."

"Thank you," I said, calming myself down, "But please don't do that again. I prefer to be with you when you are out so late at night. Remember-"

"I remember," she butted in cutting off my words. "But I refuse to live in fear of the past. I am protected," she said. "If you remember correctly, you were there to save me. What will be, will be," she said.

"If something were to happen to you, I would be lost."

"Ah," she said, "It is so nice that you care about me, but you would still have our children to worry about." She smiled.

I took the lone bag from her hand, and together we walked home. When we were inside and the food put up, I put my arms around her and just held her tight for a second.

She held me back, and it felt better than anything I could remember ever.

I said goodnight and went to my sleeping spot. I laid there awake all night. Once again, sleep was eluding me.

Light from outside was finally coming in through the window. It was time to get up. Even though I had not fallen back to sleep, I was not tired. I was ready to hit the streets.

Mama got up and fed the kids. There was enough for her and me too, although tonight we would go hungry.

There was extra paint. I wondered if I could sell it for some quick cash. That would get us dinner. After a minute or so, I dismissed the thought. It was not mine to sell. It belonged to Sam.

I walked a few blocks. All I could think of, was how wonderful it felt to be working in the shop with the boys. There was something special about working together. Maybe it was the camaraderie, or maybe just being in the company of good people. The feeling was indescribable.

Just then I heard a horn beeping. I looked up and sure enough, it was Sam.

"Hop in," he said. I jumped up and into the passenger seat. I hadn't been in a vehicle in over five years. It was nice.

"So," asked Sam, "How are my cabinets coming along?"

"We are finished," I told him.

"We?" Inquired Sam.

"Yes, we," I said. "Ben and Greg helped and then some of the other kids joined in."

"Well, what do you know," said Sam. "And how do they look?"

"Why not come see for yourself?" I said. I wanted the money. We needed it desperately.

We were at the house in minutes.

"This way Sam," I said. "We kind of made a work room inside."

As we entered the room you could have heard a pin fall into a pile of feathers. Sam was stunned. He had been a painter his whole life, and said he had never seen such a fine job.

"It was the boys mostly," I said. "I just led them a little."

"By the looks of these, I'm guessing you have quite a good crew," he said.

"Thanks Sam, I'll tell them you said that, that will make them feel great."

"Where are they now?" he asked.

A bit ashamed, I told him they were out panhandling. It was our only source of income.

"I am very impressed," said Sam. "Not only with the work you have done, but with your honesty." He reached into his pocket and gave me fifty dollars.

"I'll be by first thing in the morning," he said, "Make sure you have help to load the cabinets on the truck."

"I will," I said, "And thank you. What do I do with the extra paint?" I asked him. "There is a gallon and a half left."

"Let the kids clean up the place a little," he said, and he headed back into the truck and left.

Fifty bucks was not a lot for most, but for us it meant food, and we would eat. I stood in the workroom and looked around.

I wished we could do it again. It was great for the kids to learn a trade, and I was beginning to feel good about myself again.

I gave Mama the money. She smiled and told me she was going to go out for a while. I wondered where. I never saw her leave in the daytime before. After she left, I grabbed a brush and an open can of paint. I wasn't painting but a minute or two, when the door burst opened. It was Ben and Greg.

"What's the matter fellas?" I asked.

"It just doesn't feel right," said Greg.

"Yea," said Ben, "We want to work. We need to work."

"Grab a brush," I said smiling, "Mama is out, and it would be a big surprise for her to come home, and find this room all bright with new paint."

Before I could finish speaking, both boys had brushes in their hands, and were painting the walls alongside me. What a team we were.

We finished in no time, and it looked great. Ben and Greg did all the cutting in. Soon after, Mama came home. She had two full bags of food.

Greg and Ben took the bags, and Mama's eyes bounced from one wall to the next.

"It's beautiful," she said. "I can't believe it."

"You were gone a long time," I said. I was a bit concerned.

"I went shopping, and," she said proudly, "I went to the bank. I opened a savings account. I have a feeling we are going to need it."

I was puzzled. Why would we need a bank account? We were flat broke.

Mama began to make dinner, and the boys and I cleaned the brushes and put them back in the work room.

"Gee," said Ben, "It would be great to have a real job."

"Yes," said Greg, "I would love that too."

"You boys are young," I told them, "You'll get your chance."

The rest of the kids were back now, and Mama had prepared a feast fit for a king.

"This is for all your hard work," she said. "Every day, you all go out into the streets to help us to survive, and these past few days with this painting project, well, you all deserve far more than this."

"Thank you Mama," said the children.

"Yes," I said, "Thank you."

Sleep came easy. Even Mama got to sleep through the night.

I woke to the sound of beeping, of a truck backing up. I jumped to my feet and quickly woke the boys.

"Sam is here. We have to load the truck. Remember to be super careful with his newly restored cabinets. We don't want to mess up all that hard work."

I smiled. The kids were happy. Mama was happy. Even I was happy. Something magical was happening.

"Good morning to be alive," said Sam.

"Yes it is," I replied.

Mama, the kids and I, and Sam were all outside by the truck. Sam had a different truck this time. It was a much larger box truck.

"Joseph," said Sam, "I have a very important question to ask you."

"Yes Sam?" I said, "What can I do for you?"

He went on, "I was wondering if you would like to do another project for me?"

I looked at Mama. Her face lit up like a Christmas tree and she had the biggest smile I ever saw. I glanced around at all the children, and they too had a look of excitement written all over them.

When my eyes caught sight of Greg and Ben, I choked up and got tears in my eyes. Both had their hands folded like they were praying, and their heads were nodding up and down, as if trying to will me to say yes.

I thought of how little money we actually made. Then I thought of how wonderful working together had been for the kids. And me.

"Yes Sam," I said, "We would be honored to do any projects you could throw our way. I must be honest though, we do not pay rent, or belong in this place. We are trespassers. We could be thrown out at any time."

"I understand," said Sam, "I'll take my chances."

Everyone cheered. The excitement was overwhelming. It was like somehow, we had won the lottery or something. Just for the ability to work.

"Okay kids," I said, "Let's get the cabinets loaded."

"Hold on a minute," said Sam, "First we have to unload the truck."

"Unload?" I said confused.

"Yes," he said, "I thought you would say yes, so I brought over more supplies, and a few more items to be restored."

"Also," said Sam, "I brought some old tools that were my father's. He had quite a few stored in his basement and left them to me when he passed many years ago. It will be nice to see them put to good use again. I noticed your work room was rather large and empty," he said, "So let's fill it up."

Sam opened the truck. My jaw dropped. Greg and Ben each grabbed one my hands and said,

"Well, it looks like we have a little work ahead of us. Let's get moving Joe!"

We began unloading the truck. There was paint, brushes, primer, scrapers, drop cloths, sanding equipment, even ladders and poles for painting high places.

I turned to Sam, "Why the ladders and poles?" I inquired?"

Sam replied, "When you have leftover paint, you and the children can paint the apartment and the work shop too. It will be good for them to learn everything they can."

I smiled. Sam was a wise old man. It took almost two hours to unload the truck. He must have had fifteen full sets of kitchen cabinets in it.

After it was completely unloaded, we carefully brought out the refinished cabinets, and into the truck they went.

Sam had some nice soft moving blankets and covered and tied them down. He pulled the strap on the big truck door, and down it went.

Greg swung the arm latch into place, locking it up. We headed back inside.

"Everything is numbered," said Sam. "Start with set number one, then two, and so on. I will come every Thursday, and pick up the finished work."

"Alright then," I said smiling at him. I followed Sam back outside to the truck.

"Wonderful job," he said again. "I expect the same with all these as well."

"Certainly," I said, "They will be like new."

"Good," said Sam, "Oh and by the way, here is the final payment for this first project." He handed me an envelope.

"Thank you," I said, surprised. I had thought the fifty five he already gave me was it.

"I always pay COD," said Sam. "Cash on Delivery. And Joseph," he added, "You and those kids truly delivered a very fine product. See you next Thursday," he said and drove off.

I went inside to Mama. The kids were still in the workroom, looking over all the stuff Sam had brought.

They were so enthralled by it all, and I was in total amazement. I handed Mama the envelope. She opened it and smiled.

"I thought we might need that bank account," she said.

"Why, how much is there?" I asked.

She pulled out five crisp hundred dollar bills. I was stunned. Sam had paid us well. Very well.

Together, Mama and I decided not to tell the kids about the money, Mama just put it in the bank.

Once again we started working. No one went out into the streets today. We all worked. It was a miracle.

Ben and Greg were showing the others what to do and how to do it. They all learned fast. The days passed more quickly now than they had in years. Mama set the schedule. Each day three of the children stayed in the living area with her. They had lessons from after breakfast, until just before dinner, when we closed the door to the shop.

Of course, they and us, stopped for lunch everyday also. Mama made sure we did.

Sometimes the projects were just scraping, sanding, and staining. No paint at all. The children were fanatical with the detail they put in to their finished work.

Sam continued to come each Thursday. He took the finished items, and brought new stuff to be redone. Also, each and every week, he paid us a fair wage.

Mama went to the bank each week. She slowly bought some new clothes and shoes for everyone, including us.

She was as frugal as ever, never wasting a dime of our hard earned money. Other homeless children began to drift into our lives. We took them all in. As long as they followed the rules, (lessons, work, kindness and honesty), they could stay.

Sam, I later learned, had built one of the largest painting and finishing companies on the east coast.

When the children reached age 18, Sam offered them employment in his company, and even helped many to join the trade workers union. They became self-sufficient and full contributing members of society.

Ben was the first to leave our shop and join with Sam. He comes back on occasion, and works a day in the workroom, teaching and sharing his life experience with the new kids.

He talks a lot about how him and Greg, and the other kids, repainted the entire building and shop, in their spare time.

I remember those days. It wasn't even like work. We all had fun together, talking and laughing as we scraped, sanded, and painted. Sam had come once with a power washer, and the kids sprayed and cleaned the outside of the building.

Then they painted the trim. They did a fabulous job. The building looked great. I was always afraid we would be tossed out, but no one ever bothered us.

Mama even had the electric put on, when the kids were painting the upper floors and rooms. The kids all have rooms now. As always, they are required to keep them maintained and clean on their own. Mama's kitchen is fully equipped and functional. The money always goes to keeping up the place, and supporting our kids. They learn the trade, and most of them, when they leave here, go to work for Sam, and continue to build their lives, away from the streets.

I remember one night back before Sam passed, He told Mama never to worry about being thrown out of the building. He went on to tell her that it was his, left to him by his father.

Sam had arranged, that as long as it remained a teaching safe haven for homeless kids, for the place to be ours.

I remember the reporters coming and writing articles about Mama's operation for the homeless. She was even interviewed on television once.

Sometime after that, I received a letter from a lawyer, from where I lived before. It seemed my in-laws, had sued the hospital for negligence in the death of my wife and daughter.

They received a two million dollar settlement. They had apparently passed on a few years ago and left it to me. I guess the lawyer saw my name in an article or something.

The whole two million was still left. I, too, was now getting older and my health beginning to deteriorate. It was time for me to rest.

I bought a small two bedroom home, back in the country, close to where I had lived before, and gave the rest of the money to Mama.

Greg is at the helm now and is doing a fantastic job. He has a super business sense, a wonderful way with the kids, a really big heart, and has led many, many more out of life on the streets.

The kids learn and grow, and go from destitute poverty stricken street urchins, to full healthy functioning members of society. Many of these youths have even started their own businesses. And many still go to work for Sam's company.

Yes, laying here on the ground in the middle of the woods, just relaxing and looking up at the splendor of all that is good, is such a far cry from living on the filthy cold streets of the city, but I would not trade my experience for all the money in the world.

Thank you Sam, for renewing my faith in humanity.

Mama started a foundation with the money I gave her, solely for the homeless children's teaching center, and then she too, took leave and retired.

She moved to the country with a man in a two bedroom home. We only use one.

This story is dedicated to The Fromkin Brothers Company, and Family. Thank you for providing so many jobs and opportunities, for so many people. You have truly made a positive difference in the lives of many, and in the world. Keep up the great work. This story, although fictional, shares the vision and mission statement of a great company. Help yourself, by helping others.

Chinese Proverb: "You give a poor man a fish and you feed him for a day. You teach him to fish and you give him an occupation that will feed him for a lifetime." Thanks again. <3

Releasing the Soul
(Genre: Family/Fishing/Death)

The old man was lying in the bed, gasping for his last few breaths of life. His entire family was at his side, except his oldest son Robert, who was out on the lake fishing. His bed was in front of the window overlooking the water. He watched Robert fish.

Robert had spent most of his free time right here on the lake fishing with his dad. He couldn't bear the pain of his best friend dying. The family was angry with Robert for not staying at his father's bedside with them. What they didn't know was, an hour earlier, Robert's dad asked him to do him one last favor.

Get in the boat and go out on the lake and fish. So I can watch one last time.

Robert had looked at his dad, given him a hug and kiss, and left the house.

He rowed faster than ever to get to the best spot, where he knew his father could have the best view. His eyes were red and his cheeks stained with tears.

Robert looked toward the window, his heart being wrenched from his chest, and anchored the boat parallel with the house so his dad could see him clearly. He baited the hook and cast the line out. There was a small splash; as the bait and the small weights hit the water and began to sink.

Robert looked toward the window. He wanted his dad to pass from this life to the next happy and in peace. Fishing had always been his favorite of all things, and doing it with Robert was even better.

Robert had the pole in his hand when suddenly, he felt a bite. It was a really good tug. His dad saw the pole bend from his bed, and his eyes got wide in anticipation. He inclined his head ever so slightly in excitement.

Robert gave the pole a healthy jerk upward, setting the hook. The pole bent in half. Robert knew immediately it was big. He hoped his dad was still with him. Robert began to reel. The pole was bent hard and barely bouncing. This fish was strong. As he reeled, the fish pulled harder and the drag went zzzzzzzzzzzzzzzzzz.

Slowly, Robert tightened the drag and kept reeling. The fish seemed like it was coming in, but the water was deep, and so was the fish. It was going under the boat. Robert stood up and held the pole high and out over the side of the boat. He worried about getting tangled on the anchor line and losing it. He remembered, in that moment, everything his dad ever taught him about fishing. He reeled, and reeled, and the fish pulled even harder. After about ten minutes, Robert had the fish near the surface. He wanted desperately to get it into the boat so he could hold it up for his dad to see. It was a huge brown trout. It was the biggest Robert had ever seen in his life.

Then, with a flip of its tail, it darted back down into the depths. The fish was pulling the drag again, only this time even faster.

Robert continued to fight the fish. He again looked toward the window, hoping his dad was still with him. His dad was watching intently, and now the entire family was too.

Slowly, the fish began to tire. Robert was reeling, and gaining ground on the fish. It took another five minutes or so to get the fish to the surface and to the side of the boat. Robert sat back down, still holding the pole high. He reached for the net. It wasn't there. In his painful hurry to the water, he had forgotten it.

Robert had always used a net. His father however, many times had just reached in and lifted fish out by the gill.

Robert put his hand into the water, put two fingers under its gill, and lifted it into the boat. It was heavy. It felt, to Robert, about forty pounds. He removed the hook, and then stood up straight, directly facing the window for his dad to see.

After a minute or so, Robert lowered the fish with both hands into the water. He held it for a few seconds and then released him back into the wild.

The old man set his head back on the pillow, and with his last breath, said, *good job son.*

Robert again looked toward the window. A sudden gust of wind blew hard over the boat. The hair on the back of his neck stood straight up, goosebumps appeared on his arms, and a chill ran through his being. He knew in that second; it was over.

Robert sat back down in the boat, put his face in his hands, said goodbye, and cried.

Robert now fishes with his son. He teaches him all he can.

Thanks to Donald P Byrd for the inspiration.

The Stairway
(Genre: Death/Afterlife)

As my eyes gazed up along the winding sullen path, I saw a stairway made of rock, climbing high into the mountain tops.

It wound its way in and out through the nooks, and through the jagged stone walls. I could not see the top, as it was high up in the clouds. A figure cloaked in a black cape, was descending cautiously, as not to slip on the damp mossy surface of the cold hard stones; placed there by someone as steps, what must have been centuries ago .

Under the cape, I saw the shape of an extremely large man. As the figure got closer, I saw clearly the deep burned scars etched in his face. He seemed to me to be thousands of years old. I was frightened, but stayed my ground until he reached the spot where I stood.

"Greetings," I said, a bit uneasy. He lifted his hand slowly and stretched it toward me.

"Greetings," said the man, and we shook hands.

I looked deep into his hardened eyes. *I know this man,* I thought to myself. *I have seen him somewhere before.*

He began to speak, "I have waited many years for this moment," he said to me,

"I have waited for you, since you were just a boy." My tired old eyes filled with tears. I couldn't believe what was happening. It was my grandfather. But it couldn't be, he had died when I was seven.

"Welcome," he said to me.

He took my hand, and together we climbed the rocky stairway upward. As we neared the clouds, I became frightened.

I looked at him and asked, "Where are you taking me?"

"Be still," he said, we have a long journey ahead of us.

Once we entered the cloud cover, I might as well have been blind. I could see nothing at all. His hand tightened on mine, and we continued upward.

"Where are we going?" I asked. He was quiet. Here I was, a grown man, 78 years old, being led by my dead grandfather, to God-knows-where.

"I don't understand," I said, "You died when I was a child. I saw you in the casket. How is this possible?" He stopped walking and turned to look at me.

"Yes," he replied, "I remember you staring at me crying."

My parents and Grandma were killed in a car accident on the way home from the hospital when I was born. I survived the wreck. My Grandpa took care of me and raised me. We did everything together. He taught me everything. From eating, walking, and talking; to fishing and working in our gardens. We trapped animals for food too. Many times I remember helping him setting and emptying our traps. I was always at his side. I loved him. He was my mom and dad. He was my best friend. And then one day, it happened.

I had just entered the second grade. I enjoyed school, but I enjoyed being with Grandpa even more. Every day, Gramps would walk me to and from. We would always talk about our plans for life. All the things we were going to do together.

But this one day, when I came out of the schoolhouse, my Grandpa was not there to meet me. I walked the road home all alone. I remember being sad that he forgot me. It was the worst feeling I ever had.

When I got to our home, I found my Grandpa asleep on the floor. He wouldn't wake up.

I cried, "WAKE UP Grandpa, WAKE UP!" He didn't move.

I walked about a mile to the neighbor's house, and told them what happened. Grandpa and I would celebrate the holidays with them. They were a nice older couple, who had no family either. They put me in their car, and we drove back to Grandpa.

The Doctor said that Grampa's heart had given out. He had a heart attack. I did not understand any of it. All I knew, was that I wanted my Pop-pop back.

At the funeral, I just stood at the coffin staring at my Pop-pop, crying my eyes out. I was miserable. When we planted him into the ground, I thought maybe he would grow, like the seeds we planted in the garden together. He didn't.

The old couple wanted to take me in, but the state people said they were too old. So I was put in a foster home with people I had never seen before. They were alright I guess, but they were not my grandfather.

"How do you remember me crying?" I asked. "You were dead."

"Well my boy," he said, "Life didn't end when I died. It simply changed to another dimension of life. My spirit, like all the rest, is alive and at total peace. We cannot touch or interfere with our previous lives, but we are still here observing.

I watched you grow up. I remember just how bad you felt, on the long walk home from school, all alone, the day I died. I swore I would never let you feel that way again. So here I am. I have come to walk you, on your journey home."

"I don't understand," I said. Just then, we walked above the cloud cover.

The sky was brighter and bluer than ever before. There were people all over the place. We came to a group of people standing together. They were looking right at me smiling.

"I", said my grandpa, "Would like to introduce you to your Grandma, your Mom, and your Dad."

My head, heart, and soul exploded with such a profound love. One I had only felt glimpses of while alive. My eyes no longer had their sight. I just saw.

I could see and feel those I left behind, and those who left before me. I felt total peace. It was good. Everything was ok. No matter what had happened in life, or was happening now, it is all ok.

May you all find the peace and love that I have found, on your stairway to heaven.

Being Together

As we lay in the soft warm sheets covered with sweat, and drenched in the succulent nectars of our passion, I cannot help but to think of my enduring love for you.

My mind and soul emptied of every thought, leave the calm we share in each other's arms. Gently holding each other close, basking in the glow of our entwined bodies and hearts, and celebrating the joys of our intermingling climactic tenderness. To be one, together, for all eternity.

Walking in the moonlight on the beach. Holding hands, our naked feet massaging the warm sand for hours, as we ride the tide of love's most basic pleasure. Being together.

Sipping hot chocolate. Wine by the fire on a cold winter's night. Endlessly staring into each other's eyes, saying nothing, yet understanding it all. One love together, forever, never to part. Experiencing love's most basic pleasure, being together.

As I lay in the soft warm sheets, alone, all I think of is you. My destiny. From which direction shall you come? I will spend life's eternity, yearning to feel the awesomeness of being yours. With you, I'll find love's most basic pleasure.

Being together.

Note from Author: We all look for the perfect partners. Accept people for who they are, and work on being the best you can be. When you are working on yourself, love will find you. Peace, and Happy Holidays to all.

From Me To You

You came around when I was down,
lifted me, feet off the ground,
words unspoke there was no sound,
two souls in space together found,
a fight together, no fists to pound,
new love is formed, forever bound

You needed me, I needed you,
both in suffering is true,
in pics I saw so deep and true,
the love and strength inside of you,
it made me cry,
compassion through,
you needed me, I needed you.

Your eyes they sparkle in my heart,
never together, so far apart,
will one day come
I touch your face,
and see you dressed in white with lace?
The time will tell,
the story true,
you needed me, I needed you.

And when ours souls co-mingle so,
I hate the time when we must go,

empty, sadness, lonely, grow
it's only you I want to know.
In my heart for you to see,
I needed you,
you needed me.

Sunsets

The reason the sun setting is so warm and romantic, is because that is when the sun kisses the land, and we get to see it together.

The sunrise in your eyes melts my heart, and the full moon with you would kill me. Hiding together on rainy days, would just drive me insane.

It's you my soul longs for.

Yes you.

You!

Only you.

The Healing
(Genre: Life)

If you have never read a story written by me, or never read another of mine for the rest of your life; I implore you to read this one.

Sometimes in life, we can be made to feel really bad about ourselves, and our whole psyche is brought down to the lowest possible places. I am here to share a story with you, a true story, that I hope will help all of us to break the chains of shame and guilt; and be lifted back to the highest level that life has to offer.

We are all products of life's journey, continually being sculpted and molded, every second, of every day. Each and every interaction we have encountered from birth to this very moment, has formed us into the people we are right now.

We cannot, in reality, go all the way back to our births and start over. We can, however, start today to open a new avenue of growth and change, by sharing the truth about ourselves and how we came to be.

Hi, my name is Mike. I am just like you. I am one of billions of people living on this planet, looking for love, good health, peace and prosperity.

Who am I? I am a sixty year old husband, father of six, union floor layer, with enough dysfunction for everyone.

My passions include; harmonica, guitar, music, fishing, canoeing and rafting, camping, growing, canning, drinking, and, as of the last two years, writing short stories. My kids and Grandkids go without saying.

My financial life has always been one of playing the catch up game. Well, now that you know a little about who I am now, let's dig in a bit to see how I got to this point in life.

My earliest memory is that of being abused. When we think of abuse, don't get caught up in what kind; abuse is abuse. No matter if it's physical, sexual, or mental, they all play the same major role in forming our minds and emotions.

Some people drink too much, while others eat to oblivion, and still others turn to drugs. Many pushed by the shame and guilt become workaholics. Some strive to be the best in the world for others to see, as to hide the real them. And still others never get past it at all, and turn inward and invisible. Even bullies; they portray an image of outer strength, while dying inside. I was mentally and sexually abused.

I was a very soft and meek child who never liked confrontation of any kind. I still don't. I became a very outgoing person. No one knew what I really thought of myself. I was nothing. Well, maybe a piece of shit. That was the lowest thing I could think of myself. Growing up, I had questions of sexuality. There was some experimentation in my teen years. Guilt and shame were the strongest forces forming my being. Society had its so called normal standards. Yea right, "normal".

I always felt out of place. I know now that it was because I felt so insecure inside. My parents were good, moral people and raised us okay.

But looking deeper, there was a lot of mental abuse there too. I began drinking and smoking pot when I was around ten. It made me feel better than I really felt, but just until I was sober again.

Just like stuffing food in your mouth, the highs wore off fast, but my inner feeling were always still there.

When I was in my early twenties, my father died. My mom found God. Soon, she had me hooked too. I became a young holy roller.

Soon after, I found AA. It took some time, but eventually I began to share my feelings in the meetings. I got sober, and even quit smoking. I was getting high on the meetings. They called it a pink cloud.

It, like all the other highs, wore off and back to feeling down I went. Bouts of depression have plagued me my entire adult life. I could go months sometimes feeling up, but then like a ton of bricks, boom, down I went.

I met my loving wife when I was around twenty five. We got married two years later. We had six children together. During the time they were growing up, all my attention was on work and taking care of them.

The depression was kept pretty low during that time. When it did raise its ugly head, I smiled my way through the best I could. I know, it affected all those around me and left impressions on their growing psyche as well.

It seems dysfunction, no matter how small, has outward ripples, which if not addressed, can turn into waves in another being.

The Dr. said I had a chemical imbalance. Yea right, nothing they gave me worked to create a proper balance. Appointments and pills was their bullshit answer. I don't mean to bash, as they do help some, just not me or anyone I know.

It took a while, but I finally realized a few things which actually did help me. In AA when we shared our stories with others, I felt better. The more honestly I shared, the lighter my soul became.

I didn't need drink, or pills; I needed to share the stuff that was like a giant rock on my shoulders, making me ill.

Maybe that is where the idea of confession came from. When I was young and told my sins to a priest, it may have helped, but not enough. When I share openly with others, I get the best results.

When I share with people, they have two options. Either laugh at me and belittle me, or find compassion and empathy. I've found more times than not, people shared their story right back with me. It was the most freeing experience of my life.

I remember once, at a speaking commitment in AA, sharing from the podium about being molested as a boy. When the meeting was over, there was this large circle around me. Half the room, wanting to share back. I shared all my deathbed secrets. I am free.

I am no longer afraid of anything in my life. Although I do still have bits of depression now and then, it is minimal to say the least. I have never felt better emotionally in my life.

In the past two years, out of nowhere, I have begun to write little stories. I laugh and cry with emotion as I write them. Lots of people reply that they too, laugh and cry when reading them.

To end this simple, let me say, share your stories with your loved ones and others. We all need to share in order to heal.

I'd rather share my painful dirt with a million people, then keep it inside, and feel that crushing in my soul.

Peace to you all, and may you find the strength to stand tall and free.

Your friend, Mike

The Adventures of Mya & Jordan
(Genre: Children's Stories/Family/Adventure)

The Adventures of Mya & Jordan
Volume 1
Pop-pop's Helpers

Once upon a time there were two young children named Mya and Jordan. Jordan and Mya were brother and sister. They lived far away from their Pop-Pop, who loved them more than candy. Pop-Pop had gardens of food and fruits that they could eat whenever they wanted. He also had chickens too, and the two young siblings loved to play with the feathery animals.

One day while Jordan and Mya were playing in the back yard, Pop-Pop fell asleep in his chair under a shady tree. While Pop-Pop slept, a small red fox sneaked into the yard and was trying to get into the chicken coop to eat the chickens.

Mya heard the chickens making a clucking ruckus and said, "Hey Jordan, something is going on in the chicken coop!"

The two of them jumped up at the same time and began to run towards the coop. When they got closer, Jordan saw the fox. Being the best big brother a girl could ask for, he stopped Mya and told her to stay where she was, because she was safe there. Then, he continued to the chicken coop. When he got there, the fox was trying to dig under the wire fencing.

Jordan grabbed a long stick and approached the fox. "Go away, fox!" yelled Jordan, "These chickens are our friends!"

The fox looked right into Jordan's eyes. His heart sank a bit with fear, but then he stood up straight and ran directly toward the fox, swinging the stick back and forth to scare it away. But the fox didn't budge, and instead began to dig again.

Jordan thought for a moment and then he had a plan.

"Mya," Jordan called to his little sister.

"Yes Jordan?" Mya replied. "What do you want?"

"I need you to go by the little pool and fill the water guns, so we can shoot the fox and save Pop-pops chickens" said Jordan.

Mya ran to the small pool. She picked up the squirt guns and stuck them under the water. When they were full, she plugged the ends and ran as fast as she could to the side of coop where Jordan was waiting.

"Okay," said Jordan, "when I count to three, we start shooting the fox."

Mya looked at Jordan with tears in her eyes. "But Jordan," she said, "the fox is so cute. I don't want to hurt it!"

"But," said Jordan, "these are only water guns to scare him. They won't hurt him."

"Even so," said Mya, "I don't want to scare him either."

"Well then, what do you suggest we do?" he asked.

"I don't know," she pouted, but then she got an idea. "Wait, if he's trying to eat the chickens, maybe he is hungry. Let's give him something else to eat and maybe then he'll leave the chickens alone."

"Okay," said Jordan. "Let's go see if Pop-Pop has anything we can feed him with." The two children scurried up the deck stairs and into the kitchen. Immediately, Mya saw Sparky's bowl. Sparky was Pop-pop's lazy old dog.

"Jordan," said Mya, "we can feed the fox Sparky's food!"

"Alight," Jordan replied, "let's see what happens."

Jordan opened the cabinet and grabbed a clean bowl. Mya got a cup from the cupboard, stuck it down into the food bag, and used it to fill the bowl.

The door flew open and they were down the stairs and back to the coop in no time at all.

Mya placed the bowl on the ground as near as she could to the fox, which had by now almost dug completely under the fence. The fox looked into Mya's wide eyes, and she stared back intently at the clever animal. She said to it, "This food is for you, Mr. Fox."

The fox smelled the food and it seemed he was interested in exploring the bowl to see what it was. In a few seconds the little fox was eating Sparky's dog food from the bowl the children gave him. He gobbled it all up in just a few minutes, and then the fox slowly walked closer to where Mya and Jordan were watching him from. He rubbed up against their legs like a cat and then dashed away into the wooded lot next to the garden.

Just then Pop-Pop woke up, stretching his arms and legs with a big yawn. The kids told Pop-Pop of their wonderful adventure with the chickens and the fox.

"We saved the chickens!" Jordan said proudly.

"And" Mya added, "we made a new friend!"

"Sure you did," said Pop-Pop with a grin. "You are the best little helpers Pop-Pop ever had. I love you both so much." He kissed them on their foreheads. "Okay," said Pop-Pop, "after that adventure, I bet you two are hungry like the fox. Let's go have dinner, and you can tell me the whole story again and again."

And they did, again and again.

The Adventures of Mya & Jordan Volume 2 Berry Picking With Pop-Pop

As their car pulled into the driveway, Jordan was already working on getting out of his car seat. Summer was the best time to go to Pop-Pop's house. Just as the key turned to off, Jordan hopped from the car and dashed toward the backyard. You never knew what was happening at Pop-Pop's. He was so excited to find out, that he forgot about his mom and Mya in the car.

"JORDAN!" yelled Amanda. Amanda was Jordan and Mya's mom. "Get back here right now young man."

Jordan quickly scanned the yard with his sharp eyes and saw that nothing was happening out there, so he turned to go back to the driveway, near his mom and little sister.

Ding-dong, ding-dong, ding-dong, ding-dong…

"Okay," said Amanda, "that's enough ringing the bell."

"But Pop-Pop can't here so well," Jordan argued. "We have to make sure he knows we're here."

Just then Pop-Pop-pop-PED out the door and said with a big smile, "What a great surprise it is that you have come to see me today! I am going to pick berries to make jam, and I could use all the help I can get."

"I'll help!" bellowed Jordan happily.

"Me too!" Mya said excitedly. "We love picking berries!"

"Yes, you do," said Pop-Pop. "You both love eating them too," he laughed.

"Okay then, Dad, I'm gonna take mom shopping while you all pick berries," said Amanda.

"Alrighty-then," said Pop-Pop. "We have a lot to do kids so let's get hopping."

While Amanda and Grandma pulled out of the driveway, Mya, Jordan, and Pop-Pop, went to the shed and got some small containers for the freshly picked berries.

As the kids and Pop-Pop were picking berries (eating mostly), Pop-Pop said he needed to sit and rest. In seconds, he was fast asleep in his chair. Mya and Jordan were getting full from eating all the berries and decided to just pick the best ones for Pop-Pop to make jam.

Working their way down the line of berry bushes, Mya heard a noise on the other side of the bush. "What was that, Jordan?" she asked.

Jordan, being taller than her, could see and knew just what it was. "Take my hand Mya," said Jordan.

"Why, what's wrong?" she asked.

"There is a big black bear eating berries on the other side of the bush," said Jordan. "We need to slowly and quietly walk away."

Without another word the children began walking further down through the yard toward the horse barn down back because the bear was between them and the house.

The bear heard the children and let out a big growl. Hearing that big loud growl, Jordan said, "We have to save Pop-Pop. If we both start screaming maybe the bear will follow us, and we can run fast and get away too."

Mya and Jordan began yelling louder than they ever had before. "Here we are bear, come and get us if you can!" Then they ran again. They ran fast and hard. They ran so fast and so far that they did not recognize where they were. Ut-oh.

"Where are we, Jordan?" asked Mya.

"I'm not sure, Mya," he replied, "but we can't be too far away."

"Which way do we go?" asked Mya, feeling more scared now being lost than she was of the bear.

"I don't know," said Jordan, "but I think I know a way to figure it out. Let's be very quiet and listen to hear Bok-Bok, Pop-Pop's biggest and loudest rooster. We can follow the sound."

"That's a great idea," said Mya, and the children stood perfectly still and quiet. After a couple of minutes, sure enough they heard a crow.

"Yes," said Jordan, making a fist in triumph. But just then they heard another rooster from another direction, and then yet another.

"I guess many people have chickens and roosters around here," said Mya.

Jordan and Mya were both afraid now. Being lost is so scary, especially in the woods. All of a sudden they heard a noise, a rustling in the leaves and sticks on the forest floor.

"The bear!" cried Mya.

"No, Mya, it's not the bear," said Jordan. "It's just a fox."

"That's not just a fox," said Mya. "That's the same fox that tried to get Pop-Pop's chickens the last time we came here."

"Ya know Mya, I think you are right. It has the same white spot on his head."

The fox came close to the children, turned slowly, and then started to walk away. He turned his head back to look at them, and then continued on.

"Jordan", said Mya, tugging on his sleeve, "I think we should follow him."

With nothing to lose, the children followed the fox. In a short time Jordan was seeing some familiar sights. Then they saw the old horse barn.

"Phew, we made it back," said Jordan.

"I hope the bear is gone and Pop-Pop is okay," said Mya.

As Mya and Jordan reached the top of the hill behind the berry bushes, there was Pop-Pop, still asleep in his chair. The bear was nowhere in sight and old Sparky was wagging his tail. "Pop-Pop, Pop-Pop!" cried Mya.

Pop-Pop's eyes opened and he let out a big yawn. "So how many berries did we pick?"

Jordan and Mya grabbed a hold of Pop-Pop and gave him a great big hug. "Wow," said Pop-Pop. "I guess you two really love picking berries. Next time, maybe we can pick some plumbs and pairs. Mya and Jordan looked at each other and just smiled.

As Mya, Jordan, and Pop-Pop walked up to the front of the house, Mommy and Grandma were just getting home from shopping. Everyone helped bring in the bags, and put away the groceries. Mya and Jordan looked out the back window, and to their surprise the little fox was sitting at the edge of the wooded lot, near the garden.

"Pop-Pop," asked Mya, "may I put a bowl of Sparky's food outside?"

"What on earth for, Mya?" asked Pop-Pop.

"Just say yes, Pop-Pop," said Jordan. "I'll explain it to you later."

The Adventures of Mya & Jordan Volume 3 A Day With Grandma

Part One

It was a warm summer's day, the sky was blue, and the grass was greener then I've ever seen before. Birds were playing in the puddles from last night's rain, and the sun's rays were feeding warmth and energy to all God's creatures. The rabbits, chickens, deer, the fish. Cats and dogs everywhere were enjoying the sunny summer day.

"I'm hot!" moaned Jordan.

"I am too," said Mya. "Maybe Mommy will bring us to Grandma and Pop-Pop's house and we can go swimming in the river."

"That's a great idea, Jordan," said Mya with a big smile.

They liked going to Grandma and Pop-Pop's house. It was fun there.

"Mom," said Mya in her cutest voice, "can we go to Pop-Pop's and go swimming in the river?"

"Hmmmm," said her mom, Amanda, "That sounds so good on a day like this."

So they loaded up the car and off they went.

As they pulled into their grandparent's

driveway, Mya and Jordan were looking at all the pretty flowers growing all over.

"Strawberries!" shouted Mya, as she looked at the side garden by the driveway.

"Oh man!" said Jordan, "They are huge!"

Their seat belts flew open as soon as Amanda put the car into park, and out jumped Mya and Jordan. Right into the strawberries. The peaches were growing, apples the size of quarters, black berries, raspberries, and blueberries were growing all over.

Grandma came outside so surprised to see them. "Oh wow, how great!" she said. "You guys all came to see me?"

"Yes," said Amanda.

"And we came to go swimming too," said Mya. "It's really hot out today. Where is Pop-Pop?

"Oh goodness," said Grandma, "Pop-Pop had to go to work. They needed a couple of extra men at the shop, and he went in to help out for today."

"Come give Grandma a big hug," said Grandma.

Both Mya and Jordan looked up at Grandma, their faces and hands already stained red from the big juicy strawberries. Mya jumped up and squeezed Grandma real hard, leaving two little red hand prints on Grandma's butt. Jordan just kept picking and eating.

"Well," said Grandma, "let me get some towels and floaty toys and we can go."

"I have to run a few errands, Mom," said Amanda.

"That's fine," said Grandma. "The kids and I will be fine."

"Okay then," said Amanda. "I'll meet up with you at the river a little later on.

"Bye Mommy," said Mya and Jordan.

Amanda hugged and squeezed them both. "I'll see you soon. Take good care of Grandma you two."

"We will, as always," said Jordan.

The river was very close to Grandma and Pop-Pop's, but the long bumpy dirt road through the woods and cornfields made it seem far. As they drove through the fields, they saw all kinds of little critters. Squirrels, geese, tons of chipmunks, and even a few deer crossing back and forth from field to woods and back again, eating the corn and carrying it back to their nests to store for the winter.

Finally they reached the clearing near the water. They were the only ones there. That was surprising as it was really hot out and this was the favorite place of all the local folks. Jordan, as always, was leading the way down the short path to the river edge. There was no sand; only millions of soft rounded rocks.

"I remember Pop-Pop said once that the water, when it was real high, would cause the rocks to tumble downstream, making them oval and round by bouncing off each other and chipping off tiny pieces," said Jordan.

Grandma carried the kid's towels and a folding chair for herself. Mya and Jordan were playing in the water.

"Not too far out," said Grandma.

"I know," said Jordan. He turned to his little sister, "We need to stay close to shore so we don't get pulled in too deep by the current."

"Okay," said Mya, not really listening to him. The water was the perfect temperature. It was a little cooler than outside and it felt great.

Jordan and Mya were picking small rocks off the bottom of the riverbed and trying to throw them across the river. Then all of a sudden Jordan skipped a rock off the top of the water. "Hey Mya," he said, "did you see that? The rock bounced off the water!"

They both tried hard to make it happen again, but it wouldn't work.

After a short time in the water, Mya and Jordan joined Grandma on the rock beach. Grandma was relaxing in her chair in the warm sun and they both laid near her on their towels.

"The sun feels really good doesn't it, Jordan?" Mya asked.

"It sure does," said Jordan.

All of a sudden, Grandma started to snore. Just like old Pop-Pop, Grandma fell asleep.

Jordan heard a noise up on the riverbank,

right at the edge of the woods, nearest the cornfield. "Did you hear that, Mya?" Jordan asked.

"No," Mya replied. "All I hear is Grandma snoring."

They both laughed, and then began to scan the bank with their sharp little eyes. Suddenly, Jordan saw something move around a big oak tree.

"Right there, Mya," said Jordan.

Mya looked toward the tree and jumped up to her feet. "It's a little Indian boy!" she said. "Pop-Pop told me once that, long ago, the Minisink Indians used to live here along the river."

"Maybe they still do," said Jordan.

Just then the boy disappeared.

"Grandma is sleeping," said Mya. "She will be okay here. Let's go find him, Jordan."

Jordan led the way up the bank and into the cornfield. The corn stalks were taller than them and they could not see anything.

"Follow me," said Jordan, and he went back to the edge of the cornfield to the woods. "Give me a boost, Mya."

Mya put her hands together and boosted Jordan up to a low branch in the tree. Then Jordan stretched his arm and grabbed the next branch with his hand. Then his foot, then his hand, and another branch. Jordan was climbing his first tree.

When Jordan stopped climbing he was so high he could see the whole cornfield.

"What do you see?" Mya asked from below.

Jordan looked hard across all the tops of the green cornstalks. When his eyes reached the middle of the cornfield he was stunned at what he saw. "It's a teepee," he shouted down in excitement. A tee-pee is the Native-American name for a tent, and it is made with sticks, cloth, and animal skins.

"Oh wow!" said Mya. "I knew he was a real Indian boy!"

"Jordan used the biggest, highest trees to mark the direction they should walk through the cornfield to find the teepee. As long as he could see the trees from the ground he knew he could get very close to it. He climbed back down to Mya and then began walking in the direction of the teepee. After about ten minutes, they came to a small cleared circle in the corn, and, sure enough, there was the teepee.

"Hello," said Mya.

"Hello," said Jordan. "Is anyone here?"

No one answered.

"We should look inside," said Jordan.

"No," said Mya. "It does not belong to us." Mya was always the voice of reason.

"Yea, I guess you are right, Mya," said Jordan. "Maybe we should go and get Grandma."

The children turned to go back the way they came, and right there in front of them was the little boy.

A Day With Grandma – Part Two

The boy looked into Mya and Jordan's eyes. Mya and Jordan were looking directly back at him.

"We saw you by the river bank," said Mya. "We wanted to find you and be friends.

"Yes," said Jordan. "We want to be friends."

"I wish the same," said the boy. "My name is Running Rabbit." Running Rabbit got his name from his father, Chief Wasincharge. When Running Rabbit was born his father left the teepee and saw a running rabbit, and bam....that was it. Running Rabbit became the little boy's name.

"I am Jordan, and this is my sister Mya."

"I know," said Running Rabbit. "I have been sent to you, by the Great Spirit in the sky.

Mya looked at Jordan, "I don't understand."

"I think he means God," said Jordan.

"I," said Running Rabbit, "was chosen to watch over you and your families."

"Like a guardian angel?" asked Jordan, now all excited.

"You look kind of familiar," said Mya. "I don't think we have ever met before, but still I feel like I know you somehow.

"Perhaps," said Running Rabbit, "you remember me from your Pop-Pop's chicken coop when you fed me." Running Rabbit smiled. "Or maybe when I was eating berries near you and scared you both by mistake. Sorry for that by the way. Then I had to lead you back home to safety."

"You?" asked Mya. "You are the fox and the bear?"

"Yes," said Running Rabbit. "I am supposed to protect and help you without revealing my true self." Running Rabbit then turned to Jordan, "And yes, I am your guardian angel."

"We need to hurry," Running Rabbit said suddenly, turning his attention in the direction of the river. "Your Grandma is in danger."

The children followed Running Rabbit back toward the river. They talked on the way.

"Do you remember," said Running Rabbit, "that when you got to the rock beach, that there was no one else there?"

"Yes," Jordan replied. "There is usually a bunch of people swimming there on hot days like today."

"Well," said Running Rabbit, "the river was closed by the State Forest Rangers for today. There is a big damn up river on the Mongap

Reservoir. They are releasing all the water to repair damage on the damn, from the heavy rains last night. They must have forgotten to close the cornfield road."

The children were moving as fast as they could through the tall green cornstalks.

"Are you sure we are going the right way?" Mya asked.

"Yes, Mya," said Running Rabbit. "I grew up right here with my entire tribe long ago. I know this land very, very well."

"What will happen when the damn is opened and the water is released?" asked Jordan.

"A big wall of churning, crushing water will rush down the river, ten feet high and washing away everything near the water and riverbank."

"GRANDMA!" screamed Mya and Jordan at the same time. They ran faster than ever before.

"Hurry, Running Rabbit!" said Jordan.

"Yes, hurry faster!" said Mya.

The children came to the small clearing where the car was parked. Jordan jumped down the river bank path and saw Grandma. Mya was right behind him. "Grandma! Grandma!" cried the kids. "Wake up, wake up!"

Just then a car was speeding down the dirt road. Amanda heard about the dam release inside the General Store on her very last errand. The car came to a skid in the dirt clearing and she hopped out. By then, Mya and Jordan had Grandma's hands and were pulling her up the path.

"Into the car," said Amanda hurriedly. "We don't have much time."

Just then they all heard a thundering wave, crashing and swooshing, coming down the river. Jordan and Mya wanted to look but there was no time. Amanda put the car into drive and up the hill they went. At the top, they stopped and watched the wall of water flood the river. Like a big wave in the ocean it crashed right on the rock beach where they were swimming.

"Holy moly!" said Jordan. "We got out just in time!"

"Where is Running Rabbit?" asked Mya. She was worried about her new friend.

"Who is Running Rabbit?" asked Amanda, looking at Grandma.

Jordan immediately spoke up. "Oh, Running Rabbit is our make believe friend." Jordan remembered that Running Rabbit was not supposed to reveal his true angel self.

As the water began to settle down and the flood was going back down, Amanda backed the car down into the clearing. They all got out and hugged each other so hard.

"How did you know there was danger?" asked Amanda.

"The children," Grandma replied. "They started screaming for me, and then pulled me up the hill to safety."

"How did you know?" repeated their mom.

Jordan looked at Mya and she winked at him. "A little bird told us Mommy," she said. "Yes," said Jordan. "A little bird."

"We'd better be going," said Grandma. "I'm glad the water didn't reach my car."

Jordan and Mya got into Grandma's car, she had the car-seats. Amanda put her car into drive, and Grandma followed her back up the dirt road through the woods and past the cornfield. Mya and Jordan looked intently at the cornfield but did not see Running Rabbit.

As the cars pulled onto the main road, something in the sky caught Jordan's eye. He looked at Mya and pointed up. Mya stretched her head close to the window and looked up. There, flying high in the sky over the cars, was a bald eagle. Mya smiled at Jordan and asked, "Do ya think?"

"I don't think," said Jordan, also smiling. "I know."

Both children let out a sigh of relief and relaxed. Tired from the excitement and wonderful day, they fell fast asleep right there in the car. When they got to Grandma and Pop-Pop's, Amanda lifted them up and put them in their car, where they slept the entire ride home.

The Adventures of Mya & Jordan Volume 4 Playdate at Pop-Pop's

Part One

Sparky scratched on the chicken coop door.

"Who is it?" said a low squeaky voice.

Pop-Pop turned his head toward the chicken coop. "I must have dozed off," said Pop-Pop to himself. "I must be dreaming."

Again Sparky pawed at the door.

"Come in," said another tiny little squeaky voice.

The door opened and Sparky dashed in. Pop-Pop jumped to his feet to see. "Am I going crazy, did I hear the chickens talk? Did they open the door for old Spark to get in?" Pop-Pop began walking down the deck stairs very slowly. Sparky came out the little sliding door into the chicken run and looked up at Pop-Pop, wagging his tail happily. Pop-Pop continued down the stairs. He was a little afraid. He never heard chickens talk before.

Pop-Pop walked across the lawn and around to the big door on the chicken coop. He listened very carefully, but the chickens were only squawking. Pop-Pop reached for the handle of the door and gave it a quick jerk, opening it up fast and wide.

"SURPRISE! SURPRISE!" yelled Mya and Jordan, hopping up and down and dancing all around.

Pop-Pop jumped into the air. It took him a couple seconds to catch his breath. "You scared the heck outta me."

Just then, Kenny came around from the front of the house. Kenny was Mya and Jordan's dad. "Hi there, Pop-Pop," he said. "The kids wanted to surprise you, so we parked the car up the road a little, and, well, this was their idea."

Pop-Pop and Kenny laughed.

"That was a surprise alright," said Pop-Pop to Mya and Jordan. "I thought I was going crazy."

"Sparky knew," said Jordan.

"I see that," said Pop-Pop. "Where is Amanda?"

"Amanda went in the front door and is with Grandma," said Kenny.

"Let's all go inside," said Pop-Pop.

"Amanda and I were hoping that maybe you and Grandma would watch the kids while we go out and have some Mom and Dad time today."

"That sounds great," said Pop-Pop, as he looked at Jordan starting to doze off on the couch. "Aunt Jenn is bringing her kids here today too." Aunt Jenn was Amanda's sister. She has three children; Lilly, Christian, and Jeremiah, whose nickname is Jay.

"Did ya here that, Mya?" asked Jordan.

"Yes!" she said. "We're gonna have a playdate at Pop-Pops! Oh boy, I can't wait!"

"Well look who's finally here," said Pop-Pop, looking out the window with a big smile.

Mya and Jordan ran down the stairs and out the front door as fast as their little legs could carry them.

Playdate At Pop-Pop's – Part Two

"Stop, Jordan!" yelled Jay from the car window. "There is a bear on the side of the house!"

Mya stopped dead in her tracks, turned, and ran right back in the house. Jordan was already halfway to the car so he just kept going. Aunt Jenn grabbed up Jordan and pulled him into the car.

"Pop-Pop!" screamed Mya, "there is a bear outside. He is gonna eat Jordan!"

Pop-Pop laughed and hurried to the door. He saw Jordan safe in the car and began to walk slow and carefully to the side of the house nearest the woods. As he rounded the corner, he saw a big black mother bear and her two young cubs. The cubs were very small and couldn't have been more than a month old. The mother bear looked at Pop-Pop and slowly walked toward the front of the house with her babies following behind. Pop-Pop backed up and said quietly, "Everyone stay where you are, and watch." As they all looked on eagerly, the momma bear and her cubs walked right out in front where everyone could see them. The cubs were jumping on each other playing and couldn't care less about anyone watching them.

"Awe, they are so cute," said Lilly. "I want to pet them."

"Me too!"

"Me too!"

"Me too!"

"AND ME Too!" yelled Mya out of the house window.

Pop-Pop just smiled. The bears ever so slowly walked out of the yard and turned up toward the woods. After a short time they were gone. "Okay everyone," said Pop-Pop. "It is safe to come out now." Pop-Pop explained to the children that the mother bear is very protective of her babies, and if she feels threatened in any way, she will attack to save them.

"Well enough about the bears," said Pop-Pop. "Everyone come give me big hugs."

"Hey, Jordan," said Jay. "What are we gonna do today?"

"I'm not sure," Jordan replied. "Let's see what Mya, Lilly and Christian want to do."

The kids all talked for a while and decided to ask to go to the pond so they could feed the ducks and play. The pond was just down the street, and behind the pond was all woods.

"Pop-Pop," said Mya. Mya was always the one to ask Pop-Pop to do stuff. He could never say no to her. "Can we all go feed the ducks today?"

"Hhhmmmm," said Pop-Pop. "I think we could do that."

Mya looked up at Pop-Pop with her big brown eyes and a smile from ear to ear. "We would like permission to go by ourselves. We will be good, we promise."

Pop-Pop thought for a moment. He thought about the bears and direction which they traveled off. "Okay kids," said Pop-Pop. "The bears went the other direction from the pond so I think it would be okay to let you all go together. Remember the buddy system. Everyone stays together. You are always safer in a group, rather than being alone."

The children all agreed to stay together.

Grandma looked at Pop-Pop. "Amanda is going to be mad at you for letting them go alone."

"They're not alone," said Pop-Pop. "They have each other. They will be fine. I remember playing all over town when I was a kid."

"We'll see," said Grandma.

Finally the children reached the pond. Grandma had given the girls some old stale crackers and bread to feed the ducks with. As soon as the ducks saw the bread bag, they began to waddle toward the kids.

"Me first," said Jordan.

"No, me!" Jay argued.

"Lilly," said Mya, "boys have no manners."

"Girls go first," said Lilly.

Christian, being the youngest, was quiet. He was smart.

Jay pulled the bag away and ran toward the pond. The ducks and the kids all chased after him. As he reached the edge of the water he tripped and went head first into the pond.

"Ha ha," said Mya. "That's what you get."

"Yea," said Lilly.

Christian and Jordan were just standing there laughing very hard. "That was the funniest thing I ever saw!" said Jordan.

"The water is warm," said Jay. "We can all go swimming."

"We did not ask about swimming," said Mya with a worried look on her face. "Pop-Pop will not be happy. It is dangerous."

"But we are all together, and that is what Pop-Pop," said argued Jay.

Jordan was in the water in the blink of an eye. "Jay is right," he said. "As long as we are all together, we are safe."

The girls and Christian sat down on the grass and just watched the boys swim. All of a sudden, they heard a big splash at the wooded end of the pond. They could not see anything back there. Then another big splash. Mya stood up to see if she could see anything, but the woods were very thick. She did see that the water was starting to bubble like water in a pot on the stove. The bubbling was spreading across the water toward Jay and Jordan.

"Jordan!" screamed Mya. "Get out, get out now!"

"Get out, Jay!" yelled Lilly.

Playdate At Pop-Pop's – Part Three

Just then, from under the water, hundreds of little baby painter turtles emerged from the dark murky water, and were all around the boys. Jordan laid his hand flat in the water and two of the turtles swam right on it. "Oh they are so cute," he said.

Jay was still scrambling his way out of the pond. The turtles were freaking him out. "Get them off, get them off!" he cried.

Lilly, Christian, and Mya, just laughed and laughed.

"The turtles won't hurt you Jay," said Jordan. "They just want the bread that you fell in the pond with."

Sure enough, Jordan was right. All the baby turtles were eating the tiny bits of bread and crackers floating in the water. Jordan slowly worked his way out and up onto dry land. They watched the turtles feeding in a frenzy. As soon as the bread was gone, the babies quickly disappeared back under the water.

"I wonder where they came from," said Lilly.

"I think they came from back in the wooded end of the pond," said Jay.

"Yes," said Mya. "That must have been the bubbly looking water we saw coming toward us."

"Let's go investigate," said Jordan, already walking in the direction of the woods.

"But, but, the splash, the big splash," said Christian. "Those baby turtles didn't make that splash."

Lilly thought for a moment, then said, "And there were two big splashes."

"More the reason we should go and see," said Jordan.

"What about Pop-Pop?" asked Mya.

"We are all together," said Jay. "Now let's go while it is still light out."

The kids began to walk around the pond toward the dark woods. Jordan was first, then Jay, Mya, Lilly, and Christian. As they got closer to the woods, the pond was slowly turning swampy. The path they were on was now soggy and wet. Each step they took began to get scarier and scarier. The trees blocked the light and it was getting darker and darker too.

"Quiet," said Jordan. "I heard something."

Everyone stopped and listened.

"What did you hear?" asked Mya.

"I'm not sure, but it sounded like something big stepping on leaves and sticks further back in the woods."

"Maybe it's the bears," said Mya. "We should turn and leave right now."

"No," said Jay. "We have to keep going. We need to see what's back there."

The children all continued their journey forward, deeper into the woods. The path was now just wet and muddy. Each step they took, their little feet sunk into the mud up to their ankles. It was late in the day and the sun was heading down. The woods were getting darker and scarier than ever.

"Let's go back home!" whined Lilly.

"Yes," said Mya. "Let's go home."

Christian was really afraid, but did not say a word. He was following the big boys.

"Pop-Pop said we have to stay together," said Jordan, "and we are almost to the end of the pond." Jordan turned back toward the dark and began to walk again.

SPLASH SPLASH** SPLASH**

The girls screamed. Christian's eyes were closed tight, and Jay and Jordan...

Playdate At Pop-Pop's – Part Four

... and Jay and Jordan just froze in their tracks. Water splashed over them all.

"What did we do?" asked Jordan.

"I'm sorry," said Jay.

When they wiped the water from their eyes, they looked into the dark water but saw nothing. There was dead silence. No one made a move. Suddenly, Mya spotted a little red fox watching them from the other side of the pond. It made her heart feel easier hoping it was her old friend, Running Rabbit. "Look," she said, "the fox!"

When the children turned to look, the fox was gone. What they saw instead were the three bears; the momma and her two babies climbing out of the water on the other side. "Whew!" the kids all sighed with relief.

"I think we are safe," said Jordan, "but it is dark out and we better get home. Pop-Pop and Grandma must be worried sick by now."

As the children turned to go back, something very big was swimming toward them from the street-side of the pond. The water was churning and bubbling.

"Maybe it's the turtles again," said Jay.

"I don't think so," said Jordan. "Everybody run. Run now! Lead us out Jay, I will stay in the back of the line to keep us safe."

Jay's feet sank deep into the mud. So did everyone else's. The water level was rising and the kids couldn't move fast at all. They watched in horror as the water churned toward them, and then it past right by. Foot after foot and one step at a time, the children trudged through the mucky mud. Lilly and Christian lost their shoes in the mud, but they just kept moving toward the road.

"There it is again!" yelled Jordan.

"There's what?" asked Mya, frightened.

"The sound of something walking in the woods," Jordan replied.

The children listened.

"Oh my God!" screamed Mya. "Something is coming to get us! Move faster Jay, we have got to get out of here now!"

Everyone was moving as fast as they could. The creature in the woods was also moving faster. Then splash, right behind them.

"AAAAAAAAAAAAHHHHHHHHH!"

They all started screaming. It stood up in the water very tall but it was so dark they could not see what it was. Then the thing walking in the woods jumped out and roared real loud.

"RRRROOOAAAARRRR!"

The children were now moving much faster as the path was back to dry land, and no more mud. It was so dark that they could not see anything and Jay ran right into..............Pop-Pop. "It's Pop-Pop!" he yelled.

Everyone screamed to Pop-Pop, "Save us, save us!" Then the thing in the water came close. It was Uncle Jonny! He had on his black wet suit and his snorkel.

"Hi guys," said Uncle Jonny with a big grin. "I have been watching you the entire time. Pop-Pop asked me to sneak into the pond from the back end. The first splashes you heard were me. The others were the bears."

"What about the creature in the woods?" asked Jordan.

Just then, Uncle Ben popped out. "Ha, I was keeping an eye on you from the woods. I, too, was here all day," he said smiling.

"Grandma has a nice warm dinner waiting for us," said Pop-Pop, "so let's get going home."

"Pop-Pop," said Mya, "I'm sorry we listen very well."

"Well, Mya," said Pop-Pop, "and the rest of you too. You did all stay together and that is what I wanted. I was up the road when Jay fell in, and I just kept my distance to let you have some fun."

"It was scary," said Lilly, holding tight to Pop-Pop.

"Yes," said Mya. "It was scary."

"Yea," said Jay.

"But it was fun Pop-Pop," Jordan added.

Christian just smiled and was happy to be safe. Uncle Ben and Uncle Jonny laughed. Being little was such fun. This reminded them of when they were little.

Everyone finally reached the road. Uncle Zacky-Poo was waiting there with his big truck and everyone climbed in. They were home in a minute. The children all changed into dry clean pajamas and sat at the table to eat.

"So," said Grandma, "did you all have fun?"

"Yes, we had fun," said Mya, "and we learned a good lesson too. Next time we go feed the ducks, that's what we will do. No exploring, right Jordan? Right Jordan? Jordan?"

"Jordan," said Grandma, "it's time to wake up. Wake up little one. Mommy and Daddy are here to pick you up."

Jordan opened his eyes. "Where am I," he asked.

"You fell asleep on the couch as soon as you sat down," said Grandma. "You have been sleeping all day. Mya and I made cookies."

"But we were at the pond. All of us," said Jordan. "Me and Mya, and Aunt Jenn's kids; Jeramiah, Lilly, and Christian."

"You know Aunt Jenn doesn't have kids," said Grandma. "You must have been dreaming."

"But it was real," said Jordan.

"Well, Jordan," said Amanda, "I have some news for you. We just found out that Aunt Jenn is pregnant. She is going to have a baby."

"Wow!" said Jordan.

"Really?" asked Mya.

"Yes really," said Amanda.

"Okay kids," said Kenny, "let's give Grandma and Pop-Pop great big hugs and get moving. We have a long drive home."

"I love you!" yelled Mya, waving from the car window.

"Me too!" yelled Jordan from the other window.

Amanda and Kenny waved too as the car pulled away. Pop-Pop and Grandma waved back.

We love you all too. See you next time in............The Adventures of Mya and Jordan.

The Adventures of Mya & Jordan Volume 5 The Adventure At The Zoo

Part One

"Pop-Pop and Grandma live close to here, right mom?" asked Jordan inquisitively.

"Yes," said Amanda, as she made the last turn toward the zoo. "They live just over the mountain."

"Mom, Mom, that looks like Max in the parking lot!" said Mya.

"It is!" bellowed Jordan. "And there's Ayla too!"

Ayla and Max are Mya and Jordan's cousins. Aunt Kim is Max's mom, and Aunt Alex is Ayla's mom.

Amanda parked the car. Max and Ayla were already opening the doors to greet their cousins. "Hey guy's, you made it," said Jordan."

"Yea we did," said Max.

"We would never miss a chance to come to the zoo," said Ayla. "We love it here!"

As everyone was saying hello, the moms unloaded from the cars what they needed for the day inside the zoo. The zoo has a big fence all the way around it, and the only way out is the same way you go in. So going back to the car for lunch later would be too, too far.

"Okay everyone, hold hands," said Aunt Kim as they crossed the street.

"What does that sign say, Mom?" asked Ayla.

Alex read the sign out loud for everyone to hear. "Space Farms Zoo and Museum, Wantage, New Jersey." The zoo is located in the heart of rural Sussex County. It is surrounded by woods and farms. It is one of New Jersey's most peaceful areas. The perfect place for such a beautiful zoo.

The main entrance opens into a huge room, with an eating area, a snack bar, a gift shop, and the whole building is also a museum. It has very old toys, tools, Native-American artifacts, and stuffed animals all over. There is a stuffed Kodiak bear right in the middle, and it is the largest bear I have ever seen. Then there is the door to the inside of the zoo.

"I want a hotdog," said Max, holding his tummy like he was starving.

"Me too," said Jordan.

I want to buy souvenirs," said Mya.

"I want a nice Space Farms Zoo shirt," said Ayla proudly.

Their moms all laughed. "We can look around in here after the zoo," said Amanda. "And we already have our lunch. You boys will just have to wait."

One by one, the lady at the register stamped their wrists with the little blue zoo logo.

"That lets you go in and out all day," said the lady.

"Okay gang, here we go." said Amanda. "On the other side of that door..."

"Wait!" said Jordan, loud and excited, "We need to get bags of food to feed the animals!" Ayla smiled at Jordan, holding up a huge bag with many little bags of food inside. "Oh, okay," Jordan chuckled. "Just making sure."

"Alright," said Amanda, "on the other side of that door is the zoo. Remember the buddy system. Stay together."

With that, Max pushed the door open. Of course all four kids tried to squeeze through the door at once. "One at a time," said Aunt Kim. In just a few seconds everyone was out the door into the zoo. The sky was blue and the sun was shining bright. The grass was green and all the trees were full of life. There were birds everywhere. There were ducks and chickens running around wild and lots of other funny looking birds too. First they came to a small petting area. There were baby goats, baby sheep, and even baby pigs.

"Wow!" said Ayla. "This is already my favorite part."

"But we have just started," said her mom, Alex, laughing.

Naturally, the kids lead the way. Jordan held the small map of the zoo in his hand.

"Holy moly!" said Mya, "Look at those bears!"

Max backed up a little, somewhat frightened as he remembered the bears by Pop-Pop's house. Jordan and Ayla were right up against the fence. If they could have gone inside, they probably would have. It's a good thing there are two fences around the more dangerous animals. They all slowly walked the paths, looking at the animals along the way. There were deer, lions, tigers, monkeys, bison, pigs, horses, groundhogs, raccoons, more bears, pea cocks, kangaroos, and so much more.

About half way through the zoo, they laid out the blankets on the ground and set up for their picnic lunch. It was a good time to rest their legs, and go to the bathroom.

"So much for the boys being hungry," said Kim, watching the boys playing and running about. Mya and Ayla ate fast and were right up with the boys. Alex, Kim, and Amanda continued to sit, eat, and talk while the children were roaming around.

"Look guys," said Jordan. "That big tree has a hole in it!"

The four kids again, just like at the door, all tried to crawl in at once. "Get out!" yelled Jordan. "I found it, I will go in first." Mya, Ayla, and Max, backed up a little. All of a sudden Jordan was getting pulled into the hole and down under the tree. Max grabbed hold of Jordan's foot, but then Max was also being sucked inside. Ayla and Mya each grabbed one of Max's feet. Then swoosh! All four of them were sucked down into the hole.

Note: Space Farms Zoo and Museum Spring opening is April 1st.
https://www.spacefarms.com/

The Adventure At The Zoo – Part Two

The kids were sliding down a dark tube-like tunnel. It was a sliding board roller coaster. Up and down and all around. Twisting and turning, the children screamed into the darkness as they plummeted downward. Finally, the tube reached the bottom of the hole.

Jordan was the first to slide out, followed by Max, Mya, and Ayla. It was pitch black and they couldn't see anything.

"Okay," said Jordan, "everyone calm down. Stop the screaming and crying. We are all okay. We need to find a way out of here."

"But how?" asked Mya, still whimpering a bit. "It's too dark."

"Everyone be quiet," said Jordan. "Maybe we can hear something from the zoo."

The children all were quiet and even held their breath so they could hear better. Ayla heard a noise. "Did ya hear it? Did ya here it?" she asked all excited.

Suddenly the noise was louder and they all heard it. It was a low moaning sound.

"It sounds like a monster," said Max.

"Don't be silly, Max," said Mya. "There is no such thing as monsters."

"Yea," said Max, "then what is it huh?"

Again they heard the sound.

"It sounds like a hurt animal or person," said Jordan.

"Yes, that is what it sounds like," said Mya.

"It's a monster," said Max again.

"Let's follow the sound," said Jordan. "Maybe we can find a way out. Everyone put your right hand on the shoulder in front of you. I'll lead the way."

Ayla put her hand on Jordan's shoulder, Mya put her hand on Ayla's, and Max put his hand on Mya's. Jordan used his left hand to touch the side of the tunnel wall. As they walked, he could feel the wall and keep them from hitting into anything.

The closer they got to the sound, the more frightened they became. Jordan stoically continued to move forward in the darkness, leading his sister and cousins, hoping to find a way out of this place. The walls were wet and slimy. The air in the tunnel was warm but smelled like dirty diapers and old wet newspaper. Musty and dank.

Jordan noticed his arm was stretched out all the way from the wall. The tunnel seemed to be turning to the left. Then the wall was gone. Jordan stopped and looked to his left to try and see where the wall went. His hand felt the end of the wall and he felt that it was a corner. "The tunnel turns left," he said. Jordan turned and began to walk again, his hand firmly sliding in the slime. "Up ahead," he said. "I see light!"

"Yes, it is light!" said Ayla.

Mya and Max sighed with relieve. Maybe this was a way out.

The moaning sound had stopped and the tunnel was now much more visible. Light was coming in from small cracks in the ceiling and walls. They took their hands off each other's shoulders, as they could all see well enough to walk safely.

Suddenly Jordan smiled.

"What, Jordan?" asked Mya.

"Yea, why are you smiling?" asked Ayla.

Max could care less about Jordan smiling. There was no monster, and that made Max very happy.

"I," said Jordan proudly, "have the map the lady gave us when we came into the zoo. I put it in my pocket. Maybe this tunnel is on it." Jordan reached into his pocket and pulled out the map. After unfolding it, he searched for the tunnel. "It's not on here," he said. Then as he began to fold the map back up, he noticed a small section of the map said history. He began to read.

"Well?" said Max.

"Yes, what does it say?" asked Ayla.

"It says wait a minute until I read it," Jordan replied.

Mya looked at her big brother and smiled. "Yup, that's my Jordan."

After a minute or so, Jordan said, "Bad news, there is nothing about the tunnel written here. But, I do see on the map the path we were on makes a sharp left turn, right near where we had lunch. So if the tunnels follow the paths on the map, we can follow them down here and find the way out."

The children began walking again. Max, Ayla, and Mya, were much more relaxed now. There was some light, and some hope. And they had a great person leading them. Jordan, too, was feeling a bit more at ease. His idea of the tunnels following the paths was a good one.

Following the map, the children continued through the tunnel. The cracks in the ceiling were now gone but still every little while there was just a hint of light shining through.

"Look," said Mya, "stairs."

On the side of the tunnel were black metal bars going from the floor upwards into the darkness. Jordan climbed the stair-like metal bars. When he reached the top, there was an old wooden door. He heard noises above the door. He listened very intently. Jordan was hearing people outside in the zoo. "It's a wooden door and I can hear people outside," Jordan yelled down.

Mya, Ayla, and Max, hugged each other in joy.

"We are saved!" sang out Ayla.

Max just looked up trying to see Jordan.

Jordan tried to push the door open. It was too heavy, although he did move it a tiny bit. Jordan thought for a moment. "Maybe if we all climb up and push...No, that won't work," he thought. "There is only room enough for me. I'm going to try and call for help," said Jordan.

"Yell as loud as you can!" Ayla encouraged him.

"Yes," said Mya. "Very, very loud!"

"HELP, HELP US! We are in here!" All of a sudden there was a loud thumping noise on the other side of the door. "HELP, HELP!" yelled Jordan again. The thumping turned into a real hard scratching sound. Kind of like Pop-Pop's dog, Sparky, on the chicken coup door, only a hundred times stronger and louder. And then it came. "ROOOAAARRR!"

Jordan's heart sank. He knew that sound. BANG, SCRATCH, "RROOOAAARRRRR!" It was a door to the lions' cage. Jordan scrambled back down the stairs. The big cat was ripping at the wooden door fast and hard with its huge razor like claws. "RUN! RUN!" yelled Jordan. "RUN!"

The Adventure At The Zoo – Part Three

The children were running down the tunnel as fast as they could. When they finally stopped, they were in complete darkness again.

"I don't hear the lion anymore," said Jordan. "Maybe he gave up."

The kids were all huddled tight together. They were again safe, but in the pitch black of the dark tunnel. Mya started to cry. Ayla joined right in.

"Okay, alright," said Max. "We don't need any of that."

"We'll be okay," said Jordan. "We ran a long way! We have to be closer to the end of the path by now." Suddenly the low moaning sound started again. Somehow it was still in front of them. "Let's get moving," said Jordan. "Hands on shoulders."

Each of them grabbed the shoulder in front of them, and Jordan, with his left hand on the wall, moved forward. Mya was afraid again. So was Ayla and Max. Jordan was also worried, but knew he must be strong for the others.

The sound got louder and louder, but the children kept moving bravely ahead. Jordan saw a small bit of light up in the distance, and this pleased him very much. For some reason, the light always seemed to make things a little easier. And less scary.

As they approached the light the sound was really loud, but there was nothing there. "It's the wind!' exclaimed Jordan. "It's the wind."

"The wind?" Mya asked.

"Yes," said Jordan. "You know how at home during the storms, when the wind blows and howls like a monster?"

"Yes," said Ayla, Mya, and Max.

"Well you feel the wind right?"

"Yes," they all replied.

"It is blowing through the cracks where the light is," said Jordan, "just like a great big whistle."

"That is it! You are so smart, Jordan," said Ayla.

"No," said Jordan, "you all would have known too."

Once again feeling at ease, Jordan said with gusto, "Okay guys, let's find the way out of here!" Jordan took out his trusty map. While his eyes searched over the map, his brain was working hard. "We left the lion's cage, which is here on the map," he said, pointing with his finger, "and we stayed in this direction. If I am right, and the tunnel follows the path, we should be real close to another left turn."

With that, they started to walk again. About fifty feet ahead was another crack in the ceiling, with the dim light. And it looked like another one just ahead of that. As they reached the first crack of light, again there were metal bar stairs.

"I have an idea," said Jordan. "I'll climb up this one, and maybe we can get out here."

"No, Jordan," said Mya, pleading with him. "It could be another lion, or worse."

"I have to, Mya," said Jordan. "We need to find a way out."

Jordan climbed the stairs. The thought of another lion or maybe a bear frightened him, but he continued to the top. Instantly, Jordan knew where he was. "Ooh ooh ooh, eee eee eee, aah aah aah." They were at the monkey cage. He climbed back down and looked at his map. "Just as I thought," said Jordan. "Look, here we are at the monkey cage. If we can get to the main entrance building, which is here, maybe there is an exit from the tunnel. They must use the tunnels to get to the cages when the weather is really bad outside."

"I hope your right," said Ayla.

"It sounds great to me," said Max.

"Me too," said Mya.

"Okay," said Jordan boldly. "We have a plan."

They walked about a hundred feet and sure enough, another left turn.

"We are almost there," said Jordan.

Everyone was now happy and excited. Max was smiling from ear to ear, Ayla was humming a happy tune, and Mya was wiping tears of joy from her face.

As they walked down the tunnel toward the main entrance of the zoo, the tunnel was getting wetter. "We must be close to the big pond by the building," said Jordan. "That is probably where the water is coming from."

Mya and Ayla started to complain about the water.

"My feet are getting wet," said Ayla.

"Yes," said Mya. "This is gross."

Max liked water. It didn't bother him one bit. Jordan didn't mind either.

The further they went, the deeper it got. The water was now up above their knees and they girls were scared. Then suddenly, the next step Jordan took, he fell into deep water.

"Stop!" yelled Max.

The girls stopped and Max helped Jordan out of the water. The happy feelings went back to sad and afraid. They were at a dead end.

"Jordan," said Max, "pull out that map." Jordan took the map out of his pocket. Max and he unfolded it carefully. It was all soggy and already falling apart. "There is the main entrance," said Max. "It should be right in front of us."

Jordan and Max both thought for a minute.

"Do you think it is under the water?" Jordan asked Max.

"I believe it is," said Max.

"I will dive in and search," Jordan volunteered.

"No," said Max. "You stay with the girls. You have gotten us all the way here. It is my turn to help."

"No, Max," said Ayla and Mya. "No one is leaving. Remember the buddy system."

"We can do this together, Max," said Jordan. "We will find the way out and come back for the girls."

Max dove in first with Jordan right behind him. They opened their eyes under the water and looked at each other, then they gave each other a thumbs up and swam deep into the water. The two boys swam and swam. Just about out of breath, they saw a bright light. They both swam hard and fast right toward it. Jordan surfaced first, with Max just seconds behind him. They were at the end of the tunnel. They climbed out of the water and stood in front of a big old wooden door. There was a light over the door just like at home. There were no windows and they could not see inside.

Jordan knocked on the door hard. "Help us!" he yelled loudly, but no one answered.

Max turned the handle and it was unlocked. Slowly he opened door. There was no one inside. The room was empty, except for a piece of rope on the floor. It had two closed doors on either side of the room. "We need to investigate," said Jordan.

"We must be in the basement of the entrance building," said Max. "We have found our way out. We need to get the girls."

"You're right," said Jordan. "Let's go back and get them. They must be so scared by now."

Max grabbed the rope and tucked it into his pocket. The boys left the room and dove into the water.

Ayla and Mya were still standing in the water. The boys did not know it, but the water was now waist deep, and rising fast. The girls were going to dive in, but, after all, the boys never came back. Mya and Ayla were holding each other tight and crying.

"Maybe we should head back into the tunnel," said Mya.

"That's a good idea," said Ayla. "If the boys do make it back...oh Mya!" cried Ayla. "Jordan and Max!"

Just then, the boys' heads popped out of the water. "We found the way out!"

The girls pulled the boys from the deep water and hugged them. "We thought we were gonna die," said Ayla.

"And we thought you died too," said Mya.

"Never," said Max. "Not while Jordan and I are here. Let's do this."

"I'm gonna count to three," said Jordan. "On two, everyone take the biggest breath you ever took and hold it. On three we dive in together."

"Wait," said Max. He took the piece of rope from his pocket, stretched it, and rubbed it up and down on a sharp piece of the stone wall. The rope cut into two pieces. He gave one to Jordan and he kept the other. He looked at Mya and Ayla and said, "If either of you gets in trouble under the water, grab and hold the rope." With that, he and Jordan each tied the rope around one of their ankles.

"Good idea, Max," said Jordan. "Okay, are we ready?" Everyone nodded yea. "Okay, one, two, three!"

Splash!

The Adventure At The Zoo – Part Four

They all hit the water with arms and legs flipping and flapping. Down under the water they went. They swam deeper and deeper holding their breath. When they were about three-quarters of the way through, Mya was tired and losing her breath. Ayla too. All of a sudden Jordan felt a tug on his leg. So did Max. Ayla grabbed Jordan's rope and Mya was holding tight to Maxes. The boys used all the strength they had to help pull the girls along. Both Ayla and Mya were also kicking their legs and using one free arm to help.

Just as before, the boys were just about out of breath and bam, there was the light. They surfaced as fast as they could and brought the girls to the top also. Jordan pushed Ayla up onto the dry dirt and Max pushed up Mya. "We made it," said Jordan. "Good job everyone."

After resting for a few minutes, and taking off the ropes, they stood up and went to the door. Looking back, Max noticed the water was rising on this side as well. "We better hurry Jordan; the water is still rising."

Again Jordan knocked, and again no one answered. He turned the door handle and they all went in. Max went to the door on the left and opened it. It was only a closet. "The other door must be the way out." Jordan opened the door. It opened into a long hallway with doors on both sides. There were hundreds of them.

"Oh," said Mya, "which one will lead us out?"

Max listened closely by the first door. He didn't hear anything, so he opened it. "It is an animal stall," he said.

Jordan opened a door on the other side off the hall. "This one is a stall too."

Then Mya and Ayla opened two more doors. "Stalls," they said.

"This must be where the animals stay during the winter," said Jordan.

The children began running up the long hall opening door after door, only to find stalls. The last door was on the right side of the hall. The children stopped and listened. It was quiet. Just another stall they thought.

"My feet are wet," said Mya.

"Mine too," said Ayla.

"Oh no," said Max. The water is still rising. This door better not be a stall too." With that, he burst through the door, only to find another long hallway of doors. He let out a moan.

Jordan was now looking at the wall. He saw a line on the wall all the way down the first hall. It reminded him of the river by the cornfield where Mya and him met their friend Running Rabbit. "I wish Running Rabbit were here now," he thought.

Right at that exact moment, a ground hog ran out of one of the stalls. "It must have been hiding under the straw," said Max.

"Perhaps," said Jordan, his mind still thinking of his old friend.

The groundhog ran up the second hallway.

"Let's open the doors quickly," Ayla suggested.

"Good idea," said Max.

Jordan looked at Mya. "Mya, should we open the doors, or follow that groundhog."

Mya's eyes opened wide and goosebumps covered her all over. "Follow the ground hog!" Mya screamed. "It is Running Rabbit."

The children all ran up the second hall following the groundhog. Ayla and Max were confused. "Max," said Ayla, "that's not a running rabbit; that's a running groundhog."

As the children ran up the hall, their legs began to tire. At the end of this hall, it turned right, and another long hallway of doors. The groundhog was almost to the end of that hall when the kids turned the corner.

"My legs," said Mya.

"Mine too," said Jordan.

Ayla and Maxes legs also were getting very tired.

"We are going up hill," said Jordan. "That's why our legs are so tired." The floor was dry and no water was in sight. They stopped to rest.

"Okay," said Jordan, "let's start moving again."

It took a while to walk the many long hallways, and they were all the same. All were long, all had animal stalls, and all were heading slowly upwards. Finally, at long last, the hallways came to an end. It was a T-intersection. They could go right or left. There was only one door in each hall, and that was all the way at the end.

"Use the map, Jordan," said Ayla.

"The map was too wet to refold," said Jordan. "I left it in the tunnel." Jordan thought for a minute and then said, "We have turned left all through the tunnel. We have turned right all through the hallways of stalls. We are going back to the top. Go right," Jordan proclaimed with confidence.

The children all went to the right. They had been in the halls for quite a while now. They were all dry. It took just a few minutes to reach the end of this hall.

Mya opened the door. It was the outside! In fact, not only was it the outside, it was the entrance to the small shed, right by the bathroom, by where they had lunch. Looking past the tree with the big old hole, they saw Alex, Kim, and Amanda. They were packing up the picnic.

"Ayla," called Aunt Alex.

"Max, honey," called Aunt Kim.

"Mya and Jordan, let's go," said Amanda.

"Here we are. Here we are!"

The children ran to their moms and threw their arms around them.

"I missed you so much, Mom," said Ayla.

"Mom, you have to check this out. We got sucked down into a tree into tunnels under the zoo," said Max.

Mya and Jordan grabbed Amanda and squeezed her tight. "Thanks for being our mom," they said.

"Alright everyone," said Amanda. "Let's hop to it. It's getting late and we have to finish our walk around the zoo."

As they finished their walk down the path, they stopped and looked at the snake pit.

"Ewe!" said Mya and Ayla.

Jordan and Max climbed up on the wall to see better.

"Look," said Jordan. "There's a wooden door."

"I'm sure glad you didn't open that one," said Max.

"Me too," said Jordan laughing.

Last but not least they hit the swings for a few minutes.

"Why are you guy's not going on the sliding board?" asked Amanda.

The children looked at each other and all at once said, "We have had enough sliding boards for one day."

They all walked toward the exit door of the zoo. The same one they came in.

"I'm starving," said Max. "What about that hotdog, Mom?"

Mya and Ayla just wanted a shirt that said Space Farms Zoo and Museum. Not that they would ever forget. Jordan wanted only one thing. He wanted a new map.

"What happened to your old one?" asked the lady.

Jordan smiled. "I lost it," he said.

The woman handed him a new one and he put it right in his pocket. "Can we go upstairs in the museum, Mom?" he asked.

"Not today, Jordan," said Amanda. "It is getting late and we have to get home."

Outside the door Amanda, Alex, and Kim had the kids all sit on the big stone lion and took some pictures.

"Okay," said Aunt Kim, "everyone hold hands while we cross the street."

They got to the cars and said their fair wells. As they pulled out of the parking lot, the cars all had to stop. There was a big groundhog crossing the road. I swear it turned and winked at all the kids. Jordan and Mya smiled. They all waved goodbye, and off they went.

I hope you had a great time at the Zoo today, and I will see you the next time in...The Adventures of Mya and Jordan.

The Adventures of Mya & Jordan Volume 6 Hiking With Pop-Pop

Part One

"I'm tired," said Mya.

"Okay," said Pop-Pop. "We can stop here and rest a little while."

Jordan was happy to stop. He was tired too. After all, they had been hiking for hours now. Very early this morning, about an hour before sun up, Pop-Pop, Mya, and Jordan packed a small lunch, some snacks, a couple bottles of water, and headed out on foot to the Appalachian Trail for a hike to Sunrise Mountain so they could watch the sun rise. It was now at least ten in the morning, and they had not yet reached the pavilion on the top of the mountain.

"Please pass me some water, Jordan?" asked Mya.

Jordan handed his sister the water and a snack to boost her energy. "If I am this tired, Mya must be exhausted," he thought.

"Alright," said Pop-Pop, "time to get going again."

"Pop-Pop?" asked Jordan. "I thought we were going to see the sun come up from the mountain, but the sun has been up for a long time now. And you said it was only a short hike but we have been walking for hours."

Pop-Pop looked at Jordan. Pop-Pop had a strange look on his face. Then Pop-Pop smiled and said, "Yes, it's only a short hike." Then he turned in the direction from where they had come from and said, "Let's go."

"Mya, I think something is wrong with Pop-Pop," said Jordan with concern. "I think he is lost."

"We already went that way, Pop-Pop," said Mya.

Pop-Pop looked around, then he looked at Mya and Jordan. "Who are you two?" asked Pop-Pop. "Where are you taking me?"

Mya and Jordan just looked at him. They were frightened. Something was wrong with their Pop-Pop.

"It is us. Mya and Jordan."

"Oh yes," said Pop-Pop. "I remember you now. Let's get moving so we can see the sun come up." Pop-Pop turned to walk and collapsed onto the ground.

Mya and Jordan rushed to Pop-Pop's side. "Pop-Pop, Pop-Pop, what's wrong?"

Pop-Pop's eyes were open but he didn't say anything.

"He is still breathing," said Mya.

The kids put the knapsack under Pop-Pop's head.

"I need to go find help," said Jordan.

"But how? Where?" said Mya. "We are in the middle of the forest."

"I will hike back to the fire tower we saw this morning. Maybe someone is there now," said Jordan. "You can stay here with Pop-Pop and take care of him."

Jordan grabbed one of the bottles of water and headed back down the trail.

"Bye Jordan. Say safe," said Mya.

"You stay safe too, Mya. I'll be back with help soon. Do your best to help Pop-Pop," said Jordan as he turned and began to run down the path.

Mya was frightened, but she had to care for Pop-Pop. She got a water bottle and put the open end in Pop-Pop's mouth. He took a sip, then another. "Try and rest, Pop-Pop," said Mya. 'I will watch over you." Pop-Pop closed his eyes. He took a deep breath and then he fell asleep. Mya sat right next to Pop-Pop. She was scared and sad.

Hiking With Pop-Pop – Part Two

As Mya was caring for Pop-Pop, Jordan was hurriedly trotting down the trail heading toward the fire tower. The forest was full of animals. He saw squirrels, birds, a rabbit, two deer with a new baby fawn, and a small black snake. Jordan just kept running. All he could think of was something's wrong with Pop-Pop, and his little sister Mya is all alone in the forest with him.

Jordan stopped to rest by a small stream. He watched the water trickle down the rocks. He opened his water bottle and took a sip. In a short time he had caught his breath and rested his tired legs. "I have to keep going," Jordan thought to himself. He put the bottle back in his sack and again ran down the trail.

Mya stood up and was pacing nervously. She was worried about Jordan. He was all alone. "I wonder how far he has gone?" she thought. Her thoughts were distracted by a strange sound. It sounded kind of like a baby rattle. Like beans shaking in a plastic cup. She looked all around and then she saw it. Behind Pop-Pop was a snake.

It was a rattle snake. Mya was afraid of snakes. It was slithering all around Pop-Pop's body. Mya didn't know what to do. "What if it bites Pop-Pop?" she thought. "He is already sick, I have to do something quick."

Mya got a long stick and prodded the snake. The snake raised its head and hissed at Mya. "HHHSSSSSSSS" Then it lunged toward her. Mya whacked it right on the head with the stick. Again it lunged at her. This time Mya used the stick to lift and throw the snake a short distance from her and Pop-Pop. The snake then slithered off. Mya felt relieved and began to cry. "Please God, help Jordan bring us help!" she said out loud.

Jordan was now near the fire tower. A fire tower is a small house built on long legs, so it is high above the trees, and the park rangers can watch for forest fires. To get to the top, you must climb a ladder of hundreds of steps to the top. Jordan had never climbed a ladder before, but he did climb a tree when he was at the river with Mya and Grandma once. That was when they met Running Rabbit. And once at the zoo he climbed the metal bars in the tunnels.

Jordan looked up to the small house at the top. "That's really high," he thought, "and my legs are so tired. I don't think I can do it."

As he was thinking and looking up, Jordan saw something flying so far up in the sky it was only a black dot. He knew it was a large bird and again thought of his old friend, Running Rabbit. "I have to save Pop-Pop and Mya."

And up toward the sky Jordan climbed. Hand over hand, foot after foot, Jordan slowly ascended the ladder. He climbed and climbed. His legs were burning with pain and tired. So tired. But Jordan continued the climb. When he was just a little above the trees, he noticed the smoke.

It appeared to be coming from the direction where Pop-Pop and Mya were. Jordan's heart sank. There was no way Mya could carry, or even drag, Pop-Pop away from a forest fire. He looked up and with all his strength Jordan climbed as fast as ever to the top. He climbed over the top and onto the tower deck.

Jordan stood up. He could see farther than he ever saw before. It was beautiful. He saw the hills and valleys. He could see where the land touched the sky. He pushed through the door into the tower room. There was no one there.

Hiking With Pop-Pop – Part Three

Mya was fanning the flames. She had collected wood and sticks and used Pop-Pop's lighter to start a fire. She hoped it would keep away any more snakes and any other animals that might cause them harm. She piled leaves on the fire to help it burn, but the leaves were damp and filled the air with smoke. She didn't realize it, but Mya made a rescue fire that could be seen from any of the fire towers throughout the state forest.

Jordan sat on the only chair in the tower. He was too tired to climb down and he was running out of time.

"FIRE RESCUE ONE to FIRE RESCUE TWO."

Jordan jumped into the air. "Who said that?" said Jordan, looking all around.

"RESCUE TWO HERE, COME IN RESCUE ONE."

Jordan saw the Ranger's two way radio on the counter by the big window.

"WE HAVE SMOKE IN QUADRANT THREE BUT NO ONE IS IN THAT TOWER TODAY. CAN YOU CHECK IT OUT?"

Jordan lifted the microphone from the radio. He squeezed the button and said, "Hello. Hello?" he repeated.

"THIS IS RESCUE ONE. WHO IS THIS?"

"My name is Jordan and my Pop-Pop is hurt with my sister by where the smoke is coming from."

"OKAY, JORDAN, THIS IS OFFICER AL, WITH THE PARK RANGER SERVICE. WE HAVE HELP ON THE WAY. YOU STAY PUT IN THE TOWER AND A RANGER WILL BE THERE SHORTLY."

"I will," said Jordan.

"RESCUE ONE, THIS IS RESCUE TWO. WE SEE THE SMOKE. IT IS JUST NORTH OF THE WEST TOWER.

"OKAY RESCUE TWO," said Al. "WE HAVE A YOUNG BOY IN THE WEST TOWER LOOKING FOR HELP. HIS GRANDFATHER IS HURT AND HIS SISTER IS TAKING CARE OF HIM. THEY ARE IN THE VICINITY OF THE SMOKE."

"ON OUR WAY."

Two rangers bounced into action. They jumped onto their four-wheelers and started them up. One of them had an emergency stretcher trailer hooked on back. RRRummm ERRRr ummmm! Off they went up the trail.

"Mya," said Pop-Pop in a low gruff voice.

"Pop-Pop," said Mya. "Are you alright?"

"I think so," said Pop-Pop. "What happened?"

"You got confused and then fell on the ground," Mya told Pop-Pop.

"Where is Jordan?" he asked.

"Jordan went to the fire tower to find help," she replied.

"And who lit this fire?" asked Pop-Pop.

"I did," said Mya. "I used your lighter."

"Very good, Mya," said Pop-Pop. He tried to move, but he couldn't. "Gee Mya, I hope Jordan is okay and finds some help."

"Me too, Pop-Pop," said Mya. "Me too."

Jordan was sitting, looking out the big window toward the smoke. "I hope Pop-Pop and Mya are okay. I've been gone a long time."

RRRRUMMMM RRRUUUMMMMM

Jordan heard the four-wheelers coming up the trail. He knew that sound. "Uncle Zach has two of them at home." Jordan looked down to the ground. He had to climb back down but his legs were too weak.

"Stay there, young man," yelled the Ranger up to Jordan. "I am coming up."

The Ranger was to the top of the tower in about three minutes. She stepped onto the deck next to Jordan. "One call and we will go get your sister and Pop-Pop," said the Ranger. She grabbed the microphone. "RESCUE TWO TO RESCUE ONE, WE HAVE THE BOY. ON OUR WAY TO HELP THE OTHERS."

"TEN FOUR," said Rescue One. "WE COPY."

"That is police talk for okay, we understand," the ranger told Jordan. She then put on a small harness and strapped Jordan to her back. "Okay," said the Ranger, "are you ready for the climb down."

"Yes," said Jordan. He was happy the Ranger was carrying him down. His arms and legs were so tired he would have never made it.

Over the tower deck they went. Foot after foot and hand after hand, the ranger climbed down to the ground with Jordan safely strapped to her back. As the Ranger's foot hit the ground, she pulled a strap and Jordan slid off and onto the ground. The Ranger jumped onto her four wheeler and told Jordan to get on. Jordan jumped on and put his arms around the Rangers waist and held on tight. Just like riding with Uncle Zach or Uncle Ben.

RRRUUUMMM. RRRUUUMMMMMM. The two rangers and Jordan zoomed up the trail towards the smoke, and hopefully in time to save Pop-Pop and Mya. When they crossed the little bridge over the stream, Jordan knew they were almost there. He stopped at that stream to rest on his way to the fire tower.

"Listen Pop-Pop! Listen I hear someone coming!" said Mya.

Pop-Pop was too weak to look up. He smiled as best he could at Mya. She rubbed his head and said, "It's gonna be okay, Pop-Pop. Help is almost here."

RRRRUUUMMMM RRRRUUMMMM. The rangers pulled into the small clearing where Pop-Pop was laying. Jordan hopped off and went to Pop-Pop and Mya. Mya hugged Jordan.

"How is he?" Jordan asked.

"He woke up," Mya replied. "He knew who I was, and he asked about you. He is very weak though."

Jordan and Mya watched as the Rangers tied Pop-Pop to the stretcher, then the stretcher back in the trailer.

"Okay kids," said the Ranger, "hop on and hold tight."

With Pop-Pop in the trailer, Mya and Jordan each jumped on the back of the two four-wheelers and held on tight. RRRRuuumm Ruuummm. The Rangers drove up the trail. Up and down the hills through the forest they traveled. Some of the trail was very rocky and bumpy and they had to go slow. Pop-Pop was laying in the trailer, bouncing all around. "It could not be comfortable," thought Jordan. "but at least Pop-Pop was alive, and he and Mya were now safe."

The Rangers drove off the trail and into a small paved parking area. The sign said, Welcome to Sunrise Mountain. Jordan smiled. He knew if Pop-Pop could talk he would say, "Look we made it,'" and would laugh. Pop-Pop was funny like that.

All of a sudden they heard a thundering. WOP WOP WOP WOPPing sound. Mya looked up and said, "Look Jordan!"

Jordan and Mya watched as a big helicopter landed in the parking lot. The ranger with Pop-Pop pulled the trailer next to the helicopter. Then, two men lifted the stretcher with Pop-Pop into the helicopter. When they had him all strapped and buckled in Mya began to cry. Jordan had tears in his eyes too. "Bye Pop-Pop, Bye," they both said sadly. "We love you."

"No goodbyes here," said the Ranger. "You are going with Pop-Pop." Mya and Jordan smiled. "Get on board kids, we have to get your Pop-Pop to the hospital." Jordan and Mya buckled their seat-belts. Then the whooping sound began again, WOP WOP WOP WOP WOP WOP WOP, and up into the sky they went.

Hiking With Pop-Pop – Part Four

Jordan had thought he had seen it all. Being so high up in the fire tower, above all the trees, he could see everything, but being up in the helicopter was something totally different. He and Mya could see everything possible. They saw houses, roads, and swimming pools.

"Look Jordan," said Mya, "a school bus."

"It looks like my toy cars at Pop-Pop's house," said Jordan.

Mya giggled. They were both feeling better now. They were safe again, and most of all Pop-Pop had help. As they flew through the sky like a big bird, one of the men was caring for Pop-Pop. He put a tube into Pop-Pops arm. The man said that Pop-Pop was dehydrated and needed fluids. Mya remembered that Pop-Pop sipped the water and soon after he seemed a little better.

"What is dehydrated?" asked Jordan.

The man said, "That is when someone has not drank enough water and their body is shutting down. With the IV tube and some water, I'm sure your Pop-Pop will be perfectly fine."

Over the mountains, over the buildings and roads, over the tiny towns they flew. The pilot landed the helicopter on the roof of the hospital. A doctor and a nurse went right over to Pop-Pop. After a couple of minutes, Pop-Pop was carried off the chopper and onto a bed-like stretcher with wheels and was rolled away.

"Follow me kids," said the nurse. Mya and Jordan looked at the helicopter one last time and then followed the nurse through the big doors and into the emergency room.

"Grandma!" screamed Mya.

Mya and Jordan ran to Grandma and held her tighter than ever. Jordan was crying and trying to tell Grandma what happened. "It's okay Jordan, calm down. Everything will be okay." Jordan took a deep breath and then swallowed. As he calmed down, he told Grandma what had occurred in the forest. Mya also told her accounting of what happened. "Okay," said Grandma. "Let's go see how Pop-Pop is doing."

Grandma talked to the doctor. She was asking him all kinds of questions. Jordan and Mya slipped past Grandma and the doctor and went into Pop-Pop's room. Pop-Pop was sitting up in the hospital bed. "Hey guys!" said Pop-Pop. "Look here, I have water and juice and Jell-O for you."

"No," said Mya. "That is for you to get better. You need the fluids. The man on the helicopter told us you were dry, and that's why you got sick."

"Alright, maybe you are right," said Pop-Pop. He drank all the water, two of the juices, and ate three Jell-O cups. Grandma was back by then.

"The doctor said you were just dehydrated," she told Pop-Pop, "but they still want to keep you here in the hospital overnight for observation."

"I feel fine now," said Pop-Pop, "thanks to my two heroes. Without Mya and Jordan, I might not be here," he said. "I'm sorry kids, that we didn't get to see the sunrise from the mountain. I must have taken the wrong path. Next time I will follow the trail maps."

"That's okay, Pop-Pop, we saw the sun set, from a helicopter. And as long as you are okay, it is the best day ever."

"Say goodbye to Pop-Pop," said Grandma.

"Bye, Pop-Pop," said Mya.

"Bye, Pop-Pop," said Jordan. "We will see you at home when you get out of here. We will tell you the whole story of today."

Mya and Jordan followed Grandma to the car. The day had been long and the children were tired. They fell fast asleep as Grandma drove them home.

But, was Pop-Pop really okay? Find out, in the next episode of.........The Adventures of Mya and Jordan.

The Adventures of Mya & Jordan Volume 7 The Family Camp-Out

Part One

Jordan and Boomer were waiting in the car even before anyone else was awake. "We're going camping!" screamed Jordan loudly.

"Ruff ruff!" barked Boomer.

"Jordan? Jordan?" yelled Amanda. "Where are you?"

"Me and Boomer are in the car, Mom. We are ready to go!"

Amanda laughed. "Get your butt in this house and eat your breakfast. We have a lot to do before we go anywhere."

Jordan sighed and went into the house.

After breakfast, Ken and Jordan began packing the car. "Where is your fishing pole Jordan?" asked Ken. "I have to pack it with the rest of the gear."

"I'm getting it, Dad," yelled Jordan as he ran back into the house excitedly. "Mom," asked Jordan, "where is my fishing pole?"

"Look in your closet," said Amanda. Mya and Mom were packing the last of the food and cooking utensils. "Jordan," said Amanda, "after you get your pole, help Mya and me carry all the food to the car. We are just about ready to leave."

After the car was packed, Mya, Jordan, and

Boomer hopped into the back seat. Jordan was squeezing Mya's hand so hard. "We're going camping, Mya," he said. "We're really going camping."

Amanda and Ken locked the house and jumped into the car too. "Okay kids, buckle up for safety," said their father. When everyone was buckled up, Ken started the car. Jordan let out a loud squeal. He couldn't contain his excitement. He had heard many stories of camping from his mom and dad, and his aunts and uncles. Campfires, fishing, swimming, hiking, cooking, hunting for bugs and little critters, playing in the little streams, sleeping bags, tents, and the animals that come out at night.

"Are we there yet?" asked Mya.

Ken smiled and said, "We just left Mya. The camp ground is way up by Pop-Pop's house. It's in the same park you went hiking with Pop-Pop when you got to ride in the helicopter."

Stokes State Forest was located near High Point State Park in Sussex County, New Jersey.

"Do you remember that hiking trip?" asked Amanda.

"I sure do," said Mya.

"Me too," said Jordan. "Dad," he asked, "can we get up early and see the sun come up on Sunrise Mountain while we are camping?"

"We'll see," said Ken.

As they drove, the houses became more scattered and the land outside the car turned to mostly woods. At one point they had to stop while a long train was crossing the road. It was really cool. There was a pond right where they stopped.

"Can we go and find frogs by the pond?" asked Jordan.

"You can find all the frogs you want once we get to the campsite," Amanda replied.

Eventually Ken pulled into the bait shop near the state forest. "Okay, let's go in and see what we need."

"Ewe," said Mya. "It smells in here!"

"Ewe, yea," said Jordan. "It does!"

"That's just the bait-fish you smell," said Ken.

Amanda got some worms, while Ken got the bait fish. The shop had all kinds of things for camping, hunting, and fishing. They saw bow and arrows, guns, fishing poles, and all kinds of supplies. "It's a good thing they have all this stuff, Dad," said Jordan. "If anything happens, we can come here and get stuff."

"Yes, we can," said Ken, "but I think we are well prepared for our trip. Besides the others will all be bringing things too."

"Others?" asked Jordan.

"Who else is coming?" asked Mya.

Ken looked at Amanda. Amanda said, "You'll just have to wait and see."

While Ken paid the man for the fish-bait, Amanda and the kids went to the car and let

Boomer out so he could stretch and go to the bathroom. "Okay," said Dad, "everyone back in the car. We're almost there."

Again Jordan let out a big loud squeal.

"Mom," Mya asked quietly, "will it be scary in the woods at night?"

"We have lanterns, Mya, and we will also have a big campfire, so there will be plenty of light."

"I'm scared," Mya whispered.

"Don't be scared Mya," said Jordan. "I will be with you the whole time."

That made Mya feel better. She thought of the tunnels under the zoo, and then she remembered their old friend, Running Rabbit...

"There it is!" screamed Jordan. "The big brown sign says Stokes State Forest. This is the place we went hiking with Pop-Pop."

Ken turned right into the small road and drove down to the park office. It was closed. Ken drove back out to the main road.

"WAIT! WAIT!" said Jordan. "We have to go camping! You promised, you promised!" he cried.

"Relax, Jordan," said his dad. "We are already registered and Mom downloaded the park map on her phone. We are going to site number 16. It is right on the Flatbrook River, in the Lake Ocquittunk camping section. It has the best fishing hole among all the campsites there."

Ken drove another mile or so and again

turned right. After about two miles, he turned into the Lake Ocquittunk camping area. "See that building on the left," said Amanda. "That is the bathroom and showers. There are also small outhouse toilets right by the campsite."

As they slowly drove down the dirt road, Jordan and Mya were looking at everything. They saw the lake, some cabins on the hill, and people camping all over. Ken pulled into site 16. It was on a one way road that went in a circle with campsites all the way around.

"Hey Dad, isn't that Uncle Zach's truck?" asked Jordan.

"There's Uncle Ben and Uncle Jonny too," said Mya. "There's Aunt Kim and Max, and Ayla and Aunt Alex too, Mom!" screeched Mya. "We're gonna have a great time!"

"I thought you were scared?" asked Amanda.

"Not anymore, Mom," Mya replied. "Not anymore."

"Okay," said Ken, "let's say hello to everyone, and then we have to set up camp and unpack all the gear."

"Okay, Dad," said Jordan and Mya. "You can count on us to help."

Ayla and Max ran over to greet Mya and Jordan. They gave each other great big hugs and were so happy to see each other. "This is great!" said Max. "We are all gonna camp out together."

"I agree," said Ayla. "We haven't see you

guys since the zoo. This is gonna be really cool."

"Alrighty," said Ken. "Come on kids, we have work to do."

First Amanda put Boomer on his chain. He wasn't allowed to run free in the park. Ken and Jordan began to set up the tent. They unfolded and stretched it out over a spot with thick soft grass so they had some cushion. "Hand me the tent-poles?" asked Ken. Jordan handed them up in a flash. Within no time at all they had set up the tent. Mya and Amanda were now bringing over the sleeping bags and pillows and making the inside look like a huge sleeping room. Ken tied some rope high in the trees and hung a tarp over the area in case of rain. Jordan and Mya pulled the small wagon with the water bottles to the spring and filled them with fresh water.

"Well," said Ken, "only one thing left to do."

"I got this one," said Mom. Amanda had a great big armful of firewood and dropped it by the metal fire ring. Then she gathered some kindling. Kindling is small pieces of wood that will light on fire very easily. Amanda set the little pieces in the ring standing up like a little tent. She had a couple of napkins crushed into little balls underneath. She lighted the match and then lit the napkin. In seconds the little sticks caught fire and she began to add larger pieces of wood.

"Where did you learn to do that, Mom?" asked Jordan.

"Pop-Pop! Where else," Amanda said giggling.

"Where is Pop-Pop?" asked Mya.

"Pop-Pop and Grandma are home. Uncle Chris and Aunt Sam might bring them down for a visit tonight or tomorrow."

After the camp was set up and the fire was going good, "Time to relax," announced Ken.

Mya and Jordan went to play with Ayla and Max. Aunt Kim, Alex, Uncle Zach, Jonny, and Ben gathered around the fire with Amanda and Ken. "The stream looks like there will be good fishing," said Ken.

"Zach already caught a few brook trout," said Jonny. "Look what I brought," said Ben. He was holding a small water float board he had from the shore last summer. "I remember when I was little, riding one like this right in the river on this very site. I think the kids will enjoy it as much as I did."

"Yea," said Zach laughing. "I remember you falling off and almost drowning."

Amanda got that worried look on her face and said maybe we should put the board away. But it was too late. Jordan grabbed the board and splash!!! He was in the stream. Ayla and Max jumped in almost on top of him.

Ben told Jordan to carry the board to site 15 up the stream. Jordan did. Everyone was watching as he came crashing and splashing downstream on the board. When he hit the big water hole by the site he stopped. Max went next. Then Ayla. Uncle Zach carried the board for Mya, who by the way was terrified, and calmed her down, reassuring her it would be fun.

Mya slowly got on the board in the water. Everyone was cheering her on. As soon as she started floating down the stream, her frown turned to smiles from ear to ear. Nothing but teeth. When she stopped, she grabbed the board and started to run back upstream.

"It's my turn!" hollered Jordan.

Mya stopped and gave him the board. For the next two hours the kids just played in the stream. Up and down the stream they went. Crashing and splashing and having a wonderful time.

Everyone brought food and cooked on their own fires and camp stoves. All the food went onto one big table. There was chicken, hot dogs, hamburgers, potato salad, macaroni salad, even pickles and coleslaw. Uncle Zach cooked up the fish he caught. There were three big cooler jugs on the table too. One was juice, one was water, and one was iced tea.

Ayla, Jordan, Max and Mya sat near the warm fire drying off as they ate. Jonny and Zach were tying a garbage bag into the tree on a slide knot. "What is that for?" asked Max.

"Well," said Zach, "all the garbage goes in this bag, and at night we pull the rope and it will hang high in the tree so the bears don't get it."

"BEARS?" cried Ayla.

"Don't worry, Ayla," said Jordan. "We get bears at Pop-Pop's all the time. They want food, not us. If we see one we just walk quietly away and tell an adult."

"I want to see a bear," said Max.

"If you guys are good," said Ken, "when it gets dark, we will drive over to the big dumpster area. Sometimes the bears go there because they smell the old rotten food people throw away."

"I'll be good," said Max very seriously.

Aunt Kim and Aunt Alex were lighting their lanterns as the sun was getting very low and sinking behind the mountain. The fire was burning bright and marshmallows were on the sticks roasting in the fire. After eating a couple each, the kids seemed to have more energy.

"Who wants to go see the bears?" chimed Ken.

"I do!" Max replied.

"Me too!"

"And me!"

"I'll go!"

It seemed everyone wanted to see the bears. They took a couple of cars and all drove over to the dumpsters very slow. "Look kids," said Ken. Ahead in the headlights there were five or six big black bears. There were also a couple of really small ones too. The bears were climbing on the green dumpsters looking for a way into the garbage.

"How long will they do that?" asked Jordan.

"Not too long," said Ken. "When they realize they can't get in, they will go look somewhere else for food."

"Yea." said Max, "like our campsites."

Ayla thought about the garbage bag hanging in the tree at the campsite and knew Max was right.

Ken and the others backed the cars up and headed back to the site. When they got back to the site, everyone sat by the fire talking and telling stories, some which were really scary. Kim and Alex took their lanterns over to their tents to get ready for bed. And one by one, so did everyone else. The only light was from the campfire and that was burning low. It was pitch black outside now.

"What was that noise?" asked Mya.

"What noise?" asked Jordan.

"I think I heard it too," said Ayla.

Max sat still and listened hard.

"It sounded like someone was walking in the woods over there," said Mya.

"Bears," said Ayla. "It must be the bears."

"I think you guys are imagining stuff," said Jordan.

But still the kids got up and went over by their parents near the tents. Jordan took Boomer off the chain and put him in the tent. Everyone went into their tents and got into their sleeping bags. It felt good to go to bed. Mya, Ayla, Max and Jordan were tired, and despite being a little scared, they fell fast asleep.

The Family Camp-Out – Part Two

Jordan was having a hard time sleeping, and was rolling back and forth in his sleeping bag. He opened his eyes. "I have to pee," he thought, "but everyone is asleep." He lay there for a few seconds, and suddenly he really, really had to go. "I can do this by myself. I'll just unzip the tent and walk through the dark scary woods, to the smelly little out house, on the other side of the campsite."

As he unzipped the tent, Mya woke and said, "Where are you going, Jordan?"

"I have to pee," he said.

"So do I," whispered Mya. "Wait for me."

Boomer was awake too. His tail wagging with the anticipation of going out.

"Not now, Boomer," said Jordan. "If you get lost in the woods, we may not find you. You have to stay here boy."

Mya put on her shoes and off they went. As they were walking past the other tents, she tripped on a tree root growing across the path.

"Who's there?" asked Max softly, as to not wake anyone else up.

"It's us, Mya and Jordan. We have to pee."

"Me too," said Max. "I'll come with you."

"Not without me," said Ayla half yawning. "I've had to pee for a while, but I was afraid to go alone."

The children left the tent area and headed into the woods. It was pitch black and hard for them to see. "I wonder what time it is," Mya wondered aloud. "No one else is awake at any of the tent sites."

"Where is the bathroom, Jordan," asked Ayla. "I really have to go."

It is somewhere on the other side of the site. I saw it when we drove in this morning," Jordan replied.

Max was quiet.

"Follow me," said Jordan. "I know I can find it."

The crickets were chirping louder than ever. Strange noises, and the rustle of leaves, was beginning to scare them all. With every step they took it just got scarier. "I coulda just peed on a tree near the tent," thought Max quietly to himself. "How do I always let Jordan and Mya get me into scary stuff like this?"

All of a sudden they heard something moving in the woods. It was rushing right toward them. The children froze in their tracks with fear. "It's a bear!" screamed Ayla."

"Oh God," said Max. "I knew it! It's gonna eat us all!"

Just then, a fawn stopped running and was standing right in front of them. A fawn is a baby deer. "Well it's not a bear," said Jordan with a sigh of relief. "I hope nobody peed in their pants," he chuckled with a big grin on his face.

Mya reached her hand toward the fawn. It didn't move. She pet its head and the little deer came close to her. The children all gathered around the fawn and began petting it all over. "She seems to like being pet," said Mya.

"I wonder where her mom is," said Ayla inquisitively.

"I don't know," said Max, "but I'm sure glad it's not a bear."

"I really have to pee, Jordan," said Ayla. "Can we keep going now?"

The children said goodbye to the deer, and again began walking through the woods. Jordan was leading the way, with Mya second, then Ayla, and Max at the end of the line. They kept the girls in the middle to protect them. They came to a huge tree that had fallen across the path. Jordan climbed up onto the great big log, then he grabbed Mya's hand and helped her up. Then Ayla, and then Max climbed up by himself. When they jumped down the other side, they heard a sound, it was like a baby crying. Mya looked back over the tree, and there it was, the fawn was following them.

"It's the baby deer," said Mya. "It wants to come with us.

"It will be fine right there," said Jordan. "We have to keep moving."

Onward they trudged through the dark woods.

"We are almost there," said Jordan.

"Look," said Max. "It is getting light out."

"It is," said Mya. "It must be morning.

"No," said Jordan. "Look, it's the moon. It is coming up over the mountain."

The campground was in a small valley, in between two high mountains, which were very close together. The light from the moon would only last a short time. With the help of the moon's light, Jordan could see much farther ahead. "Aha," he bellowed. "I knew I could find it. Look," he said, "right there up ahead, it is the outhouse."

"Oh thank God," said Ayla. "I'm going first."

When they got closer to the door opening, they saw it was just an old tiny wood shack with a roof, and a hole in a small wooden seat. It was old and very rundown.

"What is this, Jordan?" said Ayla with a hint of disgust in her voice.

"Yea," said Mya, "I ain't peeing in there, that's gross. I heard Uncle Jonny tell Uncle Ben that there were snakes in there."

"Don't be silly," said Jordan. "I'll show you, I'll go first."

Mya thought for a second. "Okay, Jordan, you go first, but you have to sit down like us girls do so we can see that it is really safe."

Jordan said, "Okay," and in he went. The thought of snakes being in the hole was now inside his head, and he was a little frightened. He thought of Pop-Pop for a moment, and then he knew it was okay. He remembered stories Pop-Pop told him of using the outhouse when he went camping. So Jordan sat down and peed. When he finished, Ayla went and then Mya. No snakes. Max stood when he went, he wasn't sitting on that thing, he knew better.

When they were all finished in the outhouse, they began to walk back. The moon was already at the top of the other mountain and it would be darker again in just a few minutes.

"We are doing great," said Jordan. "We are already back to the big tree."

"Oh good," said Mya. "Is the baby deer still there?"

Jordan looked over the tree. "Oh no," he thought. "A bear." He turned them all around and whispered for them not to make a sound. "Follow me," he said.

"Why?" said Mya. "What's wrong?"

"Just follow me now and hurry," he whispered. Jordan scampered back toward the outhouse, and they all quickly followed. When they got there, Jordan told them that on the other side of the fallen tree was a really big bear.

"How will we get back?" asked Ayla.

"Yea," said Max. "How?"

"The stream is right over there to the

right," said Jordan. "I can hear it."

"Me too," said Max. "Our site is right at the edge of the stream. We can follow it back."

The children all followed Jordan. When they got to the stream, Jordan turned and headed up towards the tent sites. In a few minutes, they saw a fire glowing at one of the sites. Everyone felt better now. They were getting close.

Max heard a noise in the leaves behind him. His heart sank. He didn't want to look, he knew it must be the bear. But Max also knew, for everyone's safety, he needed to check, and he slowly turned his head. Sure enough something was there, but it wasn't the bear. It was the fawn. The little baby deer had followed them.

When they reached the first set of tents, they saw three big raccoons scavenging around the tent area, looking for scraps. "Awe," said Mya. "They are so cute. I want to go and pet them."

"Me too," said Ayla.

"Let's just get back to our tents," said Max. "I'm really tired and I want to be well rested for tomorrow."

"Max is right," said Jordan. "Who knows what our parents have planned for the day. I know whatever it is will be just awesome. I love camping," he said.

As they got closer, the raccoons scurried down over the bank toward the stream. A second later, the fawn scampered off into the woods also. When they came to Ayla and Max's tent, they said goodnight to each other. Max and Ayla went into their tent and Mya and Jordan went into theirs. Boomer was still awake and waiting for them. His tail wagging and his tongue hanging out panting as always. Everyone was safe. Mya fell right to sleep cuddling up to Amanda and Ken. Jordan laid awake for a while thinking about the night. "I wonder what we will do tomorrow?" he thought. A few minutes later he too fell asleep.

When his eyes opened, he was laying on the ground in his sleeping bag. He rolled over and only Mya was in the tent with him.

The Family Camp-Out – Part Three

When Jordan's eyes opened, he was laying on the ground in his sleeping bag. He rolled over, and only Mya was in the tent with him. "Wake up, Mya, wake up." Mya grumbled. "Wake up, Mya," said Jordan. "Everyone is gone."

Right away, Mya's eyes popped open wide. She sat up and gazed around the tent. "Where is everyone?" she asked.

"I don't know," said Jordan. "We are usually the first ones up. When I opened my eyes no one was here."

"Listen, Jordan," said Mya, a bit irritated. "I hear them."

Jordan smiled, "Oh yea, I can hear them too." Jordan unzipped the tent. He looked around the campsite from the opening, and, sure enough, everyone was outside, all busy doing things. "Look, Mya, everyone is here."

Mya crawled out of her sleeping bag and over to the tent door. She wiped the dry sleeping sand from her eyes, and looked out into the campsite. The morning air was cool and crisp, and the sky was bluer than ever. It was very bright out, even though the sun had not yet come over the mountain. "Yup, they're all here. Thanks for scaring me awake, Jordan."

Jordan laughed. "Sorry," he said, "but to be honest, I knew it would wake you up fast."

Uncle Jonny was playing with the fire, adding small twigs and dry leaves, trying to get it going. A small column of smoke was rising upward into the air from the fire ring. Uncle Ben was breaking up the dead tree limbs that Uncle Zach was collecting in the woods. And Uncle Zach, was just coming back from the woods with another big armload of branches. Ken was at the edge of the stream with his fishing pole, trying to catch some trout to eat with breakfast. Amanda was setting up for breakfast and getting ready to start cooking.

"I got one!" yelled Ken.

Jordan bolted from the tent and was at his dad's side in seconds, with Mya just a few steps behind. Amanda was smiling. "Well I guess fish is on the menu," she said.

Jonny, Ben, and Zach watched Ken as they

continued to work on the fire. Ken's pole was now nearly bent in half. Zach saw it and stood up. "Holy moly, what does he have on that line?" he asked excitedly.

Jonny and Ben also jumped to their feet. Amanda headed closer to her big strong fisherman husband. "It's really fighting hard," said Ken.

Jordan watched intently as the fish pulled the line hard, swirling and thrashing about under the water. The line was making a zzzzzzzzzzzzz sound. "What is that noise?" he asked.

'That is the drag," said his dad, Ken. "It is so when the fish pulls real hard and sudden like, the line doesn't snap." Ken slowly tightened the drag. Now the drag sound was in shorter bursts. Ken was reeling the fish in, and when he had it close to the bank and near the top of the water, he saw it. "It's a big brown trout," he said.

The three uncles were at the side of the stream now too. The fish then turned and, zzzzzzzzzzzzzzzz. He pulled the line even harder.

"You got this, Kenny," said Amanda.

Mya just stared at the water. She knew what a fish was, but never saw one caught.

Ken's pole was still bending like crazy, but not as often.

"You're tiring him out, Ken," said Jonny.

Uncle Ben grabbed the net and got closer to the water. Ken had him. As he reeled the fish in this time, it came again to the surface.

Everyone got a good look. It was a big brown trout alright, the biggest any of them had ever seen caught out of such a small stream. Ben scooped it up into the net. Ken was smiling from ear to ear. Every one cheered. "Yay!"

"Good job, Kenny," Amanda said to her husband.

"They brought the fish to the table and weighed it. Eight pounds two ounces, and it measured 20 inches long. "It's as big as a baby," exclaimed Amanda.

"Mom," said Mya.

"Yes, Mya, what is it honey?"

"When is Aunt Jenn gonna have her baby?"

"Any time now," said Amanda. "Your Aunt Jenn is due to deliver in two days."

Everyone giggled.

Ken gutted and cleaned the fish. He put it on tinfoil, cut a little onion, added some butter, two sliced lemon wedges, and a couple shakes of garlic powder. Then he wrapped it up in the foil and set it on the table.

Kim, Alex, Ayla, and Max walked into the campsite. "What's all the commotion so early?" asked Kim.

"Kenny caught breakfast," said Amanda. "A big trout."

"OH, we missed it," said Ayla.

"Well," said Aunt Kim, "if you and Max didn't sleep so late, we would have all been here."

"Hmmm," thought Amanda, then she said, "Jordan and Mya slept in too. I guess the fresh air and being out in the woods really tired them out."

The kids looked at each other smiled. Not one of them said a word about last night.

"Well we're up now," touted Ayla. "Catch another one for us to see."

Everyone laughed.

Kim, Alex and Amanda decided to cook breakfast together. They made eggs, flapjacks, bacon, pan fried potatoes, sausage patties, and orange juice. Aunt Kim even made something called hash. It was salty, but tasted really good. Oh, and let's not forget Ken's big catch. Ken cooked that. When the fire was going pretty good, he set a flat rock right into the fire, and then placed the fish in the foil wrap onto the rock. It cooked in no time at all. The grown-ups all had coffee. Pop-Pop gave Ken his camping coffee pot. He always has it on the wood stove in the winter. There is a little glass bubble on top where you can see the water turn to coffee. Pop-Pop calls it his percolator. He says it ever gets him percolating. It calls to Pop-Pop too. When the water gets hot and starts to boil, it goes pop, gurgle, Pop-Pop, Pop-Pop, gurgle pop.

After breakfast, everyone helped clean up. Mya and Ayla gathered the knives, spoons, and forks, and put them into the small dish pan on the table. Amanda had already filled it with hot water that she had heating over the fire in a large black pot while everyone was eating. All the plates and cups were made of paper. Of course Jordan and Max had that detail. They burned them in the fire. "This is the best job I ever had," said Jordan.

Max went into the woods and found a long stick. He put one cup at a time on the end of it, and then stuck it in the fire. "Look, Jordan," said Max. "I'm roasting marsh-cups." And then he laughed.

Jordan laughed too. "Good one, Max," he said.

Ben and Zach were cleaning the heavy black metal pans, called cast-iron skillets. Uncle Zach wiped them clean with napkins first, and then Uncle Ben wiped a little olive oil on them and put them away into the big blue plastic cooking box. Jonny and Ken were at the stream fishing. They said it was their job to supply food, but they didn't catch any more fish.

"Okay kids," shouted Amanda. "Let's go. Grab your towels and toothbrushes. We are going to the bathrooms."

Ayla looked at Mya. "Is she kidding, Mya? That bathroom is disgusting. I'd rather brush my teeth right there in the stream."

Mya giggled, "No she's not kidding, let's go." Mya already knew that they were going to the main bath house, and not the small wooden shack they used last night. She didn't tell Ayla that though. The kids, Amanda, Kim, and Alex all piled into the car. The men were going to do some scouting around the camp and took Boomer with them.

Amanda turned into the lot by a nice new brick building. "What is this place?" asked Ayla. "This is the main bathhouse," said Amanda. "It has hot water, showers, nice clean toilets, and mirrors."

"Mirrors," thought Ayla, "hot water, showers, and clean toilets. I'm gonna kill you, Jordan."

Mya and Max were laughing so hard, they had to hold their stomachs because it hurt from laughing so much. Jordan smiled. "You said you had to go bad. It would have taken us forever to get here on foot." Then Jordan began to laugh too. Ayla was chuckling now also.

"What's so funny guys?" asked Kim.

"Oh nothing," said Jordan. "Ayla is just being a silly girl."

They entered the bathhouse. It was clean as a whistle. It even had lights. There was three showers, four toilets, two sinks with mirrors, and electric outlets for hair dryers and such. They all took turns showering. After Jordan and Max got dressed again, they stood under the hand dryers and kept pushing the buttons. The warm air was blowing onto their heads and dried their hair in no time. When Alex called Ayla to dry her hair near the sink, Ayla stomped her foot and said, "I want to do it like Max and Jordan did."

"Hey, go for it kid," Alex told her daughter

Ayla.

Ayla smiled; she had gotten her way. She stood under the dryer and pushed the button over and over. When her hair was dry, she came outside, where everyone else was now waiting for her. Her hair was an absolute mess. It was standing straight up. She looked like a cartoon character after being frightened. Like a fuzzy haired troll doll or something.

Did you look in the mirror?" asked Alex.

"No," answered Ayla.

"Maybe you should."

Ayla went back inside. A second later, the door opened just a little, and through the crack, "Mommy!" cried Ayla. "Help me please!"

Alex giggled and went back in. She wet Ayla's hair in the sink and brushed it nice as she dried it with the hairdryer. "How's that?" asked Alex.

"Oh thank you, Mom." Ayla replied cheerfully. "Thank you so much."

"Okay everyone, back in the car." Amanda started the engine and headed back to the campsite.

"Look," said Aunt Kim. "A mother deer and her baby are drinking water over by the pond." Amanda slowed the car to a crawl so everyone could see.

"Stop mom, please," asked Jordan.

Amanda stopped and everyone got out. Mya began walking toward the deer.

"Stay by us," said Amanda.

"It's okay, Mom, I'll be okay," Mya replied.

Ayla, Max, and Jordan then followed her. The mother deer walked toward the edge of the woods, but the baby just stood and watched as the children approached. "Don't touch it," said Amanda, but it was too late. Mya had already reached her hand out and the baby was licking her fingers and palm. The little fawn let the kids rub its head and pet it. She put her head low against Mya's body and rubbed Mya back.

"I can't believe what I'm seeing," said Aunt Alex. "The fawn should be afraid of people."

"Maybe," said Aunt Kim, "it is just used to the people here in the state forest. There are a lot of campers after all."

"Maybe you are right," said Alex.

"Okay kids, let's go now," said Amanda.

The children all turned and walked back to the car. As they did, the baby deer walked up the hill to where her mom was watching from the edge of the woods.

Amanda turned the car into their campsite. There was another car there. Ken, Zach, Jonny, and Ben were all sitting by the fire. And along with them was Aunt Sam and Uncle Chris, Grandma, and Pop-Pop! The children ran and gave everyone great big hugs.

"I'm so glad you came, Pop-Pop," said Jordan. "I have lots to tell you. We are having so much fun here, and now you can have fun with us."

Pop-Pop smiled. "I can't stay right now," he said.

"But why?" moaned Jordan.

Grandma stood up by the fire. "I have some wonderful news. Your Aunt Jenn and Uncle Tim are at the hospital right now. The baby is coming!"

"Is it a girl?" asked Mya.

"No, it's a boy," said Jordan. "Remember, his name is gonna be Kiernan."

"That's right Jordan," said Grandma. "Kiernan is being born into our family right now. Pop-Pop and I are going to the hospital to be with them. We just stopped by to give you all the happy news."

"Well at least you and Aunt Sam are gonna be here," said Jordan to Uncle Chris. "We can lift rocks and find snakes, and hunt frogs.

Chris smiled at Jordan. "I'm sorry buddy, but I have to go to the hospital too. I need to drive Grandma and Pop-Pop. Maybe Aunt Sam and I will come back later on, after the baby is born."

"Okay Uncle Chris, that would be great. I can't wait.

Aunt Samantha, Uncle Chris, Grandma, and Pop-Pop got back into the car to leave.

"Tell Jenn and Tim we love them, and give the baby a big hug from all of us," said Amanda.

"Yes," they replied, then Uncle Chris

started the car and pulled away.

"We found a small lake with a beach for swimming while we were out scouting. They even allow pets," said Ken.

"Swimming? We're going swimming?" asked Max.

"I'm not sure," said Ken. "It is all up to your moms."

Mya and Jordan looked at Amanda. Max's eyes were glued to Kim's; and Ayla, she was tugging on Alex's pant leg, looking up at her, one eye closed, nodding her head up and down, signaling the answer to be yes.

"How can we say no to such cute kids? Okay swimming it is."

"YAY, YAY!" screamed the kids. "We're going swimming!"

It was close to lunchtime, but swimming would come first. The sun would soon be at its warmest as it was just peaking over the first mountaintop.

Jordan and Max ran down the beach full speed and into the water. Jordan dove first, and Max was right behind him. The grown-ups set up the chairs and blankets on the beach, and laid and sat in the warmth of the sun's rays. Ayla and Mya stood in the water ankle deep. Slowly they inched in.

"It's cold," said Mya.

"Look a fish," said Ayla. "A whole bunch of them."

There were little bait fish were swimming all over.

"They won't hurt us," said Mya. "They are in the river and in the pond by Pop-Pop's house. I have swam with the fish lots of times."

"Okay good," said Ayla. "I'm not afraid of them anyway, they are so little."

As the girls were still working their way into the water, Max and Jordan started to splash the cold water at them.

"Stop!" yelled Mya.

"Yes, cut it out," said Ayla.

Max looked at Jordan, and, without saying another word, they both began splashing like crazy, slapping their tiny hands on the top of the water and shooting at the two girls nonstop. Just then, **SPLASH, SPLASH, SPLASH, and SPLASH**. Ken and the uncles jumped in right behind the boys, making big waves almost knocking them over. Jordan turned and attacked them, splashing as hard as he could. Max was right there with him, throwing handfuls of water on the men. Laughter and happy noise filled the entire beach.

"Get on my shoulders, Jordan," said Uncle Zach.

Jonny grabbed Max and threw him into the air. Max hit the water like a bomb. When he came up from underwater, Max said, "On your shoulders, Jonny." Jonny put him on his shoulders and the chicken fight began. Ayla and

Mya just watched. The boys were pushing and shoving each other, trying to knock each other off their partner's shoulders. Suddenly from behind, Kenny grabbed Ayla, and Ben grabbed Mya and up on their shoulders they went. They moved into the slightly deeper water where the boys were, and now they had four chicken fighters, shoving and pulling and pushing, all trying to be the chicken king or queen.

Amanda, Kim, and Alex were now at the edge cheering their kids to victory. No one was falling off though. Kim Jumped in, and Alex and Amanda followed. They were behind the kids pushing and pulling at them. One by one they began to fall into the water. Splash splash splash splash. Ken grabbed Jordan and threw him high in the air. Then splash as he hit the water. Zach then threw Ayla, Jonny threw Max, and Ben threw tiny Mya sky high. Splash splash splash as they crashed into the water. Ken crouched low in the water and Jordan stood on his shoulders. Ken reached his arms high so Jordan could balance himself holding his dad's hands. When Ken stood all the way up, Jordan let go and jumped down into the water. Amanda swung Mya by one hand and one foot, around and around, and then upward before she let go. Mya flew up into the air twirling around and pow, crashed down into the water with the biggest splash of all. Ayla came flying down next, and crashed and splashed into the water. Alex smiled, she caught Ayla off guard and launched her up high into the air. Kim shot Max the highest. The look on his face in mid-air was priceless, then wham, he too came trashing and crashing and splashing down.

When Kenny and the rest of the grown-ups headed for dry land, the kids begged for more. "We're tired," the parents said. "You guys wore us out."

"And besides," said Amanda, "we have to go back to the campsite and eat lunch. It is getting late."

The Family Camp-Out – Part Four

After lunch, the adults sat by the fire, and us kids went exploring. We found our way through the woods to a small stream. Max and I were flipping over rocks looking for crayfish, snakes, and whatever else we could find. The girls were just wading barefoot in the water and talking.

"I got one!" yelled Max. He held up a greenish-gray crayfish. It looked like a baby lobster. He reached his hand out and dangled it in front of Ayla's face.

"Ewe, get it away, Max, or I'm gonna tell."

Mya just looked at him with a scowl. Max put it back in the water and the kids continued their search.

"Look what I found, Max," I said excitedly.

Max splashed his way across to where I was at the edge of the stream near some tall weedy grass. "Wow," he said. There were hundreds of baby newts swimming all around the weeds. Max reached in and grabbed a handful. He turned fast and sprinkled them all over Mya and Ayla.

The girls began screaming and shaking them off. They ran from the stream. "We are telling on you! You're gonna be in so much trouble!"

"Look, Jordan!" said Max, pointing downstream.

I turned to where he was pointing and saw that some of the newts that fell off the girls were floating, and there were fish coming to the surface and gulping them down.

I felt bad for the newts; they were really cool. I grabbed a rock from under the water and threw it toward where the fish were eating. As soon as it splashed into the water, the fish all darted away. I realized just then, that that is why the newts were in the weeds. They were hiding from the fish.

The newts were green on top and orange on the bottom, with three yellow spots in a line down their backs. "Let's leave these guys alone and keep exploring," I said.

We headed upstream until we reached the dam. It was made entirely out of small trees, sticks, branches, rocks, and lots of old dead leaves and weeds. Above the dam was a pond. Dad called it a beaver pond. He said they made the dam by chewing down the trees and branches, and dragging them to this point and clogging the stream. Then it formed the pond. They did a great job too because me and Max walked on the dam. It held us so easily, and it was holding back the whole pond.

A short distance around the pond near the edge was a huge pile of sticks mounded up high out of the water. Dad told us it was a beaver lodge.

"What is a beaver lodge?" I had asked him.

"It is where they live," Dad told me. "Their home."

I remember once on television seeing a show with Dad about beavers. They have to swim under water to get inside their house. It was coming back to me. Dad was smart. He must have remembered all about them.

"JORDAN, MAX, JORDAN?" It was Dad.

"Oh boy, Max, here it comes. We're gonna get it for throwing the newts on the girls." I yelled for him, "Here we are, Dad, over here by the dam."

"OH okay, just checking on you guys. Be careful and mindful of snakes by the dam."

"We are," I answered, relieved.

Max and I explored our way around the pond. We were at it for hours. Our pockets were filled with tiny treasures we had found on our quest. Little round rocks, shells, etc. Max even found a fishing bobber and a lure. I think it is solid gold.

We were almost around the pond, when we saw the girls headed our way. "Mom wants you both back at the campsite. It is time for dinner."

"But we're not done exploring," I moaned.

"Mom said now, Jordan."

"Oh alright." The four of us headed back to camp.

"Dinner isn't even ready, Mom," I bellowed.

"I want you to get cleaned up and dry," she replied. "And we need you and Max to go to the spring and get more fresh water."

"Okay, Mom, we will."

Going to the spring was really cool too. Max pulled the wagon with the empty jugs, while I led the way. The spring is just a pipe sticking out of the ground with water constantly pouring out. There is no faucet to turn it on or off. It just keeps on running. Pop-pop says it is the best water around. It is cold and crystal clear. He says people come from all over, just for the water. He and Grandma even come here once a week to fill their car with jugs of this water.

Max and I filled all the jugs and packed them back in the wagon. Then, together, we pulled it back to camp. Everyone was busy with one thing or another when they returned. Uncle Ben and Uncle Jonny were collecting firewood from the woods. They picked up all the driest wood they could find. They had enough to last the whole night. Ken and Uncle Zach were fishing in the deep hole, while Amanda, Aunt Kim, and Aunt Alex were cooking supper. They are great cookers.

I walked over to Dad and watched him fish. "Why do they call this The Flatbrook, Dad?"

"I don't know, Jordan."

Wow, finally something Dad didn't know.

"Anyone know the answer?" asked Ken to the whole group. No one knew the answer.

"Maybe," said Aunt Kim, "the Native Americans named it. This was their home many years ago."

What Aunt Kim said sounded right. I remember Pop-pop telling Mya and me all about the Native Americans living along the big river by his house, and we aren't far from there. "I'll ask Pop-pop when we see him again. I'm sure he will know."

I thought about Running Rabbit, him being a Native American and all. It had been a long time since I saw him last.

Just then, I heard a cell phone ring. It was the first time since they left home on Friday afternoon.

"Hello," said Amanda.

"Hi Amanda, it's Dad. Your sister Jenn just delivered a healthy baby boy. And yes, she named him Kiernan. He was eight pounds and two ounces."

"How long was he?" Amanda asked.

"Twenty inches," said Pop-pop, "and Momma and baby are doing just fine."

"Okay, Dad," said Amanda, "I'll share the great news."

"Okay hun, have a great campout, I love you."

"BBBBBut aren't you and Mom coming back here to visit?"

"Not tonight, your Mom is exhausted and we just want to get home."

"Alright," said Amanda, a bit bummed out, "I love you too, Dad. Tell Mom I love her too."

"Okay, I will baby. See ya later."

"Bye, Dad." Amanda shut her phone and shared the news with everyone. Smiles and joy filled the campsite.

After dinner, Max and I wanted to get back to exploring, but our moms said no. They wanted us all to stay at the campsite together.

The fire was getting big as we sat there telling stories to each other. The adults were the best at it, but no one was as good as Pop-pop. Max and I had sticks in the fire. When the ends would get red and on fire, we would wave them all around. Our moms didn't care for it so much, but Dad said as long as we were safe we could play with them. "But the first time you get too close to anyone, we'll take them away."

We spun the sticks around so the glowing ends could make a circle. The faster you spun, the better the circle. Soon we had the adults try to guess what we were writing. I like to write. The only thing the adults guessed right, was the "O".

The fire was not as high and bright now.

"I'm hungry," I said.

"Me too," said Uncle Ben. "I could use something to eat."

Uncle Zach went to the cooler and grabbed a pack of hotdogs.

Dad smiled and said, "Maybe you should get two packs." Everyone laughed.

Uncle Jonny was already carving the tops of a dozen sticks. Everyone got to cook their own hot dog on the sticks. It was great. They cooked really fast too.

Mom, Aunt Alex, and Aunt Kim had other

ideas. They got out the s'mores. Now there were hotdogs and marshmallows cooking, some on the same sticks. Uncle Ben put a marshmallow on his stick first, then a hotdog, and then another marshmallow. It was in flames is seconds. He ate it all anyway. He called it a flaming mellow dog.

After everyone finished snacking, Uncle Ben broke out his guitar and played for a while. He plays really good. It was the perfect ending to a wonderful day.

Dad began yawning first. Then everyone joined in. Once again bedtime seemed to be welcoming them. But I wasn't tired. I wanted to explore some more. After all, who knows when we will get to go camping again. I grabbed Max and together we made a plan.

After everyone was asleep, which didn't take long, I crawled out of my sleeping bag and pulled the tent door zipper up. One foot out on the ground and I heard the mouse.

"Going on another bathroom adventure?" It was Mya.

"Yes," I whispered.

"I'm coming too," she said.

"SSSSHHH, you have to stay here."

"Jordan," she said a bit louder as if to wake up their parent's.

I put my hand over her mouth and whispered in her ear, "Okay, you can come, but be quiet."

Together, we got out of the tent, and as we lowered the zipper, Boomer, our dog, began to whine. I gave his head a rub and he laid back down. Off we went.

"Max? Max?" I called as soft as I could.

"Over here," Max replied in an almost inaudible voice. Mya and I went to the bushes where he was hiding. Of course, he was not alone either. Ayla was up for adventure just like the rest of them.

The further we went from camp, the darker it got. Before long, not a glimmer of light from the fires could be seen. Together we forged on, back to the beaver pond. We would catch the beavers working and watch them. That was the plan. We had seen many chewed tree trunks and branches during the day, with fresh chips surrounding each one. That meant the beavers should be active.

The crickets were chirping and the forest was alive with the sounds of nightlife. We were not as afraid as we had been on the first night. We knew the area better now, and so far there was nothing threatening us. It was gonna be a fun night.

We worked our way up and over the dam, and around the pond to where we saw the beaver cuttings, only to find the area deserted. There were no beavers, or anything else for that matter. Even the crickets had stopped.

I began to get an eerie feeling in the pit of my stomach. Something was off. Suddenly there was a growl. Then two.

I couldn't see anything, but it sounded like a pack of dogs. I never heard Pop-pop say anything about dogs. I knew we had coyotes, but Pop-pop said they didn't run in packs.

Mya started crying, and I told her to calm down. "We'll be alright."

Then there were two or three more growls adding to the first ones. They were behind us in the woods, and the water was in front of us. Max and I each grabbed a chewed-off limb, courtesy of the beavers. Mya and Ayla did the same. With our backs now against the shoreline, we stood shoulder to shoulder facing the growling sound in the woods.

Out of nowhere a dog came rushing in at us. Max swung the limb and hit the dog in the head. It yelped and ran back to the pack. It looked like it had the mange or maybe it was rabid. Another one darted forward, only to be met with a blow from the limb I was holding, and then it too returned into the woods.

The moon had just popped over the first mountain, and it was quite a bit brighter. Now I could see the tree-line much easier. As the seconds passed, I began to see the glow of eyes peering at us from just behind the trees. There must have been twenty of them waiting to attack.

Ayla and Mya saw the eyes and began to

scream.

"Max," I yelled, "the beaver lodge! Take the girls into the water fast and head for the lodge! I will be right behind you!"

As Max and the girls entered the water, two more of the wild dogs came running full speed at us. I used their speed against them and swung the limb like a bat going for a home run. It cracked as it slammed the first dog, and broke the rest of the way when it hit the second. They both turned and ran back, and then I turned and dived into the pond.

I was at the beaver lodge in seconds. I heard the dogs at the water's edge, and then the splashes of one after the other.

I spoke quick and fast to the others. "Our only chance is to swim down under the water and enter the beavers' house."

"But what if the beavers are there?" cried Mya.

"It is a risk we have to take, but I have a feeling the beavers are hiding in the woods." I grabbed Mya's hand, and Max had Ayla's. "Deep breaths now, and go."

We plunged down fast and deep into the depths and came up under the lodge. I poked my head in first. Just as I had expected, it was empty. I pushed Mya up and in, and then Ayla. Then I pointed for Max to go, and up he went. I could hear the sound of water churning and getting closer fast.

As Max's feet entered the hole, I shot up as quickly as he could, and into the mound of sticks I went. It was surprisingly large inside. We could have fit two more kids if we had to.

"Okay," I said, "everyone quiet."

We could hear the dogs swimming and growling all around the mound, but none of them were trying to go under the water and get in like we had done. For the second, we were safe.

It was starting to get hot inside the lodge from our breath and combined body heat. Soon sweat was pouring down all of our faces. It sounded as if some of the dogs had retreated, but there were still a few on the top of the mound sniffing and growling, and what sounded like biting at the sticks.

"It's getting in!" screamed Ayla.

Mya cringed down and started to cry again. "I wish Running Rabbit was here," she cried.

I saw a rather large stick slowly sliding out through the top. I grabbed it to stop it, but instantly another was moving. The dogs were all on top pulling whatever limbs would move. We were finished. There was no way we could hold off the dogs for long.

Then we heard the loudest growl ever. The dogs were yelping and squealing, and then it growled again. You could hear the dogs being swatted into the water like bugs, by something big. Then my heart sank. It was a bear. And it sounded huge.

In a few minutes, everything was quiet. All I heard was the bear breathing heavily on top of the lodge. It was calm, no longer growling. The sticks began to move from the outside again. It was coming for us. But it was so calm and quiet about it. I didn't understand.

Mya was no longer crying.

"Aren't you afraid?" I asked.

"No," she said, "it's alright. It is Running Rabbit!"

The top of the lodge was now exposed by a hole about two feet wide. I looked up at the bear and into his eyes. Something was familiar about him. As his huge paws reached into the hole, I watched as his face changed into the face of my old friend Running Rabbit for just a second, and then it was Pop-pop. He pulled Mya out first and then me. "It is alright. You are safe now."

We both hugged him tightly.

I looked into his eyes. "It's really you, isn't it?"

"It is," said Pop-pop, "but I have to go now. I've been called home to live with Running Rabbit, up in heaven."

"But we love you, Pop-pop." I suddenly had tears in my eyes. "You can't leave us."

"You have your new cousin Kiernan to look after now, and soon, your Aunt Sam and Uncle Chris will also have a baby. Another cousin for you to love and care for." said Pop-pop. "Don't worry or be sad. Just know I am alright living with the angels. I'll always be watching over you. I love you both."

Pop-pop hugged both of us again, and then his face faded and turned back into Running Rabbit. He leaned down and pulled up Ayla and Max next. They looked at him speechless. He was wearing his big beautiful wings, spreading them wide.

"Jordan and Mya," said Running Rabbit, "you can now share your experiences of me and your Pop-pop with others. But wait until you know the time is right. Remember we angels are always around, even if you cannot see us. I love you guys and will see you again one day. Always be brave and remember to face your adventures head on."

As he faded and disappeared, a warm wind came over us, drying us completely and filling each of us with a calmness I had never known before. We sat at the water's edge for almost an hour talking about what had happened, and then finally made our way back to camp. It was already light out when we got there, but none of us were tired.

One by one the adults emerged from their slumber. We listened to the zippers of each tent as the adults came outside to the fire ring. Breakfast was made and eaten, and everyone helped to clean the area so it was like we had never been there at all.

As we were taking down the tents and

packing up, there was a surreal feeling throughout our campsite. A car was pulling in. It was Aunt Sam, Uncle Chris, and Grandma. Their eyes were all red and wet.

"What's wrong?" asked Amanda. "Are Jenn and baby Kiernan alright?"

"Yes they are fine," said Grandma.

"Everyone sit by the fire with us," said Uncle Chris.

Everyone sat down and Uncle Chris, choking and crying on every word, told us that Pop-pop had died of a heart attack in the wee hours of the morning. "We are going to the hospital from here to tell Jenn."

Everyone was crying.

I remembered what Running Rabbit had said, and knew it was the right time to tell them.

Jordan stood up tall and said, "I have a story to tell you, and I have to tell you now."

Everyone had their eyes on Jordan standing bravely in the center near the almost dead fire.

Jordan began, "This story is called The Adventures of Mya and Jordan. It all began in Pop-pop's yard by the chicken coop. A fox was trying to get the chickens....."

Pete's Skates
(Genre: Friendship)

I remember when I was just a young boy, around the age of nine, playing outside around the house with my younger brother and our two friends up the street. We were full of energy, and from sunup to sundown, we played. We built forts, we hiked, and we played army (using chunks of dry mud as dirt bombs that would puff like smoke when they hit the ground). We rode bikes when we had enough parts to keep them working, and we roller skated on metal skates strapped to our shoes. We played stick ball, with an old broom handle and a tennis ball, and did everything else you can think of under the sun. Climbing trees, and catching turtles, frogs and

221

snakes, even swimming in the creek without permission. The one thing I remember most was, we did it together. The four of us, were best friends. Mike, Mark, John, and myself. We could walk into each other's houses without knocking, and eat and sleep there too. There were a few other kids in the neighborhood who played with us also, but we were the team, until...

One day, a kid from a couple blocks away, came over to play near our house. He was a nice kid, but we thought him a little slow. The first thing he did, was to give me a wrapped, used GI Joe doll, and say, "Happy Birthday."

"It's not my birthday," I told him.

"Every day is somebody's birthday," he replied.

I tried to refuse the gift, but I saw in his eyes something that said it was better to just take it. We played the day away and at sundown he left. The next day he returned. Again he had a wrapped used gift, and gave it to Mark and said, "Happy birthday."

Mark, like I the day before, told him it was not his birthday. "But every day is someone's birthday," the kid replied. Mark was refusing to take the gift. I watched the kid's eyes as they began to well up and get shiny with tears. I whispered to Mark to take the gift. Mark said thank you and opened it. The kid calmed down and smiled from ear to ear. Again we played all day, and at sundown he went home, as did we all.

The third day came, and the same thing happened. And the fourth, the fifth, and so on.

After us four, and the six or so other kids all had presents, he came one last day. He had no present. He was smiling and so happy. John asked him why he had no present with him, "After all," John said, "every day is someone's birthday."

The kids' eyes glanced around the circle at all of us and he replied, "Today is my birthday."

I remember feeling horrible. I had nothing to give him, none of us did. "We didn't know," I said, "and have nothing to give you."

The boy again looked at us all. "You have already given me more than you know. Just being part of your group is the best present I have ever received."

We played the rest of the day together and had a wonderful time as always. Our new friend had become part of our tight group. At sundown, we all walked him home. His house was small, and you could tell he was from a poor family. We all were, but his was even poorer. No one said a word about that. After he went in, we left, and also went home.

On the way, we all talked and decided to all give him what we thought at the time were real presents. We took our best toys, used of course, and each wrapped one for him. I couldn't wait for the sun to come up. I don't think I slept a wink that night.

In the morning, all of us gathered in my yard and waited for our new buddy to come. It was gonna be a great surprise. We waited and waited, but he didn't show. Around lunchtime we walked to his house. Mike knocked on the door, and we waited for what seemed like an eternity. Finally his mother answered the door, unkempt and disheveled, and her eyes red from crying.

"Where is Pete?" we asked her. "We have a surprise for him."

She looked at us and began to cry again. Through her tears she said, "Peter, died last night. He was very sick for a long time," she said. "He had brain cancer." She went on, "Thank you," she said to us, "for making his last days so happy."

I don't think any of us were ever the same after that. We lost our new friend, who wanted nothing other than friendship. I think it was then, that I first realized, just how meaningless material things are. I haven't thought about those guys in a long time. I miss those days. Happy Birthday Pete! Happy Birthday Everyone. I still have the skates I was gonna give him.

The Vacation
(Genre: Family/Treasure Hunt)

It was dawn. The sky was grey and overcast. The air, cold and damp with mist from the low hovering clouds. I could hardly believe it was Summer. I looked out over the ocean but could not see a thing. Visibility was only about fifty feet. I felt bad, but worse for the kids.

Some vacation, I thought, stuck in a house on the rocky shores of Rhode Island for a whole week, with nothing but cold and rain. As I gazed at the water, I saw a ship. It was very close to the beach. It was old, ragged and tattered, and had three giant masts, but there were no sails attached. All that was left were some old torn remnants of dirty white cloth, hanging on the yardarms.

I was stunned. I couldn't believe what I was seeing. I immediately ran through the house screaming, "WAKE UP!"

I got the kids out of bed and to the large picture window overlooking the shore of the Atlantic Ocean. It was unbelievable. Suddenly, I heard the door close behind me. I turned around, and all six kids were gone. I ran out after them, and followed them down the beach to the water's edge. Like porpoises, one after the other, they dove right in and began to swim toward the ship.

The beach was eerily empty, and I had a bad feeling in the pit of my stomach. I shouted at the kids, but it was as if they were in a trance. I dove in.

As I neared the ship, the children were already aboard. There was a rope netting hanging on the side, which they had climbed up and into the boat. I grabbed a hold of it, and after quite a bit of struggle, I too, hoisted myself onto the deck. Suddenly, a wave hit the vessel, lifting it up off the sandy bottom, and launched it, and us, back into the heavy grey mist, hovering over the deep turbulent sea.

I tried to gather the children, but they were scattered about the deck from bow to stern. Jonathon was climbing up the center mast, headed for the crow's nest. The crow's nest is the small basket-like structure, built high on the mast, used by the lookout to help the captain avoid any hazards. Zachary had found a sword and was waving it all over, as if in a battle.

My heart leapt in fear. "I want you all to come here!" I yelled. It was to no avail. They were like zombies, totally enthralled in the moment. I looked for Jennifer and Amanda, but they had disappeared down some stairs, to some other level below deck. Christopher was at the helm. He was steering the boat straight away from shore, and had set his course to the open sea. I heard him holler, "Let's go, ye land lubbers. We have treasures to steal."

What was happening? They were somehow being taken over by some kind invisible force. My eyes roved the deck looking for Benjamin. He was near the stern end of the ship. He had found some old muskets and was loading them with gunpowder and metal balls.

"All clear captain," yelled Jonathon from atop the mast. "Full speed ahead."

I ran to the staircase where I saw the girls go down. I descended them four at a time, moving as fast as I could. I had to gain control of the kids as fast as possible. The girls I thought would be the easiest to bring back to reality.

I finally reached the lower deck. I scanned the area as best as I could. I didn't see them. I opened every door I came across. Most of the rooms looked like sleeping quarters. I needed to find the girls now.

Door after door and nothing. I began to panic, when suddenly, Amanda and Jennifer burst out of a large wooden door with big black metal latches on it. They were covered in jewels. Their eyes were wide and fixed. I grabbed and shook them, hoping to bring them out of this hypnotic stupor, but both at once, they turned on me, grabbing my arms and twisting them behind my back.

"To the captain!" said Jenn.

At the top of the stairs, Zach was standing, staring blindly right through me. He put the tip of the sword at my back and pushed it, making me move forward. Ben was now beside him with the musket pointed at me. Jonny climbed back down off the mast and joined the others. I was in front and they were all behind me, pushing me forward toward Captain Chris.

"Ahoy mateys," said Chris. "What have we here?"

"A traitor!" yelled Ben.

"Yea," said Jenn, "a traitor trying to ruin our fun."

"No!" I cried. "I just want to get us out of here and home safe."

"We should hang you from the yardarm and let the vultures pick your bones," said Amanda.

Jonny stood tall with one hand on his hip. He looked like a pirate. "Plank," he said.

Zach looked into my eyes. "What do you think Captain? Here's a plank walker if I ever saw one." Suddenly they all jeered. "The plank, the plank!"

"The plank it is mateys!" The captain tied the wheel secure to keep the ship, on course for the vast expanse of the mighty sea. The water was rough. I was marched over to the starboard side of the ship. Ben pushed the long plank out over the dark churning water. The waves were huge.

I stumbled back and forth trying to keep my balance, but the kids were steadfast. It was as if they had lived on the sea all their lives.

"This land-lubber won't ever ruin anyone's fun again," said Captain Chris.

They all looked at me with those hollow fixed eyes. Zach pushed the sword at my back and said, "Climb, you bilge rat."

I stepped up on the rail and onto the plank. My own kids were gonna do me in. I looked over my left shoulder toward the port side of the ship. I needed to make a getaway, and it had to be now.

I took a step forward like I was going to walk the plank, then suddenly, I spun around and jumped onto the deck, right in front of Zack. I grabbed his sword and pushed him against Ben at the same time. As they fell to the deck, I forced my way between the two girls, and scrambled toward the helm. As I reached the big wooden steering wheel, my arm came slashing downward with the sword, cutting the brown hemp rope that was holding our course. Jonny and Chris were right behind me, but I was fast, and this was my only chance.

I turned the huge wheel, steering the ship to spin sideways in the waves. Immediately a wave came crashing over the side rail, flooding the deck. I held tight to the wheel. Jonny and Captain Chris and the rest were knocked off their feet, but quickly regained their footing. I tugged the wheel hard, and as the next wave hit, the entire ship lifted out of the water and flipped over into the sea.

My eyes popped open. Oh God, I was in my bed. It was just a dream. I got up and went to the kitchen. I was shaking something terrible. I put on the coffee and looked out the picture window at the ocean. We actually were on vacation. We were on Ortley Beach, at the New Jersey Shore, and the weather was horrible these first two days. I guess that is why I had the dream. They were calling for rain today, but warmer, and the rest of the week looked promising.

As I drank my coffee, I got an idea. It was still very early, I would make an adventure for the kids. Something they would never forget. A hunt for buried treasure.

First I needed a map. I grabbed a brown paper bag and took it out on the deck, where I burned the edges with a lighter. When it stopped smoking, I took it into the kitchen, and sat at the table and drew my best, using a black pen. I sipped my coffee, and, looking out the window, saw some pretty good landmarks. I drew waves for the ocean, and I used the boardwalk for a starting point. I went across the street and even paced off and counted my steps to get to the buried treasure. I put and X on the map. I marked the spot on the beach near the red wood slatted dune fence, where I would bury it later.

Next, I went to my car. In the trunk was an old cigar box, which I used to keep a few loose tools in, in case I break down, and took it inside. Around Nine AM, the bank opened. I took twenty-five dollars, and cashed it in for all change. Dimes, nickels, and pennies. I left the money in the car. My better half took the kids to the water park in Seaside Heights, and I went to work.

I filled the box with the change. It was quite heavy. Then I covered it with tinfoil, shiny side out, and I wrapped it a whole bunch of times. I grabbed one of the kids' toy shovels, and again walked across the street to the beach. I went to the spot by the fence I had marked, and began to dig. It took me a while to get down deep enough to make the adventure last a while. Once it was buried, I put a small piece of tape on the fence right above the spot.

I went back to the house and furthered my plan. I would stick the map in the sand by the boardwalk ramp in the morning, leaving a little part of it sticking out to be seen. I was all set.

The day was warmer as the weatherman said and the kids all had a blast at the park. We cooked out on the grill for dinner and then walked the beach for a while. They were beat tired by Nine PM, and we put them to bed. Everyone was excited to go swimming in the ocean tomorrow. My brother and his kids were staying at a house a few blocks away and they were gonna hang with us on the beach too. I'm glad the cold and rainy weather was over. Now vacation could really start. I loved the ocean.

I was up at the crack of dawn and I planted the map. I sat on the deck drinking coffee and watched over the treasure. Twice I had to run to the beach and explain to the treasure hunters that this was my kids' treasure. I call them treasure hunters, people with metal detectors who scavenge over the beaches in the mornings, looking for jewelry and what have you. What happened next was just short of a miracle.

The kids were waking up and coming into the kitchen. I was watching an old man rummaging through garbage and looking all around under the boardwalk. The light bulb in my head immediately went on. I had an idea.

I made up a story about a bank robber, who stole thousands of dollars in change during the 1970's from the banks in Ocean County. I told them it was rumored that he buried it all along the beaches. He had been caught, but they never found the money.

My son Chris saw the old man out the window and said "Hey, maybe that's him."

"Well he did escape," I told them, "but I find it very unlikely that this is him." The old guy was right on top of the map. "Maybe," I said, "if it is him, he lost a map or something leading him to where he buried the loot."

Chris wanted to go out and ask him. "No," I said. "First we eat and then we go to the beach." The excited look on his face slipped away. He was the oldest of the six.

After breakfast, my brother John showed up with his two kids. "Okay, let's go swimming," I yelled, and the entire brood was heading out the door.

As we crossed the street, the kids were all looking down and over the sand.

JT, my brother's son asked, "What are you guys looking for?"

Amanda told him the story. His head, and that of his sister, Danielle, were now dragging the sand too. I saw the map sticking out as I stepped onto the ramp.

"Look good," I said.

"This is where I saw the old bank robber looking," said Chris.

Everyone looked hard. I played my part. "Okay, enough of this, we are here to go swimming," I said.

Just then Chris screamed, "I FOUND IT, I FOUND A TREASURE MAP!"

"Look," he said, "it even has an X on it."

The kids all gathered around him. Their excitement was unbelievable. I think they forgot about the ocean and everything else. Their eyes were wide and fixed. Their focus was solely on the treasure.

We set up our spot on the beach, laid out the blankets, and stuck the umbrella deep into the sand. "Help," they cried. "Help us find the treasure."

"That's up to you guys," I said, "but let me see that map." Chris handed it to me. "WOW! That sure does look like a treasure map!"

"It is, it is!" they shouted.

I walked with the map over to the ramp where I began the hunt. "Look here," I said, and pointed to a reference point on the map.

Amanda spoke up and said, "Hey, that looks like where we are, and that must be the ramp!"

"It does kind of look like that," I said. "Go find the treasure." It took about fifteen minutes and they were really close. I did give them one more clue, but just a small one.

They began to dig. Chris and JT started. They dug about a foot then got tired and moved away. Zach and Jonny jumped right in. They dug and dug. I think they got further than the older two. Then the girls, Danielle, Mandy, and Jenn also joined in the excavation. Ben was still a toddler, but he hung right by them. He was old enough to know something cool was going on.

Chris and JT got back into the hole. They lasted about two minutes and got bored. I heard one of them say, "There's nothing here." Jonny and Zach jumped right back in. They were the youngest other than Ben, but they weren't giving up. The hole was almost four feet deep now, and other kids on the beach were all hanging around the hole. Jenn, shared the story of the change bandit with them, and everyone was excited and watching. Even some adults were standing there.

All of a sudden, Zach or Jonny, I don't remember which one, caught a piece of the tinfoil in his hand. "I GOT IT!" I heard yelled from the hole. I turned to watch.

JT and Chris physically grabbed the boys and threw them out of the hole. The two of them dug like animals to get the treasure out. They lifted it up. "It's heavy!" they screamed.

"Bring it here," I demanded. Many people were now up and by the kids looking at what was going on.

Chris brought the tinfoil covered treasure box over to our blanket. I let them all watch close as Chris opened it up. You could have heard a pin drop in the sand, and then suddenly Chris grabbed a hand full of change and threw it in the air screaming, "WE'RE RICH, WE'RE RICH!"

Everyone started shouting and screaming and jumping up and down. I quickly closed the box to keep Chris from throwing any more. The crowd on the beach around us was huge. Our kids had found a treasure.

It didn't take but a few minutes before it began. "We want to go home and count it and split it up."

"Okay," I said. I grabbed the box and headed back across the street to our rented bungalow. The kids were watching me like a hawk. It was setting in. When I got into the house, I gave the box to them and said, "Count it and split it fairly. I don't want any problems."

When the counting was done, they split the money evenly. Then the complaining began. Greed. "You got more than me. I got cheated. Count it again." They argued and bickered for at least an hour. I fed them lunch and told them that if I hear any more squabbling, I would take and keep all of it. That did the trick. I guess they figured better to have something than nothing.

They all hid their money, and we went back to the beach. The weather was wonderful from there on out. We swam, played miniature golf, watched the fireworks on the beach, and even went on the rides one night at Seaside Park. What began as a miserable nightmare, became a vacation none would forget anytime soon. Still to this day, someone will mention the treasure.

Kids can be very observant too. Amanda, who was around nine years old at the time, came to me the night they found the treasure. "Dad," she said, "I thought you said the change bandit robbed banks in the Nineteen-Seventies?"

"That's right," I told her.

"Then why," she asked, "are a lot of my coins dated in the Nineties?"

I looked at her and smiled. She winked back at me and smiled from ear to ear.

After each vacation we ever took, our bills fell behind. We always managed somehow to eventually catch back up. I would not trade these memories for anything in the world, and suggest that everyone, put your family first. It is worth it. I promise.

The Legend of Mill Rift Rapids
(The Canoe)
(Genre: Family/Adventure)

Sometimes garbage doesn't stink.

I remember driving home from work one time, and along the side of the road in someone's trash, was a beat up, blue, fiberglass canoe. My ride to work was always two hours each way, and well, living by the river, I pulled right over to check it out. The front was broken out pretty bad. It looked like it hit a rock and shattered. I had patched my old fiberglass bathtub once and it was still holding, so I slid the canoe into my work van and tied the door closed on it. About two feet was sticking out the back. When I got home, the kids were going crazy. "Dad bought a canoe!" they screamed.

We had lived near the river a few years now. We rented the house. It was a big bi-level, which fit the eight of us just fine. Five bedrooms, three baths, and a good size piece of property bordered by woods for the kids to play and learn. We had taken tubes down the river once already. We were poor. On my way home a different time, I passed a garage sale that had big tractor tire tubes. Two bucks each. I had ten dollars left for the week, hahahaha that got me five tubes. There are still two left, this many years later. Anyway, I pulled the canoe out of the truck and put it in the yard. The kids sat in it and pretended to be riding the rapids in the river. I dug out the old sander, and what I had left of the fiberglass repair kit, which I used on the tub. It was rock solid hard. I promised the kids that I would have it fixed for the weekend, and began sanding the broken area down to bare fiberglass. The old gel coat paint was pretty tough to sand. I put an old wire brush wheel on my drill, and that ate it off much faster. Then I continued with the sandpaper and made it as smooth as possible.

The next day on the way home, I stopped at the hardware store and bought another kit. The kids were waiting anxiously in the driveway when I pulled in. I didn't even go inside, instead I went right to work. The children were small at the time, ranging from ages three to ten. Chris the oldest helped me spread the fiberglass cloth over the badly damaged area. When we were happy with how it was covering the hole, we removed it and began to put the gooey liquid resin on with paint brushes. Carefully we coated the entire area. Then we put the cloth back on and into the resin, and we painted it on the entire cloth, until it was completely covered. The resin soaks into the cloth, and bonds it to the canoe. When we were finished, we all went in for dinner and talked about going on the river.

After work the following day, I sanded it all smooth and gave it another coat. All I had left to do was paint it the next day. I couldn't afford the marine gel coat paint so I just used some old black spray paint we had in the garage. It worked great. The canoe was ready. I was confident that we did a good job, and it was sea worthy. It was Friday night and we were all set to hit the water in the morning. Delaware River, here we come. The oldest two, Amanda and Chris, had other plans for this Saturday, and the youngest one Ben, was a tad too small. That left Jenn, Zach, and Jonny, and me for the trip. No one slept long that night, not even me. The excitement was incredible.

It worked out better to just have the three kids and me. Instead of taking it to the rock beach down the road and taking turns, we had Mom drop us off up river, where we could hit the rapids and really have some fun. She even made us some sandwiches and drinks, and filled the small cooler for us to bring along. She drove my van into Port Jervis NY, and up the winding river road, toward the Mongap River fishing access. The day was warm, but overcast. The fishing access was virtually empty. I unloaded the canoe, put the paddles, life jackets, and the cooler inside. The wife and I carried it to the water's edge with our three youngens in toe.

"Okay," Mom said, "you all be good for Daddy. Listen to what he tells you and be safe." She hugged and kissed us all goodbye. "I'll meet you at the rock beach at sundown," she said. She beeped the horn and waved. We waved back, and off she went.

"Put on your life jackets guys," I said. They were on in a flash. I put mine on and slid the canoe into the water. "All aboard," I bellowed like an old sea captain. The kids jumped right in. I waited until they got seated, and then I gave it a big shove outward, and hopped in. It was already caught in the current and going sideways downstream. I reached for the paddle and almost flipped us over. Jenny screamed. The boys just laughed. "It's okay, Jenn," I said. "We won't flip. We are gonna have fun."

As I paddled, I could feel the canoe trailing to one side. I must have thrown off the balance with all the fiberglass and resin. But it was floating just fine. I could compensate for the trailing, with my paddle. We saw the first set of waves coming at us in the distance. The rapids looked small, until we got closer that is. They were taller than the canoe and looked kind of like haystacks. The front of the canoe went up high, and then pounded down hard in to the water.

"Yey!" yelled Jonny and Zach. "This is great." Jenn was quiet and holding on to me tighter than ever.

Wave after wave the canoe went up high and splashed back down. When we finally got through that set of rapids, Jenn relaxed. I saw a sigh of relief, then a smile of enthusiastic pleasure come across her face. She was going to be fine. We paddled some, and then we would just drift a little. We watched under the water as we floated downstream. We saw some pretty big fish and a lot of eels. "Look Daddy!" yelled Jenn. "A snake!"

"No baby," I said, "that's an eel. They won't bother us at all. They will swim away just like the fish do." She looked up at me, there were tears building in her eyes. "It's okay, Jenn," I assured her. "You know I would never let anything happen to you." The next set of rapids was approaching us fast. Jenn grabbed hold of me again but not as tight. These waves were not as big as the first ones were. The canoe lifted and fell over and over. About half way through, Jenn had let go, and was screeching like her brothers, and having fun. I smiled. I was glad she was getting accustomed to the river. It was such a blessing for our family to have a free place to fish, swim, canoe, and tube. The water got much calmer now. We decided to pull to the edge and eat, and maybe even explore a little. I was in no rush. As long as we made the rock beach by sundown, we would be just fine.

Part Two

After lunch we explored the land a bit. There was a train track following the river on the Pennsylvania side. We scouted around for about a half hour and then headed back to the canoe. When we reached the river, Zach dove in and Jonny was right behind him. Jenn looked at me. "Go ahead," I said. "It's fine."

"What about the snake, Daddy?" she asked.

"I promise the eels won't bother you." I climbed into the water with her in my arms. She screamed so hard I had to get right out. She was scared to death. I held her tight and said, "Okay, no swimming for you today," and I smiled at her. She calmed right down and played at the edge while the boys swam. "Okay fellas, time to get this trip moving again." They climbed out of the water and we all got back into the canoe, and off we went.

Jenny was the oldest of the three. She was seven, Zach was six, and little Jonathon was only five. She may have been the oldest, but she was also the smallest. The water began to get shallow and the boys and I got out of the canoe. Jenn wouldn't budge. I waded through the ankle deep water while the two boys pushed the canoe along. Jenn was smiling. "Home, driver," she said like a rich snobby person. Zach tilted the canoe to one side and Jenny grabbed the side and started to scream. "Alright fellas, that's enough of that," I said. Jenn settled back down and we continued through the shallows. The water gradually got deeper. When it was about a foot, we hopped into the canoe and started paddling downstream. It was eerily quiet on the river. Usually there are a lot of folks floating along on rafts, canoes, and kayaks, but not today. So far we had only seen one other canoe with an old man and woman. They passed us when we stopped for lunch.

The sun had been slipping in and out of the clouds most of the day, but now it was hidden behind the heavy grey blanket covering the sky. The temperature dropped about ten degrees. The wind was picking up, and I realized a storm was brewing. I hoped it would be a short one, but by the looks of the sky I knew it wouldn't. I knew the river pretty good from fishing when I got the chance, and I knew we had two more sets of rapids before our trip would end. The rapids change in size depending on the weather and the water level. At lunch, I had checked the canoe and the repair was holding well. I was a little worried about the oncoming storm, but we had no choice. We had to finish the trip.

"Listen, Dad," said Jonny, "I can hear the rapids coming."

"OH YEA," said Zach excited, as he pushed his paddle hard into the water trying to get to them faster.

The rain started. It got bad really fast. It was pouring like crazy, and the wind was tossing the canoe from side to side. Now I was nervous. The rapids were just a short distance ahead. Jenn was pulling my arm. "Look, Daddy, look," she said. I turned my head toward her and she was looking behind us. As my eyes looked back I saw a swell in the water completely across the river from one side to the other. It was coming at us fast. I tried to paddle out of the current toward shore, but the wind was driving me back toward the oncoming rapids. The canoe's reactions were also sluggish due to the repair. The trailing was helping the wind and current keep us out in the middle of the river.

"Everyone hold on tight," I said. The boys grabbed the side of the canoe and with their other hands grabbed the seat. Jenn grabbed me. I used the paddle as a rudder. I hung it out the back and held us straight in the water. The swell went under the boat, lifting us up about five feet. I watched the river's edge as the water went up while it passed us. I didn't know what was happening. I had never seen this happen while fishing, and I fished in some pretty bad weather. After the swell passed the water level stayed high. The rapids just ahead now sounded like thunder. I could see the turbulence. It was all white water. I was now frightened. I should never have taken the little ones out here alone. *I must be stupid,* I thought.

I took a deep breath and calmed myself down. "Okay kids, hang on tight. If anything goes bad, just float. You have your life jackets on, we will get through this." Jenn looked into my eyes. I tried not to show any fear. I forced a smile onto my face and whispered to her, "Just hold me tight and don't let go." The front of the canoe hit the first wave and we were launched into the air. We crashed back down into the water. Then up again. Water was everywhere. We splashed down and into the next wave. It came up over the canoe, soaking us, but luckily only an inch or two entered the boat. "Hold on tight!" I yelled again. Wave after wave bashed us and our canoe. As we were nearing the end of the rapids, Zach and Jonny were yelling and screaming, "YAHOO YAHOO!" Here I was scared to death, and they were having the time of their lives. Jenn just held onto me as tight as she could not making a sound. I steered the canoe with my paddle rudder out of the current and toward the edge. The canoe was half full of water but we were upright and alright. The boys and I tipped the canoe and emptied the water out.

"That was fun," said Jonny.

"Yea it was," said Zach.

Even Jenn now had a smile on her face. The rain subsided a little and we got back into the canoe and headed toward home. The only thing between us and the rock beach, was one more set of rapids. I felt better. We made it through this far, one more is a piece of cake.

Part Three

"There's water coming in through a tiny crack!" yelled Zach.

"Where I asked?" He showed me this minuscule hairline fracture. It was on the opposite side of where the old hole was, right at the tip of the boat. It did look like some water was seeping in, but with the rain it was hard to tell. "It's probably just the rain catching on the little crack in the gel coat," I said. As I looked, I could see thousands of these small cracks. I didn't notice them when I fixed the canoe. I looked over at the repair and it was in great shape, however there were the same star shaped cracks all over the canoe, except on the spot we re-fiber glassed. "It will be okay," I assured them. "We only have one more set of rapids and we are home free." The last set of rapids was closer to where I did most of my fishing. Down by the train trestle at Mill Rift. They were not as big as these others and I felt we could navigate our way through no problem.

The rain and wind were picking up again. Even with the drop in temperature earlier, it was still around eighty degrees. We were wet, but we were warm. I let Zach and Jonny paddle while Jenn and I again glared into the water intently, watching the rocks on the bottom and trying to see fish. Everything Jenn saw looked like eels to her. The weeds, sticks, even the rocks lol. Soon I heard the faint sound of rushing water. The current had picked back up and we were being sucked into the middle again.

"Give me a paddle," I said. Jonny handed me his, and again I used it as a rudder. I wanted to have control of our craft just in case. Within a few minutes the faint sound of gurgling water, had become a thunderous clashing of water crashing over the rocks in the river. I forgot about the water suddenly becoming so high, and the effect it would have on the rapids. My confidence dropped instantly, and fear and panic set in.

"Paddle hard left, Zach!" I yelled. "We need to get to the edge and get out of the river." My stomach had this terrible feeling. We paddled hard trying to battle the current, and the wind was once again our enemy. We were stuck in the middle and being drawn right into the biggest waves I have ever seen in the river. The wind was blowing so hard it turned the canoe sideways. We were dead for sure.

"Paddle hard right!" I screamed to Zach, as I used the rudder to get us straight. The first wave was big but we had managed to turn the canoe right in time. Up we went, then BAM! We splashed back down into the water. Up again, and BAM! Back down. Each wave seemed bigger than the one before it. The canoe was holding together, and the kids were holding on tight. *Please God,* I said to myself, *help us through this.* Coming down from the top of one wave, I saw ahead, the biggest one of all. The dam thing was at least twelve feet high, it looked like it could stop a bus. My heart sank. "Hold on tight, and remember if you fall out, to keep your legs up high in front of you, and just float with the current until you get to calm water."

"Okay," said the boys. Jenn began to cry.

"It is okay baby, we are going to be fine." I used every bit of calm I could muster, to sound confident enough to comfort her. "You will float," I said, "like a little beach ball." She looked at me and I saw her face relax. Waves were now crashing over the bow and the canoe was filling fast with water. It was getting heavy and not going up so high on the waves. Here it was, the bus stopper. Up we went. The wave carried the canoe the full length to the top, but this time it didn't launch us into the air; we were filled with water and too heavy. Instead the front of the canoe turned straight down towards the water. I was in the rear way up in the air. "Hold on kids, Daddy loves you."

The bow of the canoe came down fast and hard, and CRASH, BAM, SPLASH; it hit dead center on a big rock. All three kids were catapulted and launched out of the canoe, thrown far out in front and into the water. I saw them for a second, floating, but then I too, hit the water and rocks. The back end of the canoe smashed me in the head, and it was lights out. I must have been unconscious for a minute or so. When I opened my eyes, I was in calm water with my leg stuck under the seat of the canoe. I looked ahead for the kids.

"I have the paddles, Dad!" yelled Zach.

"And I have the cooler!" squealed Jonny.

Both were just floating freely in the water unharmed. I looked for Jenn, she wasn't by the boys. I scanned across the surface and she was not there. I turned my head back toward the rapids. My heart fell.

Part Four

My eyes searched over the rapids desperately trying to find her or some sign of where she was. Did she get caught on a rock, or sucked under in an eddy behind a rock? I was frantic. My brain was reeling back and forth. I was sick to my stomach and almost threw up. Just then Zach and Jonny had swam to my side.

"What is wrong, Dad?" they asked. "Are you alright?"

I turned to face them horrified. "Your sister is gone," I cried.

"What do you mean?" said Zach.

"Yea," said Jonny pointing his finger. "The old people have her over there on shore."

My eyes followed the direction of his finger and came to rest on the most precious site I have ever seen. There was the old woman holding Jenn safely in her arms. The old man was standing right next to her. I did not see their canoe, and there was no house around. They boys and I headed over to them pulling the canoe along with us. Jenn put her arm out to me and the woman gently handed her over to me. I held her so tight.

"You were right, Daddy," said Jenn.

"Everything is alright just like you said it would be."

I thanked the woman and her husband for their help, but they didn't speak. The woman's eyes had a soft glow about them as she looked at Jenn. Her and her husband's faces were kind looking but very solemn. "If there is anything at all I can do for you, just say the word," I said. The old man and woman turned away and stepped into the woods without a word, and were gone. I squeezed Jenn again, kissed her, and set her down alongside her brothers.

"We made it," I said.

"We're not home yet," chuckled Zach, looking at the canoe. The entire front end was smashed to bits and the only thing holding it to the rest of the boat was the fiber glass cloth we had applied with the resin. What I failed to realize when I found the canoe, was that it was very old, and very brittle from the elements. We still had about a mile to go. "We can walk the edge of the river to the rock beach," I said. The three kids looked at each other and got into the canoe. "Okay," I said, "we're gonna finish this trip in style." I tore off the rest of the loose broken end and set it in the middle of the canoe. I pushed the canoe out a little into deeper water, and climbed in the very back, and sat on the small triangular tip at the very end, and put my feet behind the back seat. Then Jenn and Jonny sat on the seat, and Zach sat on the floor right up against their legs. He handed me a paddle and hollered, "ALL ABOARD!"

With all our weight in the back, the front end of the canoe was up and out of the water. We had won the battle with the river. The storm was over and the sun was popping in and out again. As I paddled, I thought about the old people who helped us. I wondered who they were and where they went in the woods. As we came around the last bend in the river, there was my wife waving from the rock beach. What a site it must have been for her to see, the front end of the canoe missing, with her husband and kids still inside, paddling down the river. When we reached the beach, she hugged us all and told us she was so afraid. When she got to the dirt road that we use to get to the river, she said it was closed. Due to the pending storm, there were multiple dam releases up river and there was no canoeing or rafting allowed today. I never saw anything posted where we entered. I guess that was where the huge swell of water came from.

Jenn looked up at me and said, "Daddy, when can we go again?"

"Yea!" chimed in the boys. "That was the best ever!"

We loaded the canoe and headed home. After dinner I told my neighbor about our day on the river. He asked if I was gonna ditch the boat, if he could have it. I told him it was shot but he wanted it anyway. He went on to tell me a legend he herd long ago when he moved here. It was about a mother and father who lost their daughter in the river. They never found her and never gave up looking. He said that there were other stories like ours, of the old man and woman, saving children in the river. The stories began back in the late 1700's on the upper Delaware. When I told the kids about the legend, they asked me if it was the old people we met. "Maybe," was all I could say. Jenn and the boys, and Amanda, Chris and Ben, still use the river today with their kids. My neighbor restored the entire canoe. It still has a slight trailing to the right...

A Love Story For You
(Genre: Romance/Suspense)

I walked along the water's edge. The river was high and muddy from the recent rains. I needed to clear my head. I was by myself now, and I was lonely. This was my favorite place to come and think, in the woods by the river, with just Mother Nature and me.

I remember back when I was just a young girl, when my mom would take me here to swim on those hot sticky summer days. Oh the fun we had. Splashing and dunking each other, and then laying in the sun on our towels, just relaxing and talking for hours. Some days, if we didn't want the water to cool off, she would take me to the stores, and we would window shop in the cool air conditioning. Whatever we did, we did together. We were best friends. My dad had died just after I turned seven, and we were alone. Just the two of us.

Mom worked as a cleaning lady for other people. If I was sick and had to stay home from school, I would go with her. Unless I was very sick, then Mom would stay home and take care of me. She was a great role model and teacher. I learned everything from my mom. I guess that's why I miss her so much now. The last few years, she fell ill. She had cancer. It was a battle right up until the end. Mom was okay with moving on. She would tell me that, almost every day. I, however, was not. I wanted her alive, and here with me. She was all I had.

I never went on dates, or had many friends. We lived in a very rural area. When school let out, I took the bus home. We were the last stop on the route. The closest neighbor was two miles away. Her name was Lizzy. She had a brother named Jake. Their family was poor too. We didn't have cars like some folks, but every once in a while on a Friday, my mom would let me sleep at Lizzy's, or Lizzy would sleep at our house. We would use the school bus as our ride. Then on Saturday, Mom, or Lizzy's mom, would walk to our respective house and get us, and together, we would walk the two miles home. Sometimes, we would all have dinner before we left. It was great fun. I never told anyone, but I had a crush on Jake. They moved away and I never saw them after that. It was in sixth grade.

I thought about my life and what I was going to do. I had the house, my job, and my good old Chevy Impala; that was about it. I bought the car when I started working. One of the families that Mom worked for had it just sitting in their driveway, and they let me have it for two hundred dollars, which I paid them twenty a week until I paid it off. It was in very good condition.

I listened to the water gurgling over the rocks. It was making me miss her even more. I heard a noise in the woods and twisted my head around to see. It was a deer coming down to the water for a drink. I watch quietly as it waded in the water and drank. Then she saw me and bolted back up the little trail. *Maybe she is all alone too,* I thought.

I wondered about love. Not the kind I had with mom, but love with a man. Would anybody want me? I was now in my mid-thirties. I thought about what I'd missed in life. Kids. I always wanted one of my own. Travel. That would be okay I guess, but I think settling down and having a family would be nice.

I remember a little of how it was when Dad was alive. We would eat at the table and play games. He would take Mom out on dates. They would pack some food, and on special occasions, a bottle of wine. They would walk through the woods and just enjoy nature. I think I know now a little more of what it was about. I guess after Dad passed, Mom must have been very lonely also, but she never said a word or complained. I'm glad she at least had the chance to love and be loved. A chance I did not see in my future.

Suddenly, a group of about eight deer came running past. They jumped right into the water and began to swim across. I wondered what had spooked them so bad. I have lived here my entire life. *The only thing I know that scares them like that,* I thought, *are humans.* The hunters used to hunt here by the river and drive the deer. Sometimes the deer out smarted them by just crossing the river. It wasn't hunting season, and I've never seen a poacher around here. If it was humans, I had no idea who it could be. I got a bit frightened. *I wish my mom was here.*

I turned from the water and began to walk back up the trail toward the house. A man stepped out of the woods, startling the heck out of me. He said, "Hello." I looked him over good. *I could probably take him*, I thought. If needed, I know I would try my best and he would be sorry.

I responded back and said, "Hello." He asked if I lived around here. "I do," I said. "My husband is right up the trail by the house."

"How nice," he said.

"Where may I ask are you from?" I said a bit coldly to him.

"I," he said, "lived just a short distance away from here when I was a kid. I used to know the family that lived in that cabin. But that was years ago."

"Oh," I said, "what brings you here now."

"Well," said the man, "I came here to try and find some answers."

"Answers?" I asked.

"Yes," he said. "Living here was the happiest time of my life. Ever since my family moved from here, I have been empty inside. I thought perhaps returning to my roots, I may find some peace in my soul."

"I'm not sure what you mean," I said.

"I am lonely," he replied. "My mother and father have passed, and my sister moved out to the west coast a few years ago. I just needed to get close to nature again," he said.

"I understand that," I said. "I lost my mom recently and I too come here a lot to think. What is your name?" I asked him.

"My name is Jake. And yours?" he added.

I smiled at him and said, "Sarah."

"That's quite a coincidence," he said. "I had a crush on the girl who lived in that cabin back there when I was just a young boy. Her name was Sarah."

"That would be me," I whispered just loud enough for him to hear.

His eyes welled with tears. "Sarah? It's you?"

Part Two

"Yes, Jake, it's me."

Jake instantly moved forward to hug her. Sarah's eyes, now also filled with tears, glanced up the trail toward the house. Suddenly, Jake stopped his advance. "Oh," he said, "I'm sorry. You said you are married."

"I didn't say I was married. I said, my husband is up the trail by the house."

"Well that sounds like married to me," said Jake, now beginning to back away.

"There is no one by the house, I lied. I was being protective of myself. I did not know it was you."

"So you're not married?" he asked.

"No," I told him, "I am not. I never found the right person. I stayed with my mom ever since your family moved away."

"Well," said Jake, "she did a fine job raising you. That was very clever of you. I thought for sure he was up there."

I wanted Jake to hug me, to hold me in his arms, but it seemed the moment had passed. I thought quickly and stepped toward him lifting my arms gesturing him on. He again stepped forward and put his arms out and around me.

"Sarah," he said. He held me tighter than ever. I melted in his arms. Here he was, my childhood crush holding me tight, and my name on his warm breath. I was in heaven.

My emotions and my entire body were squirming with the excitement. I had never felt like this before. Jake put his hand on the back of my head and turned my face toward his. I closed my eyes in anticipation and seconds later his lips touched mine. He was forceful and I loved it. I kissed him back passionately. I felt like a teenager being kissed for the first time. I couldn't believe it when he stopped. I didn't want it to end. I could have stood there in his arms forever.

"We should talk," said Jake.

I knew in my soul he was right. We did not even know each other. Yea, we had memories, but from so long ago. Did we even like the same things? Did we want the same things in life?

Slowly we walked up the path toward my house. After I opened the door, Jake looked at me. "Are you sure you want me to come inside?"

Was he kidding? My mind was still reeling from his touch, from the feel of his lips pressed to mine. Of course I wanted him to come in. Come in and never leave again. "Yes Jake, I am sure. Please come inside."

He followed me through the door. "Wow Sarah, it is just like I remember it." He gazed around the room, and a picture on the shelf caught his attention. It was of both our families having dinner together. He walked closer to the picture. "I remember this picture," he said. "I wanted you even then."

In the picture, I was staring at him. He looked back toward me and deep into my eyes. Could he see my love? Did he know I yearned for him all these years? I felt flush and very warm.

"Why were you staring at me?" he asked.

I swallowed hard and leaned close to him, put my hand behind his ear, and whispered gently, "I have always loved and wanted you, Jake, and now, more than ever." Our arms wrapped around each other, and once more we kissed. I had never had these sensations coursing through my mind and body before, but it is everything I imagined I would feel with Jake.

After our embrace, Jake asked me if I would like to go to dinner. *Dinner,* I thought? *Is he crazy? Here we are meeting for the first time, touching and kissing each other, and he was thinking about dinner.* "I can cook here," I said willingly, not wanting to leave the cabin. "I am a great cook." I didn't want the mood to be broken. What if it didn't come back?

When he spoke it was as if he dropped a bomb. "We should take this slow," said Jake. "I would like us to get to know each other."

Yea me too, I thought, but that wasn't gonna happen in a restaurant. Suddenly it hit me. I was on fire with lust. I was alone and so lonely for so long, that I was desperate to feel a man. And Jake was the man. He was right. We needed to get to know one another. Mom always told me that relationships were not built on sex.

Relationships were forged with love. The intimate knowledge of learning each other's strengths and weaknesses. Mom said lust was what attracts two people, but love is what keeps them together. I remember her telling me that the initial fireworks in every relationship don't last. They are to blind us to the bad parts of the other until the love bond is stronger than the faults. Without the lustful attraction, no one would take the time to get to know each other. Well I had enough lustful feeling for Jake to last a lifetime.

"Alright," I said, realizing the public arena may be a better place to become reacquainted. My bedroom would have to wait. "I would love to go to dinner with you, Jake."

My old Impala was in the driveway. I went for the door and Jake grabbed my hand and turned me fast, face to face. His lips hit mine like lightning and his tongue pushed through and into my mouth. I almost fainted with desire. My hand came off the handle and I held him tight and kissed him back as hard as I could. My legs went weak. *I wish he did this while we were still inside. I'd have given myself to him right then and there.*

He slowly pulled his lips from mine and, looking deep into my eyes, said, "I love you, Sarah."

Tears rolled down my cheeks, and I tightened my grip even tighter, if that was even possible. I looked up, "I love you too, Jake."

Jake's car was parked down the road near the deer path leading through the woods and to the river. He wanted us to take his car. "Okay," I said, "mine is old and beat up anyway."

As we walked to his car, I was walking on air. I couldn't believe this was really happening. When I saw his car, I almost fainted again, but not from a lustful feeling this time. It was a chauffeur-driven limousine. I looked at Jake. "I'm rich," he said smiling at me.

I couldn't wrap my head around what he was saying. He was in jeans, work boots, and a flannel shirt. "What do you mean rich?" I asked.

"I have done quite well in life," said Jake. "Everything I touch seems to turn to gold for me. Except with love. I have never found happiness. That is, I think until now. I can give you anything your heart desires," said Jake.

"I have already found my fortune in life," I said to him. He looked at me puzzled. "You, Jake." Our lips met again with more ferocity than the last time.

"Madam, Sir," said the driver, holding open the car door. My eyes opened, Jake's were still closed tight, but I could see him looking at me inside. I pulled my mouth from his and squeezed his arm as I did.

"After you," said Jake.

I was never in a limo before. It was huge. There was even a small bar and a television.

"Where's the pool," I asked. Jake looked at me. I smiled and laughed. "I was just kidding."

"It is in my house," Jake said smiling back. "Where would you like to eat?"

I felt ill at ease about picking a place to eat. For me, the local diner was about the nicest place I ever ate at. Mom and I went there on the first Saturday of every month as long as we had the money. "You pick," I said.

Jake leaned up to the driver still holding the door and whispered in his ear. The driver said, "Very good, Sir," and then closed our door. He got in the driver's seat and off we went.

I was stunned when the driver pulled into the local diner. Jake looked at me. "I have never been happier in my life," he said. "Will this place be okay?"

I thought of my mom. I knew she was watching over me. I mean really. He was rich, but we came here. "I couldn't be happier," I told him. "This place is just perfect."

The driver got out and began walking toward my door. Jake motioned something to him and he got back into the car. Jake got out and walked around the car. He put his hand on the handle to open the door for me, and WHAM! A car hit Jake and the side of the limousine. He was there and then he was gone. The limo shook hard and the driver was leaning sideways unconscious.

I screamed, "JAAAAAAAAAAKE!!!!!!!"

Part Three

I jumped out the door on the opposite side, and up onto the sidewalk. I ran toward the front of the car, and there was Jake, lying on the ground right behind the parked car in front of us. People from inside the diner were already pouring out the door. "We called the ambulance," I heard one man say.

I crouched down next to Jake; he was out cold. I put my hand near his mouth, and I felt his breath on my wrist. *He's alive.* I called his name loud and abrupt, but no response. I saw a bone sticking out of his right leg, straight through his jeans. His pants were soaked with blood. He looked alright other than that, although his head was laying kind of crooked to his shoulders. Then I saw a small trickle of blood coming from his ear, and a small puddle forming by the back of his head.

"Out of the way, folks," said the medic. I was about to move when he pushed me hard away from Jake. I scrambled to my feet and began crying. One medic was at the car checking on the driver, who was just waking up. The other car was kind of crushed into the driver's door, angled toward the front. Another medic was tending to the guy driving the car which hit us. He was put on a stretcher and they covered him with the white sheet. I later learned that man had a heart attack, and that was what caused the crash.

I sat in the Emergency room with Jake for hours. Even though he was breathing, they did a tracheotomy and hooked him up to a respirator. They did an MRI and a CT scan. Jake was in pretty bad shape. He had a compound fracture to his right femur, a Jefferson burst fracture in his neck, and a head injury. "He must have tried to get out of the way from the car," the policeman said. "The car bumper struck his leg, pushing him forward and into the rear end of the parked car, head first."

I stood over Jake just looking at him. My heart was in agony. "Wake up, Jake, please just wake up." I closed my eyes and kissed his lips softly, and I heard movement. My eyes darted open expecting to see his, but they were closed. It was only a technician coming to check his vital signs.

They worked pretty fast on him considering what I knew about hospitals. With Mom, everything was as slow as trying to pour molasses out of the jar. But with Jake, it was different. Maybe because he was young and hurt so bad, or maybe they knew he was rich. Either way, they acted fast. He went from the ER to surgery and they fixed his leg. A titanium rod had to be inserted. It would stay with him for the rest of his life.

After surgery, he was put in to the intensive care unit, or as a lot of people call it, the ICU. He had a hard plastic Aspen collar around his neck, and a bandage on his head. He was still unconscious. The doctor said that Jake's head injury had caused severe brain trauma, and only time would tell if he would recover. Being in a small town hospital, doesn't always offer the best treatments like you get in the big cities.

I woke up in the chair around nine in the morning. Jake was lying in the bed exactly the way I left him. Nothing had changed. Again I called his name hoping to stir some kind of response. Anything at all, would have been great. Nothing. I just sat there all day, waiting, expecting him to wake up because he loved me and I loved him. This wasn't the movies, though; if he was to wake up, it would be when his brain said so. I decided to go home and shower, and get changed into some clean clothes.

It felt like a life time since yesterday on the riverbank. I looked at the picture on the shelf. I had waited all my life for Jake and didn't even know it. He was the one. My one and only. I held the picture against my heart and cried. I was also Jake's one and only true love. I realized right then, that we were soulmates.

I had to get cleaned up, and I did so in a flash. I was in a hurry to be by him no matter what. If I stayed by his side, I thought, he would be fine, and we would live out our destiny together. I had to get back to the hospital.

I grabbed a water and some crackers, and climbed into my old Chevy and started it up. *What if he doesn't remember me when he wakes up?* I thought. I dismissed the idea and zoomed out of the driveway and toward the hospital. *If Jake wakes up, I need to be at his side. He will see me, his love, and we will be together.*

It had been almost five hours since I saw Jake. I wondered if he was awake yet. I thought of Mom again, and how she always told me that my Mr. Right would show up when I least expected it. She always seemed to know everything. I bet she never thought it would happen like this.

I turned into the hospital parking lot, and pulled into the closest spot I could find. I hurriedly walked inside and up to the ICU. Before I could press the button to ask the nurse to open the door to the unit, it opened, and a cleaning person came out. I slipped in and dashed to Jake's room. It was empty. It was all clean and ready for a new patient.

I think my heart stopped beating. I ran to the nurses' station. "Where is my Jake?" I asked in a panic.

"Who are you?" she asked me.

"I am Jake's girlfriend," I said. "I was here all through the night by his bedside. I just went home to get cleaned up. Where is he?" I persisted.

"I am not allowed to give out any information," she told me. "Only to immediate family members."

"Is he dead?" I asked, starting to cry.

"No," said the nurse.

"Then where is he? What is going on?" She could see I was genuinely distraught.

"How long have you two been dating?" she asked me.

I looked into her eyes and shared the whole story. I watched as tears began to fill her eyes too. The nurse pulled me into the linen closet and said, "They flew him to another hospital better equipped to care for him."

"Where," I asked. "What hospital?"

"I do not know what hospital," she said, "but it is somewhere out west."

I went to the hospital administrator's office and demanded to know where Jake was flown. "I'm sorry, Ma'am, but by law I cannot release any patient information without the patient or legal guardians consent."

I told him the story of how Jake and I came together after all these years, hoping to get him to be sympathetic. But he was cold. "I'm sorry Ma'am," he said. "It's the law."

After trying several other offices, I gave up and left. I sat in my car crying for hours. "Oh Jake. Oh my precious Jake." *Out west? Jake said*

Lizzy moved out west. I wonder if that is where he was sent. Out by Lizzy. That made some sense to me, but how would they have known?

I decided to drive to the police station. They must have police reports. I was involved in the accident. They had to give me copies. "No, Ma'am, the reports will not be ready until Tuesday."

"Tuesday," I barked at him. "That's five days away."

"I'm sorry," he said. "You can come back then, and we will make your copies."

I had no choice; I would have to wait.

I was a wreck. My whole life was turned upside down and twisted inside out. Finally, I had my true love, my one and only, my Mister Right, and poof he was gone.

I lay on my bed crying for days. *If only I had said no to dinner and just stayed here, we would be holding and loving each other right now.* I cried even harder.

As each day passed, I felt a little better. The pain in my heart was still strong, but I stopped crying. I was a woman, not a little girl any more. I would forge on. Tuesday came and I picked up the police reports. They even had the nerve to charge me a dollar per page. I sat in my car and opened the envelope. It had to have Jake's name and address; after all, it was his car.

I read through the reports; Jake's name was there, but no address. He was listed as a passenger, as was I, in a vehicle owned by Lexi's Limo Service. It was not Jake's car; it was a rental. There was no other useful information in the report.

I decided to drive to the diner and get something to eat. I probably lost ten pounds this week and I was hungry. I asked the waitress if I could use the phone book and she brought it right over to me. I looked up Lexi's Limo Service. There was only one listed in the state and it was 100 miles south of here. I went to the payphone on the wall and dialed the number.

"Lexi's Limo's," the man answered. "How can I help you?"

"Hi," I said, "I was wondering if you could help me."

"What do you need, Ma'am?"

"I am looking for the address of one of your patrons, a Mr. Jake Morgan."

"I'm sorry lady, but we don't give out our client's information, it is against policy."

"But," I said, "I was the victim in a car accident with him in one of your limousines in Prattsburgh last week."

"Oh, that car," he said. "I'm sorry, Ma'am, that car was reported stolen a week before the accident. You will have to contact the police department for any information."

My jaw hit the floor. *Stolen?* I was numb. My brain was all over the place. *Who is he? I hate him, no I love him. Oh god, Mom, please help me!*

Part Four

I pulled into a gas station off Route I-86. The trip was almost two hours long, and I was about half way there. The Elmira Airport was in the middle between Prattsburgh and Sayre. Sayre was actually in Pennsylvania, but very close to the border. I was glad they decided to advertise in the state phone directory. I guess when you are so close to the state line, you get customers from both sides.

I put the nozzle into the tank and went to pee. Forty five miles and I was already peeing. *It must be my nerves,* I thought. I hadn't had any coffee since last week at the diner. I didn't even eat the food I ordered. After calling Lexi's, I got light headed and sick. I went to the bathroom and threw up. I drove home and went to sleep. It felt so good to lie in my bed. I stayed there for days. Depression was overwhelming me.

"Mom is that you?"

"Yes, Sarah, it is okay. Everything is going to be fine.

The plane landed and I got off. Mom was waiting in the driver's seat of the Limo. She got out and opened the back door for me, and there was Jake. I climbed inside and she slammed the door hard.

The sound jolted me awake. I was still in my bed; I was dreaming. The room lit up and then boom, the thunder. It was one in the morning and I was wide awake. I paced the house for an hour trying to think, but the dream had consumed my every thought. I decided to drive to the limo shop. By three, I was showered and in the car. The ride was good. This early, there were no cars on the road except mine. It was as I passed the airport that I noticed my gas tank was nearly empty, so here I am.

I paid for the fuel inside the mart, and grabbed the local newspaper and a coffee. I would be at Lexi's in an hour, and they were not open until seven. I could read the paper for a while to steady my nerves while I waited.

Gas tank filled, I headed back down the highway toward Sayre. I don't know what I was going to find out, but I had to try and find out about Jake. Anything at all. I had to know. My soul was twisting and tearing inside me. I needed answers. Even if I couldn't have him, I needed to know something; I needed closure.

As I drove, I thought about my dream. I was in a plane, and my dead mom was waiting for me in a limo, with my love inside. *Why did I dream this? It must mean something.* They flew Jake away in a plane. The driver of the other car was dead. My mom was dead also, but alive driving the limo. The only thing that made sense to me was Jake. He was there in the back of the

Limo. I was confused and tried to shake it all from my mind. The coffee was refreshing and welcomed. I sipped it as I drove.

Welcome to Pennsylvania. It wasn't much further now. The next sign said four miles to Sayre. My stomach started to have the butterflies. I felt a little panicky too. *Maybe it's the caffeine*, I suggested to myself, but I knew better. I was afraid. *What if Jake stole the car?* I didn't care if he was rich or not, but the lying, that would be unforgivable. Especially in the first hours of our miraculous reunion.

I began to wonder if he set me up. *Had he known I was alone and still lived in the cabin? Was I his next mark? Maybe he saw Mom's obituary and decided to prey on my emotional sadness and weakness.* My mind plotted crazy scenarios. I slapped my face. I remembered how Jake stopped us from going all the way. He said he wanted us to take things slow. I wondered. The only thing I had of value was the cabin, and that wasn't much; I wouldn't think enough to try and scam someone. Jake, maybe he was a conman after all.

I turned onto Canal Street and immediately saw the big lighted sign. "LEXI'S LIMO'S". I pulled into the lot and parked. It was just past six in the morning. I had an hour to wait. Between the coffee and my nerves, I was fully awake. I reached over and took the newspaper off the passenger seat. The seat looked like I felt, empty and alone. Even so, I was determined to get some answers. I needed to heal.

I put my seat back and lifted the paper to read. My thoughts interrupted every sentence and made it hard. I was on maybe the third page, when the parking lot lights went out. It was daybreak. I turned on the interior light to keep reading. A small headline on the next page caught my eye and my interest.

"LIMO DRIVER ARRESTED IN FATAL CRASH". I shook my head in disbelief, it couldn't be. It was.

Apparently, the limo driver had worked at Lexi's. He stole the limousine and used it to pick up clients at the airport in Elmira. He had been working the scam a little over a week when the crash occurred. It went on to say that the accident left one dead and one critically injured. Two others were treated and released. The driver was picked back up and arrested two days later. *It wasn't Jake, it wasn't Jake. Surely they would have said he was involved if it had been him.*

A car pulled into the lot behind me and I put the paper down. A man came over to my car and asked if everything was alright. "Yes," I said. "I came to talk to the manager."

"That would be me," he said. He opened the door and turned on the lights. "Now how can I help you?"

I explained who I was, and that I needed any information he could give me.

"OH, I remember you," he said. "You are the lady on the phone last week."

"Yes," I told him.

"I'm sorry you drove all this way. I told you before you need to speak with the police."

"I know," I said, "but did you know they caught the man who stole your vehicle?"

"Yes of course. I was notified immediately. He was a former employee of mine."

"What else can you tell me?" I asked him.

"I know nothing more than that," he said. "My car was stolen by an ex-employee, and involved in a fatal accident."

"Yes," I said, "and my boyfriend is in critical condition."

"Well shouldn't you be by his side then?" he said.

I looked at him with tears in my eyes and said that is all I have been trying to do. "No one will help me." The tears came fast and strong. I was crying hard again. "No one will help me."

"Calm down Ma'am, calm down. Everything is going to be fine. I don't know if this helps, but my driver, when he worked for me, always picked up his clients from the Elmira Airport."

Tears slowing, I choked out a few words, "I read that in the paper. How can that help?"

"Well," said the manager, "his job was to only pick up clients from privately-owned planes.

They pay the best and he knew that. Maybe your boyfriend came off a private jet."

My eyes popped open wide. I jumped up and threw my arms around him. "Thank you, oh thank you1" I said excitedly. "That must be it. Thank you. I have to go now, I have to go!" I rushed to my car away I went.

I was on the highway and speeding back toward the airport. *It never dawned on me that he flew here, and rented the car.* "Let's take my car," he had said. *It was his car; his rented transportation.* What a fool I was, how could I have not trusted him? Our short time together was just too intense to be fake. *No, my Jake is real and I am going to find him.*

The airport was quite large. I did a lot of walking and asked many people a lot of questions. After going from one place to another for almost two hours, I wound up at the base of operations office. The young man working there was very nice. Handsome, too, I might add. He was about my age, well perhaps a year or two younger than me.

"My name is Fred," he said. "How can I assist you?" I told him my whole story. He looked at me the entire time I talked. He listened to every word I had to say before he spoke. When I finished, he wiped a tear from his eye, and vowed to help me. "That was the saddest, most loving story I have ever heard," he said.

He took my hand in his and led me to another room. As we neared the door he slipped his other arm around me and his hand gently rested on my side. He gave a soft squeeze and then took it away and opened the door. It was a file room. "All the flight manifests are filed here," he said. I think he was just trying to be comforting. I won't lie though, his touch felt good and stirred something deep within me. "It will take me some time to look through all these files," he said. "If you give me your phone number, I'll call as soon as I find something."

His eyes were soft and honest looking.

"Alright, that would be wonderful," I said. I gave him my number and he walked me all the way back to my car.

"I am very touched by you and your story," he said to me. "I wish you all the luck in the world finding him." He put his arms out as if to comfort me. I was not uncomfortable and I let him hold me. "I'll find him, Sarah," he squeezed me. "Don't you worry." He let go.

"Thank you," I said. "I'll be waiting for your call." He opened the car door for me and I got in. "Thank you again Fred," I said, and drove toward the exit to go home.

I don't know why, but for some reason, I found myself thinking about Fred. It was like there was some kind of connection between us. He was a good man, and he was going to help me find Jake. I drove the last forty miles in quiet, just reflecting.

Time began to pass. I was back to work and back to my usual routines. Loneliness was my life. I wondered if Jake was even alive. It had been months since our encounter by the river and my feelings were once again going dormant. All I could do was wait.

The young man at the airport, Fred I believe his name was, promised to call if he found anything, but so far no call. I walked by the river a lot more these days, hoping and longing for a sign, or maybe what I really wanted was love. *Maybe Jake had passed,* I thought. *Will I spend my life alone? Well there are no men lined up at my door so I guess I will have to be content with my memories of my Jake.*

I was so lonely. I missed Mom a bunch. I thought of her and Dad, having their dates out in the woods, just them and Mother Nature. It made me smile. *If ever I get the chance, that is how I want my relationship to be. I think Jake wanted that too.*

RRing Brring, RRing Brring.

I jumped up, startled by the phone ringing. My old phone hasn't rung since after Mama's funeral. "Hello," I said.

"Hi, is this Sarah?" asked the voice on the other end.

"Who is this?" I asked.

"It's me, Fred, from the airport."

My heart leapt into my throat. The lump was there and my eyes began to well up. "Yes, Fred, it is me, Sarah. Have you found anything?"

"I was calling to see if you have found Mr. Morgan?" he said.

"No, nothing yet," I told him. "I was actually waiting on you. You are my last hope."

"I have spent a lot of time looking through those files," he said. "It's going to take time to get through them all. But I was wondering if you might like to have dinner with me sometime?"

I thought about him for a second and how nice and caring he was toward me and my plight. "Yes, Fred, I would like that very much."

I flashed back to Jake, the dinner and the accident. I shook my head, *I need to move forward.* "When would you like to go?"

"How about Friday night?"

"Okay," I said, "where shall we meet?"

"I know a great place," said Fred. "It's closer to my house if you don't mind the drive."

"No, not at all. Give me the address and I'll meet you there."

"Is eight o'clock alright with you?" he asked.

"Eight is fine," I said. "I'll see you there."

"It's a date then," he said and hung up.

A date, I thought. *I just made a date with a man.* I was alone and the companionship would do me good. Besides, he was doing me a favor spending all his break times looking through files to find Jake's plane registration and address. He was a good hearted man. I remembered him wiping the tears from his eyes when I told him my story. "A date it is," I said out loud.

I felt better than I had in a long time. It was Friday, I was done working for the week, and I had dinner plans. I was feeling a little smug. Happiness was creeping slowly back into my life. God knows I needed it. I got home and took an extra-long shower and cleaned extremely well. I groomed myself, the first time in months. Damn I needed it. I dried my hair and used the curling iron to give it a little pizzazz. I put on my only evening dress; I had to get it for a function at work once. It was beautiful. It felt superb to get all dressed up, and to be going out on a date with a nice guy. A date with anybody!

I thought about Jake while I was driving. I wondered if he was awake, in a coma, alive or dead. I hadn't heard from him. "I will find you, Jake," I said to myself. "I promise." I wondered if I was cheating on him going on this date. *If he was alive and awake, he could have contacted me if he wanted. Right?* I asked myself. I was doing this for him and that's that. This wasn't cheating. Besides, it is just dinner with a friend.

It took me just under an hour to get to the restaurant. The Elbow Room, in Elmira. Fred was standing at the door waiting. I was late. Only ten minutes, but none the less, late. "Hello, Fred."

"Hello, Sarah. You look beautiful." He put his arms around me and held me tight for a second and then released me. It was good. Just a healthy hug. "I have a table for two waiting for us." he said. "How was the drive?" he asked.

"It was fine," I said, not wanting to get my brain back on the cheating thing.

Fred held the door and I went in first. The hostess led us to our table, where Fred, being a perfect gentleman, held my chair as I sat down. He pushed me in and then put his hands on my bare shoulders. They were strong and warm. I felt myself quiver. *I hope he didn't notice.* I saw other woman eyeing him. He was handsome. Just the way he carried himself, and holding my chair, I think they were jealous.

The menus were already on the table. The place was cozy and had a comfortable family atmosphere. "Your waiter will be over shortly. Can I get you something to drink while you wait?"

I ordered a glass of wine. "Make that a carafe, and two glasses," Fred told her.

"I'm not much of a drinker, Fred, and I do have to drive home. It will probably be wasted."

"That's okay," he said. "If we want it, it is here."

I smiled. That seemed reasonable enough to me. Growing up poor, I learned that you don't waste anything. If he didn't mind wasting his money, who was I to argue?

We talked about Jake at first, but then the subject was about me. Fred wanted to know everything about me and I just kept talking like a chatty school girl. I didn't realize it, but by the time the food came, half the carafe was gone. We ate and talked. He made some jokes that were actually pretty funny. He had me laughing so hard. I was having such a good time with him.

When dinner was finished, so was the wine. I excused myself to go to the ladies room to pee. Fred took care of the check while I was gone. When I came out of the bathroom, we left the restaurant. I was more than tipsy. I was drunk.

Part Five

I couldn't drive like this. *What am I gonna do?* "Jake," I said. He looked at me. "Fred," I said, "I'm so sorry."

"It's alright, I understand," he said softly. He really was a great guy.

"Fred I can't drive, I'm drunk. I need to get a room."

"You can stay with me in my apartment," he said. "I promise to be a perfect gentleman. And best of all, I live right down the street so we don't have to drive."

I thought for a second and said, "Agreed, I'm sleeping with you." I slurred the words. I was feeling very woozy from all the wine.

It was only a block, but I was getting drunker as we walked. When we got to the door of his place, he fumbled with the keys, dropping them on the floor. We both went for them at the same time and bumped heads. When we came up he had the keys, and his eyes were fixed on mine. He put his arms around me again and pushed his mouth on mine. My tongue went into his mouth kissing him back.

He felt soooo goooood. I couldn't help myself. We went inside and he turned on a dim light in the living room. I sat down on the couch and he sat right down next to me. His hand was under my dress in seconds. "Oh, Jake," I said. "Yes, I love you."

"I love you too, Sarah," he said. His mouth found mine again, and our tongues swirled around and around and around. I could see Jake's face even with my eyes closed.

"Yes, Jake," I said again. His lips were life fire on mine. I felt his hand sliding up my leg, "Oh Jake," I said, opening my eyes to see him. "NOOOOO STOP NOOOO. NOT YOU! You're not Jake. Stop. Stop!"

Fred pushed himself closer. He was not going to stop. I grabbed the low lit lamp and smashed him over the head. He fell to the floor unconscious. I went to the kitchen and splashed cold water on myself. *I need to get sober and get out of here.*

I heard Fred moaning on the floor. I grabbed a long knife from the kitchen drawer and went back to the living room. Fred was on his knees. "No, please don't kill me!" he said. "I have the file right here. I was going to give it to you in the morning."

"Yea," I said, "after you gave it to me tonight. You are a pig."

"I am," said Fred. "You are so beautiful, I just had to have you. I knew if you were lonely enough you would be easy to seduce. I found the file the same day you came to the airport."

"You're worse than a pig," I said. "You should be in jail."

"I'm sorry," said Fred. "Here is the file."

I took the manifest from him. I glanced inside and saw Jake Morgan written on the top. I threw the knife toward him, almost hitting his arm, and I turned and left.

I walked back to the restaurant where my car was and went inside and ordered a coffee.

"Is everything alright, Miss?" asked the hostess. I wondered if I should call the police. After all, he planned this whole thing. He was just some creep taking advantage of girl in a weak state of mind. I remembered thinking that about Jake once. I was wrong about Jake, but this guy? "Yes, everything is fine," I told her. "I just had too much to drink and made a bad decision. I'll be fine. Is there a motel near bye?" I asked.

"There is one a few miles closer to town," she said, "but we have a few rooms here, that we rent to our patrons when they have had a little too much to drink. They are forty dollars for the night."

"Wonderful," I said, "I'll stay here."

She led me to the office and I got the key and went up to my room. I laid on the bed. I couldn't believe what almost happened. I opened the folder. The manifest was blank other than Jake's name. *That son of a bitch,* I thought, *he even faked the manifest.* I guess that was going to be my parting gift. Oh what a sucker I had been. No more!

I left work early today. I was feeling down and wanted to go to the river. It's been two years to the day since I met Jake in the woods. He was still consuming my thoughts, but I have no means of finding him. I guess he probably died, or remained comatose in a hospital bed somewhere. Maybe he and Mom were looking down watching me together, waiting for the one day I will be with them forever.

I was tired of being lonely and alone. I thought a lot about the river. The rains were heavy all month and the river was high and muddy, just like that wonderful day. I drove toward home. I was going to leave a note at work because no one would ever go to my house and find it, but I didn't. No one cared any way. The water would be rough and the current strong. *Far stronger than me.* It would be called an accident. *If you only knew my pain. My desire to be loved and to love that one and only back. My hurt and loneliness have brought me to the end. I can't go on alone anymore.* That's what my note would have said if I had written one.

I pulled the car into my driveway for the last time. I changed into my heaviest jeans, sweater, and work boots. I slowly walked down the path toward the river. *I give up God.* I could hear the roar of the river. I would not hesitate.

As I came around the last bend in the trail, there, standing alone on the river bank was a man in a t-shirt, his leg was a bit crooked.

"Jake!" I screamed.

He turned toward me. "That would be me," he said, just loud enough for me to hear.

I ran and jumped into his awaiting arms. I threw my arms around him and he held me tight. "Hold me and never let me go again, Jake."

"I won't," he said, "I promise."

We walked back up to the cabin and went inside. I grabbed him and pushed my lips on his and my tongue into his mouth. He squeezed me hard and kissed me back.

We were standing in the doorway to my bedroom, his back facing my bed. He pulled his mouth from mine and said, "Sarah, we need to…"

I put my fingers over his mouth and said, "Shut up, Jake," pushing him back and onto my bed.

They remained in the cabin by the river. The forest was their playground. Jake and Sarah were together for all eternity.

Labor Day Memories
(Genre: Health/Friendship)

Part One

It was a beautiful Monday morning; it was Labor Day. The sun was already shining bright with blue skies and a temperature of around 70 degrees, of a 90 degree forecast for the day. I had just opened the coops to let the chickens and ducks out, and was on my back deck having coffee and eating my breakfast, when I heard the engine sputtering in and out.

It sounded very close. At first, I thought it was the kids down the road playing with their mini-bikes, but then I remembered they were still on vacation at the Jersey Shore. Suddenly the sputtering stopped and it was quiet. All I heard was the peeping of the baby chicks and ducklings, and the wild birds eating the feed of the ground inside the run.

I lifted the mug, and tilted my head back to take the last swig of coffee, when suddenly, right over my head, just missing the rooftop, was a small plane, heading straight towards the stable yard further down back. My head flung wild and I dropped the cup, spilling the last sip all over my face. I stood up in horror and watched the final seconds of its decent to the ground. If it could clear the trees, I thought, maybe they could land safely. It seemed the engine had quit, and the pilot was guiding the gliding craft the best he could.

I grabbed my phone and bolted down the stairs. I watched the small plane as I ran. With the trees now in the way, I could not see them. All I heard was the cracking of tree branches, and the screams of what sounded like a young girl. I continued to run, my heart pounding with fear.

When I reached the lower part of the yard, near the stable, I saw the plane in the middle of the fenced-in oval paddock. The pilot had somehow managed to land the plane safely, even after taking down an old dead tree. He was climbing out when I entered and finally reached the tiny plane. It was a very small homemade, single-engine ultra-lite.

"Are you okay?" I asked in a panic, still breathing heavy from the run.

"I am," he said.

"And how about the girl? I heard her screaming."

"There is no girl, or anyone else with me," said the man. "My plane only has room for one, and that one," he said smiling, "is me."

I looked over in the direction of the barn. The two girls whose dad boards their horse in the stable, were there cleaning out the stall. They were walking through the field heading our way.

"Was it you I heard screaming?" I asked.

"Yes," said the younger one. "I thought he was going to hit the stable, and all the horses are still inside. We just arrived to feed, clean, and let them out. I am sorry I scared you," she said.

"Oh that is perfectly fine," I said. "This man scared us all."

After talking for a minute or two, the girls went back to do their chores. I turned my attention again toward the pilot and his plane.

"My name is Mike," I said. "I'm glad you are okay."

"Yes, me too," he said. "My name is Milan."

"I heard your engine die?" I told him. "What happened?"

"It's a long story," said Milan. "It was my own fault. I hadn't planned on having such a strong headwind when I calculated the amount of fuel it would take to reach the airport. I guess I came up a bit short."

"Well," I said, "if you were trying to reach the Sussex Airport, you came very close. It is about five miles further as the crow flies."

"Yes, I saw it on the map," he replied. "I thought I was gonna have to put her down in the river back there, and then I spotted this farm."

"Well ya did great," I said.

We looked under the plane and there was just one broken part where he had caught on the top of the tree. "Thank God that tree was so dead or you may have been as well," I told him.

"Yes, I believe you may be right about that," Milan replied. "I need to fix my plane and re-fuel. I have to get back home before dark," he added.

"I have some tools up at my house," I told him, "and the gas station is only a couple miles away. I have plenty of containers we can get filled."

"Your help is much appreciated," he said.

We headed up the hill to the house. There, we loaded the containers into my pickup and off to get gas we went. I asked Milan why he needed to go back so quickly, and why the trip in the first place? He gazed out the truck window for a second, and then began to speak. "The reason for the trip," he said, "has been a life-long dream. I grew up on my grandfather's farm in Czechoslovakia until I was ten. My grandpa always wanted to fly in a plane, but never got the chance. When he died, I promised him I would build him his own plane. About a year after his death, my parents sold the farm and we moved to America, where my dad started a farm of his own. My parents are both dead now too, and I am the sole owner."

"Where is your farm?" I asked him.

"It is just outside of Prattsburgh, New York. It is one of the largest farms in the area. I have many workers and the local economy depends on us."

I looked at Milan. He wore a dirty white t-shirt, grubby old jeans, and a worn out pair of work boots. I don't know why, but I was thinking he was embellishing just a bit.

"Anyway," said Milan, "I have been building this plane in my barn for the last ten years. I made a promise to my grandfather and I was not going to break that promise. So here I am," he laughed.

"That is a very interesting, and touching, story," I told him. "But now, how will you make it back with the same amount of gas?" I asked.

"Faith my boy, faith. I will have a tailwind going back and should have more fuel than I need."

We pulled into the barnyard, and over to the plane. Milan grabbed my tools and fell down to the ground and under the craft near the wheel mounts. Within minutes, he popped his head up with a big grin on his face and said, "All fixed."

We filled the fuel tank to the top and still had a small jug left. "Would you like to take it just in case?" I asked him.

"No thank you, Mike," said Milan. "I am sure that I will be just fine."

"You were five miles short of your destination," I persisted. I wanted him to take the extra fuel just in case. He refused.

We hooked the ultra-lite to the hitch on my pickup, and I towed him to the very end of the field. "Is this going to be enough for lift-off?" I asked him.

"It will do just fine, Mike, relax."

"Alright," I said. I admired his confidence. He had a steadfast way about himself. So sure, yet throwing caution to the wind. Kind of like an old sea captain. "Before you take off, can I offer you some lunch?"

"I am hungry," he replied. "Better to fly on a full stomach."

We hopped into the truck and drove up the dirt road back to the house. I made a couple of chicken sandwiches on white bread with a little butter, salt, pepper, and mayonnaise. "What would you like to drink?" I asked him.

"Water would be just fine, Mike," he answered.

"Water it is," I said.

We both ate rather fast. I guess when you spend your days constantly working, you learn to save time where you can. We talked a little about my home and gardens. He was curious to know what I did for work, and how I survived. I was truthful with him. I told him of my daily struggle just to keep afloat. I talked a lot about my garden and my chickens and ducks.

"Is this sandwich from your flock?" he asked.

"Not this one," I said, "but when things are tight, I do indulge occasionally. Mostly I use them for eggs, and for company," I told him. "And they keep the bug level down."

"Oh, I know," he said. "I have my own on my farm too."

We finished eating, walked down the deck stairs, and headed to his plane. When we shook hands, he grabbed me and said, "Family hugs," and hugged me like I was his brother. I hugged him back.

Milan climbed into the pilot's seat, the only seat, and started the engine. I stood back and watched as he moved the throttle forward and the small craft began to move. He cleared the tree line by about a foot. He circled once and waved goodbye. I waved back with tears in my eyes. Never had I been so touched by a stranger before. Well, I thought, another memory; another story to file away in my brain.

When he was out of sight, I headed up the hill and into the house. That was five years ago today.

Part Two

About three years ago, I was working nights on a job in New York City, when I had a pain in my chest. It was Two AM, and I was leaving the building and headed for my car, when suddenly it felt as if someone had reached into my chest, grabbed my heart, and was squeezing it as hard as they could. I stood in the middle of the street frozen, almost as if I was turning to stone, like in the movies. In a few seconds it stopped. It scared the hell out of me.

I had a two hour drive back home to the country, and I was alone. I got to my car, got in and began to drive. I felt better as the pain was gone, but I was beginning to worry I was having a heart attack. I made the long drive home without any more pain. *Just gas, or maybe a cramp,* I thought. I was glad I didn't waste time at a hospital. *I'd still be there and would owe them my soul.*

It was Friday night, well actually, very early Saturday morning. I went to bed and slept fine. Around Eight AM, I woke from a sound sleep with the pain again. This time it was worse. I looked up and said, "No, if you are taking me, you do it while I sleep."

As the painful cramp, like a charlie-horse in my heart, dissipated, I went back to sleep. I slept until Two PM. I felt great. I ate last night's dinner for my breakfast, and went out to tend the gardens and the animals. The pain was gone. I made it through the rest of Saturday and Sunday, and no more cramping. I was relieved.

Monday night I headed out to work, again in the city, just off Time Square. I started at Six PM, and worked until Two AM, just as I had the previous week. Around Eleven-Thirty, I began to feel a little shaky. I had the jitters. I was alone on the eleventh floor. Small little pains began striking me in the chest. I opted to leave and go home.

When I got outside and near the car, the squeezing got really bad. It was the worst yet. I breathed like a pregnant woman giving birth, and once again it passed. I got in the car and drove home. I went to bed feeling no pain, but I was scared.

I slept through the night and woke up at Nine AM. I still had no pain, but decided to shower and dress for work, and go to the emergency room. If nothing was wrong, I could leave for work right from the hospital. I entered the ER.

Newton Memorial Hospital. I told the on-duty nurse I thought I was having a series of small heart attacks. I explained them as I did here in the story. She immediately put me in a small room and gave me an aspirin. She hooked up an IV, and the EKG monitor. The Doctor, an old white-haired grumpy guy, asked me what was going on. I explained to him in detail everything that was happening. He ordered a few test and kept me there about four hours. They did an ultra sound, an EKG, blood tests, and a chest x-ray.

The doctor, and I use that word lightly, came back into my room and told me I was fine. He checked all the results and could find nothing wrong with me, and I could go home. I said okay and began to put my work boots back on, when I thought, *Am I stupid? There is something definitely wrong in my heart.*

I looked up and he was still in front of the room. "Hey Doc," I said. "I'm not leaving. There is something wrong with my heart." He got all nasty and said that the only thing they could do was admit me and monitor me over night. "Well," I said, "you're going to have to do that because I am not leaving."

A short while later, a woman administrator came into my room and again came the words, "What's going on?"

Again I explained my symptoms in detail. She then told me that if I was not admitted, there would only be a one hundred dollar charge. I told her I didn't care about the damn charges, I was in trouble. After a short heated exchange of words, she said she would send in a cardiologist to see me and see what he thinks.

"Fine," I said. "I can live with that. Literally!"

A short time later, a young black doctor named David James came in. He was well spoken and very meek. He asked me those very same words again now for the fourth time. "What's going on, Mr. Wright?" I again explained in detail what had happened each day since Friday. He looked at me stunned. "They were going to send you home? From what you have explained to me," he said, "you are a textbook case of blocked arteries."

Dr. James had me immediately admitted. He scheduled another ultrasound that he himself administered. He then said he wanted to do a nuclear stress test in the morning, and an angiogram if need be. I said, "Okay. You are the doctor."

"Okay, Mr. Wright, I will take good care of you." We shook hands and he said, "I'll see you in the morning, Seven AM." Then he left.

I was in a regular hospital room by about six pm. I called my wife, who was now home from work, and filled her in on everything. I hadn't told her about the pain as to not worry her, but if I didn't come home tonight, she'd be even more worried. They brought me dinner, I ate, and fell asleep.

I woke up to the sound of her voice and her rubbing my head. I opened my eyes and she kissed me   "Hello. You should have told me," she said.

"I didn't want to worry you," I said.

"Well I'm worried now," she said to me.

I laughed. "I'm okay," I said. "This doctor seems like he really knows his stuff."

"I hope so," she said.

I asked her to please not worry the kids. "Just wait until after all the tests and then we can tell them." The kids were all out on their own and had struggles of their own, trying to survive in this world.

"Okay," she said. "I'll wait until the tests are finished."

"I'm tired," I said, "and want to sleep."

"Do you want me to stay?" she asked.

"No, I would feel better if you went home and took care of Sparky and the animals."

"Alright," she said. "I'll see you in the morning. If anything happens, please call me."

I smiled and said okay, figuring if anything happens, the hospital would be making the call.

Seven AM on the dot, Dr. James came into my room. He told me he thought a lot about the stress test during the night. "If it were to show nothing," he said, "we would still have to be more invasive and do an angiogram. I would feel better if we skip the stress test and go straight to the angiogram. It will give us more definite answers, and be less stress on you and your heart."

"You are the doctor," I said. "Whatever you think is best."

"I will set it up now. If it shows any significant blockages, we will send you to Morristown Medical for the surgery."

"Let's get this over with," I said.

I called Janet, my wife, and filled her in.

"I'm on my way," she said. "I'll be there in forty minutes. I love you."

"I love you too," I said, and hung up.

I trusted this kid, my doctor. He reminded me of my son-in-law, Ken. He is confident and very mild mannered. No sooner than he walked out of the room, the nurses came in with the mobile bed. Upstairs we went.

I was awake during the procedure. He talked to me the entire time.

"Hey Doc," I said, "anyone ever die from an angiogram?"

He looked at me and said, "The likelihood is one in a thousand, but that is generally for people with more serious heart issues."

"Has anyone ever died on your table?" I asked, somewhat nervous now.

"I've done over thirteen hundred procedures, and yes, I did lose one patient."

So the odds were one in seven hundred for me.

I could feel the camera moving through me. After a few minutes of it roaming through my veins, he reached the heart. "Oh boy," I heard him mutter. "Not good news," I said questioning him.

"You have three major blockages on the left side of your heart," he said. "We need to send you to Morristown."

"Okay," I said. "Just make sure my wife knows."

"She is already here and in the waiting room," he said. "I will tell her the results as soon as I leave you."

When he was finished searching through my heart, the good doctor gently pulled the camera out of my arm. "My associate, Dr. Godkar, will be doing your surgery," he said. "He is one of the best."

I was moved to a recovery room for about ten minutes, in which time I saw my wife. "They are going to put three stents in my heart," I told her.

"I know," she said.

"Don't worry, it's all gonna be okay. I'm fine," I said. "Either way, I'll be good. It's you and the kids I worry about."

"Your ride is here, Mr. Wright," said the nurse. Janet kissed me and left for the other hospital.

The EMT's moved me onto yet another stretcher and out the door we went. Through the halls and down the elevator, and out the main doors to the ambulance. After locking my stretcher in place, the engine started I was rushed from this hospital to the next. I was brought right in and saw my wife, daughter, and grandson for just a minute as they rushed me straight into surgery. Again I was drugged, but awake, during the procedure. They went in through my groin area into the femoral arteries, and like the angiogram, slowly found their way up and into the heart where the blockages were.

There was no pain. I did, however, at one point feel like I was leaving. I told Dr. Godkar I felt weak. He responded quickly. I heard him say that I was grey and ashy looking, and ordered atropine. I was awake and alert again in seconds. When the surgery was finished, he left the tubes inserted for about twelve hours. One was in case they needed to go back in, and the other was a balloon assist pump, to help keep the heart beating good. It hurt a little when they removed them.

I recovered in a reasonable amount of time and was home again. I was, however, very tired and weak for some time to come.

Part Three

The gardens got far out of hand, and the place was getting run down fast. When I was able to go back to work, it got very slow and I was laid off. Who needs a sixty year old with a bad heart, when the younger guys are like bulls? I did work here and there, but not enough to pay the bills.

I worked more in the gardens and hatched more chicks. With little money, we needed everything we could do to survive. Then I broke my ankle. There was no work, no garden; I couldn't even care for my birds that well. Things were getting very bleak. The mortgage fell behind five months and foreclosure proceedings had begun. The electric and water bills were also way behind. Somehow though, I managed to keep them on at least.

My ankle took almost six months to heal, and we were financially in dire straits. It was

Labor Day once again and I was sitting on the deck looking at the over grown vegetation covering the entire property. The poor chickens hardly got out of the run anymore because I couldn't handle the stairs.

I thought about Milan. I looked up from my chair into the sky and saw his plane in my mind. He had fulfilled his dream of flying with his grandfather. I had a dream too. I wanted my grandkids to enjoy our little slice of heaven. I wanted them to play with, and tend, the chickens and ducks. I wanted them to be able to eat the fruits, berries, and veggies we grew right here. I wanted them to know what roots really mean. My dreams would vanish into thin air as our home was retaken by the big banks. I had failed myself. I felt miserable. I tried so hard in life. I guess the old saying is true; nice guys finish last.

It took almost a year for the banks to foreclose. I had the property back up to snuff with fruits and veggies galore. More chickens and ducks than ever before. If I was going down, I was going in style.

I was in the garden when I heard the mail truck. I was hoping my social security check was here. It was only six hundred dollars, but that was electric, water, and what food we needed from the markets.

I walked limping to the box. As I went through the mail, there was a letter from a Lawyer in NY. *Oh great, what now,* I thought.

What more could be put on my plate this late in life. I went in the front door and right out onto the deck to read the bad news. My social security check was not there.

The letter began:

Mr. Wright, my name is James P. Stoll, Attorney at Law. I am writing you in reference to the estate of Milan Strakeda. He has passed away, and it seems he has left you one-fifth of his estate. His entire farm was left to his workers, and his cash assets are to be split among yourself and three others. Two million dollars each. His Will mentions you.

'It is with my sincere thanks for your help in fulfilling my life-long dream. I hope this can help you to fulfill yours. Signed, Family Hugs, Milan.'

Please contact me at your earliest convenience so we can issue you your inheritance. Happy Labor Day, Sincerely James P. Stoll.

As I wiped the tears from my eyes, I looked again toward the sky.

A Parent's Worst Nightmare
(Family/Tragedy)

Part One

On September 10, 2011, my wife and I went to bed as usual. It was a Saturday night around ten o'clock. Do you know where your children are? Chris, Amanda, and Jenn were already living on their own, and Jonathon was away at college in Rhode Island. Ben and Zach were the only two still living home. Zach had just turned 21, and Ben 14 the month before. They were good kids.

Ben's friend, Ty, was sleeping over, and the boys were all in Ben's room, playing games on the computer. Zach had just bought a pizza for the three of them, and they appeared to be settled in pretty good. I locked the doors, and said goodnight. I told them there was no more leaving the house, as their mother and I were going to bed.

"Okay, Dad," they said.

We went to bed and soon fell fast asleep. Around Two AM, the phone rang. My wife answered it. It was Tyler's dad. He was camping down by the river, and had received a call from Tyler, that he and Zach had crashed the dirt bike.

"No," said Janet, "they are in Ben's room, at least they were."

Janet and I scurried to Ben's room. It was empty. I hollered for the boys but got no response. I ran out the back slider door and they were not there either. As we hopped in the car to go search for them, a young kid named Roger came out from the side of the house.

"Where are the boys?" I asked excited.

"Zach and Tyler are on the dirt bike, and I'm waiting for my turn. They've been gone a while," he said.

"Where is Ben?" I demanded.

"I don't know," he said.

I told him to stay in the house and to keep the boys there, should they return before we got back. Zach was an excellent rider. He was always safe and usually careful. The moon was full, and everything was well lit, except, for where there were a lot of trees that is.

Janet and I drove street after street looking for them. We live in a rural area, and there are not that many roads they could have been on. After scouring every road and not finding them, we were going back to the house to see if they had returned.

We rounded the corner to our hill, and there was Ben. He was headed home.

"Where are Zach and Tyler?" I screamed at him.

"I don't know. I was walking my friend home."

"Friend? What friend? I told you guys to stay in the house."

"Yea, well he just showed up and I told him he had to leave. I walked him halfway."

"Get in the car, Ben," I said frantic. I was hoping the boys got up and shook it off, and were now at home. As we pulled into the driveway, I jumped out and went to the door. Roger was still alone. I got him into the car, and off we went again searching. I was more worried than ever. I knew they must be hurt, or Zach would have come back.

"Where were they riding?" I asked Roger.

"It sounded like they were up behind the Country Club?" he said.

We headed in that direction. About a half mile up the road, we came to another car and we both slowed down. It was Tyler's dad.

"Where did he say they crashed?" I asked him.

"Ty said River Road," said Glen. I told him Janet and I looked all over, and they are not there either.

Just then an emergency vehicle approached. He stopped and told us, "It just came over the radio. They found them inside the Country Club, follow me."

We followed him and came to a large washed out part of the road. It was twenty feet deep and about thirty feet across. It was washed out by hurricane Irene, and was not yet fixed. It only had sawhorses and two-by-sixes blocking the immense hole. On the other side was a fire engine and two ambulances.

I jumped from the car and looked down into the huge gully. I saw Tyler laying on a big drain pipe, and Zach was at the bottom. Ben looked too, and got sick to his stomach. He sat down on the ground and put his head in his hands.

The medics were working on Zach. I heard him moan as they got the board under him. I heard Ty as he tried to answer the medic. It was a low inaudible whimper. It looked like a war zone. There was steam coming up from the hole. There was water running through the bottom. The bike was just a bent piece of metal. It was a Kawasaki KX 150 power-band type. But worst of all, the boys were both in very bad shape.

I heard the helicopters flying above us heading for the municipal parking area. It is the only place they could land. It took quite a while to get the boys up out of the hole, and into the ambulances.

The wood barrier was broken in half. They had come around the corner fast, broke through the barrier, and slammed into the wall on the other side, head first.

We got into the car and followed the ambulance to the helipad. When the boys were loaded into the choppers, we dropped Roger at his home, and drove the fifty miles to the medical trauma center, as fast as we could. It being the middle of the night, the roads were empty and we made great time. When we entered the emergency room, they would not let us right in. I saw their helmets on the floor. The left side of Zach's was completely crushed in. Ty's was cracked almost in half.

Part Two

After about fifteen minutes, we were allowed to enter the ER room. Tyler was on one side of the room and Zach's empty bed was on the other. A long curtain divided the room.

Ty was awake but in a lot of pain. Zach was up in X-Ray having an MRI. When he came back to the ER, Tyler went up. Zach couldn't talk. The left side of his face and head was so swollen we didn't recognize him. He was conscious. He responded with his right eye as the other was swollen shut.

The doctor came in and told us the results from the x-rays. His left femur had a compound fracture, he shattered his cheek bones, broke his jaw and nose, broke his left hand, and fractured some of his ribs. He was immediately put on a ventilator because the swelling was so severe.

When Tyler returned, the doctor told Glen his results. He suffered a broken wrist, a ruptured spleen, and if I remember correctly, a punctured lung. Both of them were put in the Intensive Care Unit. There was one unit for adults, and one for children. Ty was only fourteen so he went to the one for kids. We didn't see him again until he was in a regular room about a week later. He was recovering quickly.

Zach had some troubles though. He was in the ICU a bit longer. The leg had been repaired the first morning in the hospital, but he needed surgery to repair the facial bones. They couldn't operate until the swelling went down. It took the better part of a week. When the doctor finally gave the word, Zach headed for surgery.

It was a fifteen hour wait. I'm still amazed how the doctor was able to stand at the operating table for so long. But he did. He rebuilt Zach's facial bones with tiny strips of titanium. His jaw was wired shut, and his eye socket was rebuilt using some kind of Teflon, so the eye could slide around easily. His hand was not caste. For some reason, it just had to heal on its own. His brain, thank goodness, was fine. He stayed in the ICU another four days, heavily sedated. The nurses were wonderful. I stayed at the hospital 24/7, until he was released to the rehab center.

Tyler had a chest tube draining the blood and fluid buildup inside. He healed fast, and was released and sent home. He stopped by often asking about Zach, and to hang with Ben.

Zach worked hard in rehab and was out in no time. When he came home, he needed a lot of help for quite a while. The leg had a titanium rod inserted and he was not allowed to put weight on it. He used the crutches as best he could, but the broken left hand didn't help. We used the blender to puree all his food. He ate anything we gave him with no complaints. We even did pizza once.

In time he got better, though he did limp a bit. At about the ninth month, he was able to go back to work with my brother. He was now twenty-two and lost nearly a year of his life. His friends, Rachel and Ray, came and visited often. He was back. He worked all week, and on the weekends he and Ray would hang out. They either stayed at our house, or went to Ray's to swim in their pool and ride the four wheelers. All was going good.

On August 4th, just short of one year since the bike accident, Ray and Zach left my house to go to Ray's. They had plans on going to dinner at a friend's, and then to a beach to swim. I felt at ease when they left, as they were both great young men. They obeyed the law, and were very mellow, never giving us any reason to worry. The first time was a fluke. Kids being kids.

It was again a Saturday night. My oldest son Chris slept over because we all planned on going fishing on the river Sunday morning. At Two AM, there was a hard knock on the front door. Sparky began barking and going nuts as he usually did when someone came to the door. I opened it and standing in full dress blues, were two NJ State Troopers.

Part Three

One male and one female officer.

"Can I help you?" I asked.

"Are you Mr. Wright, Zachary Wright's father?"

"Yes I am," I replied.

"Sir, we regret to inform you, your son was involved in a multi-fatality car accident, and did not survive his injuries."

The female officer then handed me a card and said I needed to go to Chilton Hospital and identify his body. In shock, I closed the door on them and went upstairs waking everyone up.

"Zach is dead, Zach is dead. We have to go to the hospital and identify his body."

It was all I could manage to say. My wife looked at me sullenly. Chris, Jenn, and Ben were frozen in disbelief. We all got dressed and drove to the hospital. This one was forty miles away. All the way there the kids and my wife were praying and hoping it wasn't him. I kept telling them the entire way, that the police had to have Zach's license and it was him. I needed them to be ready.

When we pulled into the parking lot and parked, we got out and stood together and said a prayer. "Please God," said Jenn. "Please no."

I asked God to give us all peace. With that, we entered the hospital through the emergency exit. I told the policeman who we were. I had everyone stay in the waiting room while I went with the policeman. I didn't know how bad he looked and wanted to spare them that if at all possible.

I entered the room. The boy on the bed was Zach's best friend, Ray. He was like a son to us also. I held his hand for a second and talked to him for a second. My heart was heavy. I told the cop that this was Ray, and followed him out the door. He turned toward the waiting room.

"My son?" I asked him.

"The other fatality is a girl, the driver," he said. "Your son must be the boy in Morristown Medical in critical condition."

We gave the officer and the hospital staff Ray's parent's contact information, and rushed off to Morristown. When we got there we rushed right in. Zach's eyes were partly open, his hands and legs spread out wide across the bed, and his tongue was hanging out. I thought he was dead, but then I saw his chest moving and knew he was alive and breathing on his own.

A technician followed us into the room.

"What's happening?" I asked.

He summoned the doctor, and he immediately came into the room. "Your son," said the doctor, "has a broken neck and a bad contusion on his head. His right femur is shattered in a couple of spots."

"Is he paralyzed?" I asked.

"We don't know; he has not woken up yet."

We all talked to Zach and kissed him gently on the forehead. It was like deja vu all over again.

Chis was leaving for Florida to be married. His wedding was in five days. I told Chris I was sorry, but I was staying here. "You go get married," I told him. I told my wife and the rest of the family that there was nothing they could do here. The best thing they could do was to continue on with their plans and head to Florida also. I would call every day with the latest updates.

We all went home. It was Five AM. I showered and headed right back to the hospital. The others slept, or tried to anyway.

When I got to the hospital, Zach had just gotten to ICU. Again. Some of the nurses knew him, and me all too well. "You just missed him," said the nurse.

"What? What do you mean?" I asked.

She informed me that Zach had woken up and responded. He knew his name and even squeezed her hand on command. "He also wiggled his toes," she said.

I stood there crying when she turned off the medication in the IV and called his name loudly. "Zachary, Zachary wake up." He made a sound. "Someone is here to see you," she said.

"Zach," I said, "do you know me?"

"Dad," he replied.

"That's right," I said, "and don't you give up or go anywhere. We have a ton of wood in the driveway to split and I'm not doing it by myself."

"Alright," he said, and slipped back asleep. I saw the nurse turn the IV back on. They kept him in a medically-induced coma for a couple days. Janet and the others came back that night, and the next morning before they left for Florida. They were back in a week and he didn't even know they were gone.

His neck was braced with an Aspen Collar. They did not use a halo. The spinal surgeon said he had shattered the C-1 and C-2 vertebrae of the spine, and he badly tore the ligaments in his neck. His head had a bad contusion on the back. "We believe when he was thrown from the Jeep, his head hit a tree."

Again Zach healed. A little slower than the first time, but he healed. His leg was healed again in eight or ten weeks. The collar was on for six months. I remember in early Spring splitting that wood. He helped. He now works with Ben, Chris, and I in the carpenters union. Zach misses his dear friend and talks about him often. Chris and Samantha celebrated their 6th anniversary yesterday.

Yes, life has many trials. Zach gets the Give Me Grey Hair award. I am a lucky old man to still have all my children alive, healthy, and together. My heart goes out to all who suffer loss. I lost my kid sister when I was in my twenties. Time does seem to heal and hide the pain, but memories are forever. May you all find peace. Your friend, Mike.

My Dog
(Genre: Pet/Family)

I sat down in my chair to write a story for you but my mind was blank today. I tried so hard to think of something to write about, but my mind was just lost.

I thought about life and death, love and happiness, even sadness and pain, but nothing.

I remember when I was a much younger man, and we had our first three children. Amanda, Jennifer, and Christopher. My dad had just died and we rented the upstairs of my parents' home from my mom. She lived downstairs.

I was in the flooring business, you know, the carpet guy who carpeted your house or office, or installed your kitchen floor. The kids were young. Chris was five years old, Mandy was four, and Jenn was two. The girls shared a room, and Chris had his own. I was changing the carpet in their rooms and decided to be a bit playful for them. I put grey carpet in his room with a brown runway from the door to the head of his bed. On the runway, I seamed in a big dinosaur out of green carpet. Its eyes were black and white with nice black eyebrows. It had a red tongue that hung out like a puppy dog. I enjoyed making that for him.

Next I did the girls room. The main area was eggshell white. Not a good choice for kids, but I was young, who knew. I also seamed in a runner to their bed. It was a bright red carpet. I inserted a white cross at the top. Still it seemed something was missing. One night while loading up at the store for the next day, I saw carpet samples being tossed out. I took them home. I put all different size pastel colored hearts all throughout the white carpet. They loved it, and so did I. We didn't have a lot, but they had something that all their friends thought was the most awesome thing going.

It was around this time our dog had died. Her lame was Lady. She was a small beagle who had been abused and very scared of people. It took a while to get her to even trust us.

She got out one night and didn't come back. We searched for a few hours but we couldn't find her. I left for work about five AM the next morning. I kept my eye out for her. When I got about a mile away and just near the highway, I found her. She had been hit by a car. We were all devastated.

A few days later Janet, my wife, said it would be okay if I went to the shelter and got us a new dog. When I got to the shelter there was a lone dog outside in the run. I went inside, and there were many, many more. I walked up and down checking out the dogs to see which one wanted to come home with me, and become a member of our family.

One dog, kind of large, a Shepard/Collie mix, came to the front of the fence and licked my hand right through the cage. It was the one that was outside alone. I continued up the cage line and then came back to Hershey. That was her name. She was all light, with dark brown swirls from head to toe.

The girl who ran the shelter told me she needed to be fixed and that it would cost around two hundred and sixty dollars, and that I could not take her until that operation was performed. I was gonna just blow it off and pick another one, when I noticed on the little card by her name, someone had drawn and colored a bunch of little hearts, all pastels and all different sizes. I immediately thought of the girls' room. *Okay, I'll take her.*

I gave the girl a deposit and told her I would be back the next day with the rest of the money. As I left, I looked back at the outside kennel and there was Hershey. The only dog outside, watching me leave. I got out of my van, and went to the kennel cage, bent down, and told her I would be back and that she would be coming home with me. I let her lick my face through the cage and then I left. I felt bad leaving her there like that.

The next day at work, I asked my boss for a small advancement of the week's pay, and he gave me the money to get the dog. About a week later I was allowed to take her home. When I got to the shelter she jumped all over me like she had been mine forever. We got in the van and home we went.

When the front door opened and these three little kids came out, she went berserk. She ran all around them and rubbed up on them all. But she did not jump on them. It was like she knew they were too small. She was ours, and there was no denying it. She played with the kids all the time, and better yet, she was the best protector ever. Even when I would throw the kids around playing, she would get up and in my face. No one got near those kids with Hershey around.

We fed her table scraps mostly, and dog food when I could afford it. She was strong and healthy, and, I might add, happy. She lived just over twenty one years with us until one sorry day, we had to put her down. She was very old and in pain.

But she lives on in my memory and in the memory of my kids. She even took them on a sleigh ride on Cranberry Lake once. Five kids, all on one long sled.

I tied the rope to her collar and she pulled them all over the ice. She was a great friend for all the kids, and for Janet and me too.

Sparky is our dog now. He is a great little buddy. As the kids are all grown, he gets to protect the ducks and chickens. He is ten years old now. He too lives mostly on table scraps, and the occasional steak.

I could not imagine living life without a dog or cat in the house. We have had other pets also, but none have ever had the love of our dogs.

Well I know this isn't much of a story, but it does bring back some very warm memories for me.

Peace to you all and have a wonderful week.

Your friend, Mike

Summer's End
(Genre: Seasonal)

The cool breeze was blowing over the sand, as I walked calmly along the now quiet and lonely shoreline. Footprints in the sand, filling behind me, vanishing, with drift, and others washed away never to be seen again.

The bright moon, hidden behind the now rainy and overcast sky; and the waves crashing hard, over empty beaches. Bungalows closed and bundled up, readied with love, for the promise of tomorrow.

One for now, one for then, the Winter's harsh, slowly, creeping in. Mountain homes; cold, and empty. Children unwillingly trudge back into schoolrooms; and parents, back to the jobs they wanted so much to forget.

The wind blowing through my soul, the hair on my neck standing high.

Circuses closed, carnivals gone. Send in the clowns.

New love and friendships, forged on those warm sunny days; and nights, oh, those nights...now lost, and fading into yesterday's threat of snow.

Again the crash of a memory of waves; the lakes and rivers, left to the power of ice, and wind. Sleet, covering the roads in every direction; a hindrance, a hibernation, a sleep. A rest for new life, a journey into tomorrow, or the promise thereof.

My blood was pumping as I walked. My head was swirling with the memories of each past day. What was next? Where was I to go? To who, to what, when?

I walked and thought of you.

The Fireman
(Genre: Family/Non-Fiction)

The fire was really hot. Even from the other side of the road where we were standing, it was too hot to stay long without the heat burning your face. The building was five stories and engulfed in flames. Firefighters were blasting it with water from the long fire hoses they carried. It took four men to a hose due to the tremendous water pressure. I saw fourteen trucks in all, and two of them were hook and ladders. They are the long fire trucks with a driver in the front, and one in the rear. There were countless other emergency vehicles covering the entire block. The chief had a bull horn and was shouting the men orders, as they fought the blaze. The hook and ladder trucks, had their ladders extended to the roof, and were rescuing as many people as they could. I couldn't even imagine just how hot it must have been right up in that fiery blaze.

We watched in horror as one wall gave way, caving in and crumbling down into the fire.

"Look," said my mother, pointing to the far side, "there is your father."

All six of us had our eyes now fixed on Dad. He was at the top of one of the ladders carrying people down to safety, then climbing right back up to retrieve another. He was in full gear that must have added at least an extra fifty pounds of weight. I never realized how strong he truly was. I miss him, my mom too.

There were eight of us in all, plus our dog Tippy. He was brown all over, except on the edges. His paws and the tip of his tail were white. Hence we named him Tippy. We lived in a small urban town in New Jersey, just outside of New York City. Our mom didn't work outside the home until we were a lot older. Taking care of the six of us rambunctious hoodlums was more than enough work and stress for anyone. And let me tell you, we were a handful.

Dad was a full time fireman. He worked shifts. One week on days, the next it was nights. If memory serves me right, they were twelve hour shifts. That put Mom as the primary care giver most of the time, but Dad wore the pants in the family. What he said was usually law back then. He worried about us all the time. He did soften up as we got older.

Early one evening, while Dad was working, Tippy came home smelling like smoke, and his hair was a little singed. Mom put him in the tub in cold water, and was pouring the cool water over him when the phone rang.

"Hello," I said.

"Hi, this is Mr. Yasko. Is your mom there?"

"Yes, Sir," I said. "Please hold on while I get her." I turned and yelled, "Mom, it's Mr. Yasko!" He was our friend's dad. He was a fireman too. They lived about a block away from us across from the school.

It was weird. Mom flew out of the bathroom and to the phone. She grabbed it from me fast and hard, and her first words were, "What's wrong, John? Did something happen?"

He told her everything was okay, but that Dad would not be home. He was working on a big fire and had to pull a second shift.

"Where is the fire?" she asked.

"On the corner of Highland and Lincoln," he told her.

Mom hung up the phone and rounded us all up.

"Where are we going, Mommy?" asked my little sister, Laura.

"We are going to see your father."

I didn't realize it then, but I sure as hell understand now. Mom was worried sick about dad.

We didn't own a car. The firehouse was just ten blocks away. It was near the apartment building my grandma lived in. She was the Super there. The fire was in between our house and hers. We walked about two blocks and then began to see all the action. The closer we got, the more hectic it became.

"Stay close," Mom ordered us. She had us all hold each other's hands. Standing there in that heat and watching our dad, I think gave us all, including Mom, a new sense of respect for him.

At one point when the people were all out, Dad got a short break. One of his firemen friends told him we were there, and he came over and hugged Mom. I saw tears in her eyes. Then he knelt and opened his arms wide and hugged all six of us at once. He smiled and said, "I love you guys." He looked at Mom. "I think Tippy is gone," he said. "He was here and chased me as the ladder went up. I heard him bark, then yelp, but I had to get to the people up top."

Mom told him our dog was home and okay. It was an odd thing I thought; here was Dad in the midst of chaos, and he had a look of relief on his face. I guess he counted on Tippy to help watch over us while he was gone. "I'll see you when I get home," he said. "Be good for your mother."

"We will, Daddy," we all said.

He hugged Mom and went back to work. He was now holding the hose with the other men, and blasting the fire with water. Mom seemed to feel better now, and we all walked back home.

About six years later they passed a law, that firefighters could live out of town. They had to live in the state, but did not need to live in the town they worked. Dad and Mom sold the house, got a car, and quickly moved us all into the country. Dad saw a lot of the goings on in town, and wanted to give us a safer place to grow up. Less congestion meant less crime and, more important, less drugs. He incorporated a long commute to work for himself, but to him, it was worth it to keep the family safe. To be honest though, there was less violent crime, but drugs were still easily attained, even here.

We started school in September and made new friends. My two oldest brothers had friends with driver's licenses. They would come and visit sometimes. My brothers would also go back to the city and sometimes stay at their friend's houses overnight. Yea, the city didn't prove to be too good for them. Luckily Dad and Mom had instilled good morals and values in all of us. After some trouble and a near death experience, they began to stay in the country and around home. Dad took us fishing a couple times, and the older boys hunting. It was the best thing he could have ever done. It really helped save their lives I think.

When I was about sixteen, the house was getting emptier. One brother out on his own, one in the navy, and my older sister was just married. That left us three younger ones. My little brother and sister, and me. We were very close in age and had a lot of the same friends. We all hung out together too. Mostly, we all lived in the same neighborhood, and even rode the same bus to school. Mom now worked. She had a job in Ma-Bell. Dad still commuted to the firehouse all the time. Life was alright. My parents did not have to struggle as hard now with two incomes and a few less mouths to feed.

Over the years, I think we all forgot how brave and courageous Dad really was. We began to fight against his rules all the time, thinking he was just a tyrant. Looking back, I know he just wanted us safe.

One night in late fall, Dad had just come in from hunting. His shifts at work had changed up, and he was off for three days. Mom had dinner ready and we sat down to eat. It was about 7:00pm.

"So Dad," I said, "how did ya do hunting?"

"Oh," he said, "I saw a couple but nothing large enough to shoot." I could see he was exhausted from being out in the cold all day.

Suddenly Mom screamed. "FIRE!"

I got up and stood next to her looking out the kitchen window. Down the hill was lit up like a giant candle. It looked like everything down there was ablaze.

Dad jumped from his chair and into his boots, dashing out the door in only his cotton thermal underwear, which he wore under his clothes hunting. I can still see him running down the hill. We, of course, were all following him. As we reached the bottom of the hill, I saw it was my best friend's house. It was an old converted summer lake house. Newspapers and straw were half the insulation. The house was totally consumed.

Our neighbor Jim was the cop on the scene. The first firetruck had just arrived and started shooting the water on the house.

"Is anyone inside?" yelled my dad.

"The mother and one son are out. We don't know about the father and the other boy," said Jim.

"Wet me down!" screamed my father to the firefighters.

"You can't go in there like that, you'll die," one of them responded.

My dad looked at Jim.

"He is a paid city fireman," yelled Jim. "Do what he says."

The volunteers hosed him down and he disappeared into the house. It seemed like he was gone an eternity. People watching began looking at one another. It didn't look good. Finally, my dad came out of the house. "The father is gone," I heard him tell Jim. "It's too late. He is on the side porch dead. Wet me down again," he yelled.

Again they soaked him with the hoses and in he went. They turned the hoses onto the side porch, thinking he was going to get the dad I guess. After another excruciating few minutes, he came out. "There is no one else inside," he said, and collapsed.

They turned the hose on him for a just a second to cool him, and then back onto the fire. The medics put my dad into the ambulance and gave him oxygen. He was okay. He suffered from some smoke inhalation. He refused to go to the hospital. The fire slowly got lower and lower until finally it was extinguished. My friend came home toward the end of it all. I told him about his dad, and took him to where his mom and brother were. His mom broke her hip when she had jumped out the window and into the yard. I left him there and went back to my dad and family over by the other ambulance. After Dad had rested a bit with the oxygen on, we all went home. It is a night I will never forget.

Nine years later, Dad went on to retire after suffering a couple of bad heart attacks. He died two year later. He lived through the Korean War, and through a lifelong career of putting others before himself. To most others, he was just a fireman, but to me, he was a Hero. Thanks Dad!

Snowy Sun Birds
(Genre: Romance)

"Bob, if you don't stop calling, I am gonna call the police. This is ridiculous. I will not allow this to continue."

I heard Noreen on the phone. It was Bobby again. He had called at least three time a week for two whole months now. I wanted to talk to him so badly. I loved him, and he loved me. Our families were keeping us apart. They treated us like little kids. It was cold out now, but a couple of months ago we were at the shore for the summer. That was where we met.

Each year, our family rents a bungalow at the ocean. It is a family tradition. We stay a few weeks every summer, and it's fun in the sun for everyone. This year was extra special for me, I fell in love.

My name is Barbara. Everyone calls me Barb. Except Bobby, he calls me Barbie. I love it when he calls me that. It makes me feel like a beautiful little doll.

I was out walking on the beach one evening after dinner, it is something I love to do. I trudge along barefoot in the sand, and just think about life. Where I've been, and where I'm going. Just pondering life in general. The waves seem to calm my mind and soul, and it is so wonderfully peaceful.

This one evening, as I was kicking along through the sand, I watched as he walked toward me from the other direction.

He too was barefoot, just stepping in the sand near the water's edge, it seemed, watching his footprints melt away with each step closer he took. He was mesmerized watching the water gently swirl the sand back to a smooth surface leaving no trace he had ever been there. He had no idea I was even here.

We were nearly ten feet apart when he finally looked up and saw me. Our eyes met, two lonely souls getting ready to pass like ships in the night, never to see each other again.

My eyes looked down at the sand, and I gazed at my feet, a bit embarrassed that he saw me starring at him. Slowly we passed, step by step. I turned my head backward to see him, and he was already looking back at me.

"Hello," he said.

"Hello," I replied softly.

"Nice evening isn't it?" he asked.

"Yes," I said, "It is." I turned back around and took another step.

"The water is as warm as the air," he said. I turned back. "Oh? I hadn't noticed."

"That's because your feet are walking in the dry sand. Come closer to the edge and let the water run over your feet as you walk. It is very relaxing", he said.

I looked into his eyes. Something inside me was drawing me toward him. I stepped to the edge, and let the end of the wave trickle over my feet and through my toes. It swirled the sand around like silk on my feet.

"You are right," I said, "It does have a relaxing feel."

He was not shy. "My name is Bob...May I ask yours?"

"I am Barbara", I replied.

"I've seen you walking the beach the past two evenings," he said.

"Oh, and how is it you saw me?"

"After dinner, I sit on our porch and watch the waves. The sight and sound of them crashing on the beach relaxes me. It is a great way to unwind after the long day."

"Yes I suppose it is," I replied. "That is why I walk."

"To be honest," he said, "I came out walking tonight, hoping to see you again and perhaps meet you."

I looked up at him, "Meet me?" I asked inquisitively.

"Yes Barbara. The first night, as I watched you, it was as if you were floating across the beach on the water. The second, I just couldn't take my eyes off of you. Something in the way you moved along had my full attention. I was imagining you were an angel, gently drifting past in the wind. I have never seen you here before. Do you live here or are you just visiting?"

"I'm here with my family for a couple of weeks on vacation," I said. "How about you?"

Bob smiled. "I am here with my family too. They rented a house down the beach."

"So we are neighbors," I said.

"I guess we are," he replied back quickly.

"I have to be going," I told him, "They will be worried if I am not back soon."

"I understand. My family is full of worrywarts also. May be we could walk together tomorrow evening and chat a while?"

"I would like that, Bob," I said.

"Please, my friends call me Bobby."

"Alright then, I'll see you tomorrow evening Bobby."

Bobby smiled. "That's great Barbara, I'll see you then."

"Bobby?" I said.

"Yes Barbara?" he answered.

"My friends call me Barb."

"Good night Barb," he said, "Until we meet again."

We both turned and headed for home.

I laid in my bed. I couldn't stop thinking about Bobby. He was so nice. I enjoyed the short time we spent together, more than anything I could remember in a very long time.

He seemed to be gentle and kind. There was just something about him that made me feel very comfortable. I didn't fall asleep until very late. My mind was running scenarios of what tomorrow would be like.

In one, we would be walking and then swimming together. In another we held hands and had ice cream cones. Still in another, he was kissing me goodnight. Imagine that. Me, kissing some guy. I laughed at myself.

I didn't say a word to anyone about Bobby when I got back. Noreen would have locked me in the house. She always thinks she knows what's best for me. No, I kept him my little secret.

Bobby and I spent the next three weeks walking and talking for that one hour each night. Those scenarios, by the way, all did happen.

Well we didn't swim, but we did get ice cream and hold hands, and at the end of the second week he kissed me goodnight. I enjoyed his company so much. I felt happy and alive.

The third week we stretched our time an extra half hour. No one seemed to notice.

We had so much in common. His family like mine, was over protective of him. It was as if we were kindergarteners or something. We had brains in our heads, we could think for ourselves and make our own decisions. That extra half hour each night flew by.

The second-to-last night he looked into my eyes and said, "Barbie. You are my Barbie, because you're such a doll."

I melted like butter on a hotplate. He held me tightly and put his lips to mine. We stood there kissing for what felt like an eternity. I was as high as a kite in love with him and him with me.

Then the crash. Tomorrow night was the last night of our vacation. I had to leave.

We met right after dinner, and talked. We made plans to get together after we were home. I gave him my address and phone number, and he gave me his.

We kissed more that last night, and there were stars in the sky.

When it came time for us to part, Bobby held me by my waist, looked deep and hard into my eyes, and said, "Barbie, I love you."

Immediately, and without reservation, I uttered the same to him. "Oh Bobby, I love you too."

During the long drive home I mentioned Bobby. Just as I had expected Noreen flipped.

"Are you crazy?" she said, "What's wrong with you? What would daddy say?"

Blah, blah, blah.

"I'm not a baby," I argued, but Noreen wasn't having any of it.

I closed my mouth, and like many times before, became quiet and just sat there. When we got home I went straight to my room. I even cried a little.

Not even a day had passed, when the phone rang and Noreen answered it. It was Bobby asking for me.

She yelled at him a number of times, and even hung up the phone on him.

I snuck to the phone twice and called him, but I got the same treatment from his family.

Time went by, and I was feeling depressed. I missed him terribly. If I could just hear the sound of his voice, I know I would feel better. What is wrong with people? Standing in someone else's way of true love. Then it came.

Noreen handed me a letter. It was from an old school friend that moved away. Sandra Rudi. I opened it right up. Maybe it would help take my mind off of Bobby.

It started, *My dearest Barbie Doll.* I almost fainted. My heart jumped and skipped a beat and began working double time. It was from my Bobby. He was so smart. He had remembered the story I told him about her moving away, and he used her name on the envelope.

He told me how he tried to call and how Noreen had shut him down. He had formed a plan so we could at least talk through writing letters to one another. He gave me one of his friend's names that I would use on the envelopes I sent to him.

We began a campaign of letter writing. It lasted through the winter and into the spring. We couldn't wait for summer vacation though, we had to see each other now. We made a plan.

It was early on a Sunday morning when I slipped out the back door just after breakfast. I figured I had a couple hours before anyone noticed me missing.

I hopped the bus and headed for Pittstown. Bobby also was on a bus headed there. It was halfway between our homes. When the bus pulled in to the station, I got off as fast as I could. I got there first. I hid behind a wall by the side of the building and waited.

It wasn't but a few minutes when I saw my Bobby getting off his bus. I kept hidden and watched him. He was like an angel floating gently on the breeze heading to the station door.

He went in. He came out a second later and looked around.

I saw him wiping the tears from his eyes, and I jumped out from behind the wall like a sixteen year old prankster.

"Barbie!" he said as he burst into tears. Our arms were around each other in a flash.

"Bobby!" I cried, tears also rolling down my face. We held each other tight.

"Never let me go," I said.

"I won't, I promise," said Bobby. "Are you ready?"

"I am," I answered.

He got down on one knee and took my hand in his. He looked up at me and into my eyes.

"Barbara Jones... will you marry me?"

"I will, I will! Yes, I will!" Bobby slid the ring on my finger and off we went.

The chapel was only two blocks away. The preacher asked if we were sure we wanted to do this. "Look at us," Bobby said, "what do you think?"

The preacher began. *Dearly beloved... I do, I do too.*

Bobby grabbed me tight and swirled me down low holding me in his arms and put his lips to mine. We kissed and kissed. The reverend finally had to cough a bit to get us to stop. We were married. Husband and wife. And there was nothing Noreen or anyone else could do about it.

We spent the night at a motel right there in Pittstown. The next morning we got on a bus together, and headed to my house.

Bobby thought it best that we go there first. He was my husband, and I knew he was right. They would be frantic, and losing their minds wondering where I was. They would probably even call the police. I didn't care. Bobby and I were together, until death do us part.

We walked from the bus stop to my house. When we got at the end of my street, we saw three police units, and some other cars that Bobby said looked like his family's.

When we got closer we saw that he was right. His family and mine, and the police were all outside arguing and crying. We walked hand in hand up the street.

"They must have found the letters," I said.

"Who cares," said Bobby, "We are married now."

I smiled. They were so busy fighting and blaming each other, that they didn't notice us.

"Ahem!" Bobby cleared his throat. Everyone went silent. They looked, and saw us standing there together.

"Mom!" yelled Noreen.

"Dad!" yelled Bob's daughter. "Oh my god you're both alright!"

"Of course we are alright," Bobby said, "We aren't little kids no matter what you think.

We are not senile either. But we are husband and wife."

I grabbed him, and in front of our kids and grandkids and even two great grandkids, kissed him and kissed him good.

"BBBUT," said Noreen.

"But nothing!" I said. "Meet your new daddy, this is my Bobby."

"And," said Bobby to his family, "Meet your new mother, this is my Barbie doll."

The police canceled the Silver alert and Barb and Bob set themselves up in an apartment in an assisted living center so their kids didn't have to worry about them anymore.

They all lived happily ever after.

Happy Veteran's Day

For those who stood and fought and served,
and brave in battle held the line,
one day, just not, enough deserved,
when came home dead, and maimed and blind.
For freedom though in mind so real,
less truth deception honest hold,
of leaders who, the devil's deal,
all spoils owned, dread deep dark gold.
Our heroes strong continue on,
for all of us safe broke at home,
a story deep, to ponder one,
courageous now, so all alone.
God bless our families, the sacrifice,
and remember the honest true,
our brothers fought, and suffered so,
for black, red, white, and you.
May all our Heroes be lifted high.

Our Family Miracle
(Genre: Family/Miracle)
Non-Fiction

The story you are about to read is true. It happened to us. Well, to our youngest child, our two year old son.

My name is Mike Wright. I have a wonderful wife and six fabulous children. Four boys and two girls. Their ages at the time, were fourteen down to two. And let me state, for the record, Miracles are real.

It was fall of 1999, and late in November. The temperatures outside were normal for that time of year. Our wood stove had been going since Halloween, and I was downstairs working on the coal stove.

The fire brick was broken and needed to be replaced. It was a custom made stove that I had bought a few years earlier, second hand, and I could not find any premade brick to fit inside. I ordered a dry mix of caste-able refractory, in order to make my own.

It was early Sunday morning, and my wife Janet, took our two girls, Amanda and Jenn, on a scouting fundraiser being held at our local Shoprite. If I remember correctly, it was a bake sale, to raise money for Christmas presents for those in the community in need.

I was home with the four boys. Chris, Zach, Jonny, and Ben. The girls left before breakfast, so I made Jelly pancakes for the boys and myself. After breakfast, I told them I would be downstairs working on the stove.

The Friday night before, I had made forms, mixed the refractory, and made the bricks. They were good and dry now, and ready to be installed.

I had all but one brick in, and the last one would not fit. I went to the garage and got my grinder. The boys were all sitting on the couch watching TV and getting along. Getting along was unusual.

I squeezed the trigger on the grinder, and started to grind the brick. Within a second, it made a big blast of white dust and I immediately stopped. I opened the door to upstairs and the door to outback to let the dust get suck out. I again started the grinder. This time the three oldest boys were at my side in a flash. They liked when stuff was going on. I stopped and sent them right upstairs.

"This dust is poison," I said "You can't breathe it. Is has silica, and that is very bad for our lungs. Especially for you guys," I said.

They ran back up and began to watch TV again. I continued grinding until the last brick was just snug. I tried to get it in, but it was just a hair tight. I thought, I know, I'll tap it in with a hammer.

I remembered seeing the hammer upstairs on the TV. I had used it to make the forms on Friday, and the kids helped. I went up, and as soon as I got off the landing, I glanced at the couch. Only the three boys were there.

"Where is your brother Ben?" I asked.

"We thought he was with you..." they replied.

I called his name loudly. No response.

"Benjamin!" I screamed at the top of my lungs. Nothing. My heart sunk.

A few day before, the older ones came home from the pond with two huge carp they had caught. They asked if they could put them in the pool. The pool I had gotten from a neighbor and set up this past summer. It was old, but it made the season.

I did not have a cover, or the money to buy one. After all, it was gonna come down anyway. It was shot. I told them sure, go ahead. They put the carp in the pool and we fed them dough balls. A bear, or a coon, came one night and tried to get them. His claw ripped the lining at about the three foot level. So the water was about two and a half feet deep.

I screamed again, "Benjamin!" as I headed back down the stairs in a panic. The boys right on my heels.

Zach said he heard a moan from out back. No one else heard it. But then I knew.

When the boys had first come downstairs, Ben must have walked straight out the door and down back to the pool to see the fish.

That was almost thirty minutes ago.
I dashed out the back door and ran down into the lower part of the yard where the pool was.

I saw his body as I got closer. He was in the water, on his back. I jumped the edge in a leap, and into the icy water I went.

He was on his back, stiff, with his tiny hands clenched tight into fists. He was blue, even whitish, frosty, like on a TV show.

I grabbed him and put him on his stomach on the decking. I climbed out and ripped my shirt off and ripped his clothes off and held him on my bare skin.

I rushed into the house and Chris got me a blanket. I wrapped it around us both and held him. He was still, stiff, and made no sound at all.

He was breathing very, very shallow, and slow. Having no other car, I ran across the street holding him tight to me in the blanket and kicked the neighbor's door.

My neighbor came out, and then rushed us to the hospital in the next town. They took him right in and put him in warming blankets. His internal temperature was 86 degrees. He was still blue and stiff.

They slowly warmed him up. After what felt like a lifetime, (It was about thirty more minutes), his color went to deep purple, and then slowly to pink.

My neighbor had left and went to ShopRite to inform my wife. She and the girls came in just when he began to cry. And he cried louder and louder. And so did I.

A little while later, my neighbor was back, with my sons. We all waited. He was crying, and that was a good sign.

Janet and I were in the ER room with him. Soon, he was calm and talking. They let all the kids in with us. He was now talking and jumping around like nothing ever happened.

The doctor said he was a very lucky little boy, and told him he was proud that he thought to float on his back, which kept him from drowning.

Ben looked up at the Doctor and said, "The Angels were holding me up."

One of the nurses gasped and held her face. Tears flowed. I think even the Doctor was stunned. Benjamin was fine.

Today he is twenty years old, and works in the carpenters union with myself and two of his brothers. Our entire family, two nurses, the Doctor, and our neighbor, are here to testify to this.

No one will ever tell me that miracles are not real.

God bless you all, and please share your miracles with others.

I believe in miracles; they have happened in our family. More than once.

PAID, Thank You
(Genre: Inspiration)

On Friday morning, I headed out to do a little grocery shopping. I had to cross the bridge over the river to get to the store. There is a dollar toll to cross the bridge. I had only seventy-five cents in my pocket. I sat at the booth and searched the car for another quarter. I found two dimes and five pennies. I gave the girl the dollar in change, said, "Happy Holidays," and continued on.

After getting what I needed at the store, I was using my debit card to pay. It asked if I wanted cash back. *I never take any, but this time, I thought. I know, I'll take twenty dollars, and the next time I come into town, I will pay the toll, and then pay for the next nineteen people, and have the attendant just say Merry Christmas to them.* I packed my bags into the car and headed home. Of course while unpacking and putting away the food, I realized I had forgotten a few things. I do that a lot more these days. I decided I would go back the next morning, and get the items I'd forgotten.

I woke up, showered, had a cup of tea, and left for the store. I immediately noticed my gas was very low, so first I drove to the closest gas station. I needed what was left on the card for the food. My bank account is always lean. It is a week to week life here for me. I reached into my pocket and gave the guy the twenty that I got back at the store the day before, and was back on my way. I was half way across the Milford Bridge when it dawned on me, *I don't have a cent left to pay the toll.*

When I approached the end of the bridge, I slowed and stopped at the booth. The little light came on and said, *Paid, Thank you.* I looked up at the woman a bit embarrassed and said, "I'm sorry, but I don't have any money to pay the toll."

She smiled at me and said, "NO, NO, it's alright. The car in front of you paid your toll, and told me to wish you a very Merry Christmas."

I said thank you to her, and Merry Christmas, and proceeded on my way with tears rolling down my face. Oh yes, there is a power far greater than any of us. Merry Christmas and Happy New Year to all.

The Hunt For Christmas

'Twas the night before Christmas,
no food in our house,
I grabbed hold of my rifle,
gave a kiss to my spouse.
I said,
With some luck, I'll be home with some grub,
She smiled and said
With God's help and His love.
On with my coat,
and boots off the floor,
in a quick dash, I slipped out the door.
I got in the car and drove 'bout a mile,
on the edge was a deer, and I started to
smile.
Jammed the car into park
and snuck into the woods,
in search of our dinner,
if only I could.
Stepping so quiet, avoiding the leaves,
to the small clearing; below all the trees.
When I got there I saw,
down low by a tree,
a buck and a doe,
and a fawn, there were three.
When I looked through my scope my eyes
couldn't believe,
not a deer; but a family,
on Christmas eve.

Mother and father,
a small baby boy,
a light so so bright,
and so full of joy.
The woman, a queen,
looked into my eyes,
her message was clear,
wow what a surprise.
My eyes started tearing
and my heart filled so fast,
I left the woods food-less, the deer got a
pass.
I drove toward our home
and the closer I got,
the lights were so bright,
like in the woods, on that spot.
What I saw was a mansion,
not our small wooden shack,
my wife in the doorway,
bright light at her back.
We have visitors for dinner
she said with a smile,
a mother and father
and their newborn boy child.
The cupboards are packed,
and the woodshed is to,
lets visit the child, for his story is true.
He's given us everything our hearts can
desire,
come now dear husband, and sit by the fire.

MERRY CHRISTMAS TO ALL
May the true meaning of Christmas fill all hearts.